Also from STARbooks Press

Boys Will Be Boys – Their First Time
An Erotic Anthology Edited by Mickey Erlach

I0647984

Boys Caught in the Act

An Erotic Anthology Edited By
Mickey Erlach

STARbooks PRESS
Herndon, VA

Published in the United States STARbooks Press PO Box 711612 Herndon
VA 20171 Printed in the United States

Many thanks to graphic artist John Nail for the cover design. Mr. Nail may be
reached at: tojonail@bellsouth.net.

Herndon, VA

CONTENTS

BACKYARD BUTTFUCK
By Jay Starre

I'd been out jogging that September morning. Muddy and hot, I came into the backyard from the wooded ravine that cut through our suburban California neighborhood. After splashing through puddles left behind after a violent rainstorm the night before, my jogging shoes and shorts were soaked.

Once in the backyard, I grabbed the garden hose and sprayed off my legs and shorts. The water in the hose was warm from sitting in the sun all morning. It felt great. In fact, it felt so good that as I hosed off my muddy crotch, I got the wild idea to shed my shorts and hose off naked.

My parents were gone for the day at my younger brother's soccer tournament, so I had the backyard to myself. Another wild notion popped into my head as I hopped around on one foot tearing off my shorts and jockstrap. I was going to peek through the hole in our fence into Tom's yard again, just as I had the day before!

The warm sun and warm water from the hose on my naked crotch got me horned up right away, and my dick popped up into a boner. I couldn't help stroking it, while recalling the nasty scene I'd witnessed the day before.

With my stiff rod in one hand, I crossed the lawn and shoved the branches of the bushes aside to sneak into the shrubbery that lined the fence between our place and our neighbor's. I easily found the knothole at chest-height and bent over to stare through it. Slowly stroking my boner, I gazed at the empty backyard through the hole in the fence and remembered what I'd seen from that same spot.

I'd been kicking the soccer ball around by myself when it flew into the bushes. In my search for it, I noticed the large knothole and out of curiosity checked it out. Just on the other side, there was my next-door neighbor, Tom. Sprawled out on a chaise lounge, his swimsuit pulled down as he pumped furiously at a big hard-on!

I gasped, both turned on and frightened. Tom and I were not exactly friends. We'd been neighbors for almost five years, but he'd totally ignored me all that time. Through high school, he was on the football team, and now that we'd started our first year at the local college, he was on the football team there, too. He was big and kind of mean. He was very big in fact, his size alone intimidating enough – if he hadn't also been quiet and aloof. He acted like he was too good for the rest of us.

Only the fence separated us. He was about three feet away, and straining to pull a load out of a huge, nasty boner, his legs spread wide and his hips up off the lounge chair as he grunted and thrust into his slick palm. I noticed every detail with breathless excitement. He'd obviously lubed his dick; it gleamed wetly in the bright sunshine, and his slick fingers made a slapping noise as he stroked faster and faster up and down the stiff shaft. The head was wide and purple, as if it was full to the brim and about to blow.

It was, and it did.

A geyser of cum erupted from the slit in the big bulb. Tom's beefy thighs, huge hams of white flesh, tensed and flexed as he shoved his hips upwards like he was fucking the sky.

That was yesterday. Now today, I leaned over and stared through that hole again. He wasn't there, which was disappointing, but I recalled the spy-feast from the day before with vivid accuracy. I remembered how stiff and solid that big rod had looked. Picturing that tower of fuck meat, I unconsciously spread my legs and felt my butt crack open up. I was totally horned up, conscious of my naked ass and dangling balls hanging free. I stroked my dick slowly as I fantasized about Tom's huge shaft and imagined it rubbing against my spread ass.

That was fucking exciting! Even without Tom there now!

I bent over further and planted my feet wide apart. Air caressed my naked crack. I felt the air against my bare asshole and shivered. I thought of Tom's boner rising up into the afternoon sunlight, slick and hard, spewing cum all over his hefty football thighs. I thought of that giant meat rubbing and pushing against my crinkled hole. I shuddered

2

and stroked my dick a little faster. I squatted down, and that opened up my asshole. God, I was feeling so horned up!

Naked from the waist down, wearing only my tank top and jogging shoes, I felt vulnerable and nasty. I thought of my tight asshole and willed it to open up, arching my back and pouting the snug hole's lips outward, feeling sleazy and completely unashamed of it.

My dick was torrid-hot and so hard in my hand. I pumped it a little faster as I imagined Tom's huge meat rubbing against my tender ass lips, now distended and open to the afternoon air. I almost laughed at my bizarre exhibitionism, but I knew I was alone and hidden in the bushes, so I really got into it. I flexed my butt cheeks and rolled my hips, pretending Tom's dick was riding up and down my bare crack, teasing the tender slot as it crossed back and forth over it.

Maybe he would return to lie down in the lounge again! That thought only made me more horned up.

I was about to cop a feel of my own asshole when suddenly, I felt something clamp over one of my writhing butt-cheeks!

"I saw that white butt waving at me from the bushes, and I had to come see what was going on." A gruff voice identified that clamping hand on my naked ass.

Tom!

A shudder crawled up spine. I froze in place as he continued speaking in a low growl. "What a nice little surprise, my cute stuck-up neighbor jerking off while he spies on my backyard through a hole in the fence. Did you see something nasty yesterday you liked? Did you see my big rod and my juicy load shooting all over the place?"

I was totally mortified. Not only was I caught jerking off, but also caught spying on him while I pumped my dick in the bushes like a total perv!

But there was a hand on my ass, a sweaty paw gripping one cheek as another suddenly clamped hold of the other. My dick lurched in my fingers, and my asshole clamped shut and then spasmed open, confused and horned up just like my spinning head. What the hell was I supposed to do now?

3

Tom and I had never even had a conversation before; now he had his hands on my naked butt!

"How'd you like my dick shoved up your ass?"

"What?" I sputtered out.

Regardless of my embarrassment, or inability to admit out loud what I really wanted, my body spoke volumes. Those ham hands slid into my crack and roamed up and down it possessively. Fingers strummed my vulnerable asshole, sending waves of heat up and down my trembling body. I arched my back and shoved my ass into those fingers, letting out a sluttish moan that sounded almost like a "yes."

"I came over to borrow your mower because ours is fucked up," Tom whispered throatily behind me. "No one answered the door, so I checked out the backyard to see if someone was here. I spotted your cute white butt squirming around in the bushes like it was getting fucked good. And that's what you want, isn't it? Your ass getting fucked good?"

I hardly heard his explanation. My mind concentrated on those fingers rubbing the tender lips of my asshole. Big, blunt and insistent, they pawed and poked at it.

And, I was absolutely loving it. ·

I shivered and grunted and actually bent over further, offering my ass in a gesture of total capitulation.

"Lucky for us, Dan, I always carry condoms in my wallet. You never know when you'll come across a sweet ass ready to get fucked," Tom hissed behind me, and then laughed.

I imagined a sneer on his cute face, but that image did nothing to cool my nasty heat. I wanted him to fuck me. I wanted it more than anything in the world! I didn't care if he was arrogant or snotty. His dick was big, and it would feel great sliding up my hungry hole.

At least I hoped so; I'd only had a few fingers up there before, although they'd felt pretty fucking good. I felt as if I should say something, but my tongue was frozen. Not so my body. I wiggled and shoved my ass back into Tom's hands like a total perv. And, I started whacking away at my dick again, too far gone in heat to care how totally embarrassed I was.

4

For a moment those hands abandoned me. I heard a zipper being undone, and the thought of what was behind that zipper sent another wave of irresistible desire washing over me. I felt faint! I couldn't resist turning my head to sneak a peek at what was coming.

There it was! Jutting out from Tom's waist as he dropped his shorts to the grass and stepped out of them, a humungous boner bobbed up, lined with veins and capped by a swollen head that twitched and leaped as Tom quickly began to roll a condom down over it. He seemed to know what he was doing. I hadn't even thought of a condom, even though I knew I should have.

"Don't worry. I've fucked a few pussies, and a few assholes. I know my prick's fucking gigantic, but I was gonna jerk off after I mowed the lawn, so I got some lube along with the condoms. Lucky you, Danny-boy."

Tom's matter-of-fact tone was oddly reassuring. I was half bent-over, with my naked butt wide open and my hand stroking my dick. That would have been embarrassing, but he was naked now, too, with a hard-on in his hand and talking about fucking pussies and asses as if it was an everyday occurrence.

I braved a look up into his eyes. Bright blue under dark brows, they gazed at my butt with such bold greed, I suddenly felt as if all the uptight bullshit between us was just that. Bullshit. He wanted my ass. I wanted his dick.

"Fuck me then. I can take anything you can dish out, football brain," I hissed, staring back at him with a daring smirk.

His eyes went wide, and he looked down at me. He saw my grin, and he burst out laughing. "Okay, you smart-ass, blond punk. I gotta admit I've been checking out that tight ass of yours for a long time. Whenever I saw you jogging, I imagined those sweet bouncing cheeks riding up and down my stiff shaft. Now we can both get off."

"Okay, then. Do it. Do it now," I urged him. Just looking at that huge dick had my guts churning. I wanted to feel it up inside me!

He was still grinning as he rubbed a handful of lube up and down the giant rod. I was thankful for that; I knew my snug butt hole would need a greasing if it was going to take his monster meat. I was willing, which I knew was a big part of it. He'd have to do the rest.

5

Tom's eyes went back to my ass, and that look of hunger resurfaced. The expression of nasty need on his handsome face transformed it. No longer arrogant, he looked like a big eager puppy dog. I turned away and rose up slightly to place my hands on the fence in front of me and prepare for the anal assault. My asshole twitched and clamped. I bit my lip and willed it to open up. I wasn't totally ignorant, at least. Although I hadn't been fucked, my imagination was vivid. I'd read a few steamy porn stories that explained in raunchy detail the joys of butt-fucking. I'd shoved two fingers up my own asshole many times – and loved the stretching, aching feel.

Suddenly I was feeling the real thing!

Tom rubbed his enormous dick up into my crack. I planted my feet wide apart and focused on the feel of that solid piece of meat sliding around in my parted crack. I could feel it throb against my ass-crack, full and lengthy. He rubbed it up and down slowly, while I shivered and my asshole twitched nervously. He held the thick column there while he gripped both cheeks of my butt. I could feel it pulse.

"What a sweet ass! It's so fucking firm, like a smooth rock or something. All that jogging I guess. Shit! It feels so fucking good!" Tom muttered from behind me. He wasn't sounding so matter-of-fact now!

He continued to rub his dick up and down my crack, slowly and teasingly. It felt awesome. The whole length of the thing lay against my crack, from his balls to the crown. It pulsed against my crack, slippery and heated. Although my fevered imagination lusted to have that big pole reaming my guts, I was oddly content to let him rub it slowly back and forth without poking it in.

The big football stud did that for a long time, moaning between comments on how much he loved my hot ass. I leaned against the fence and said nothing. My whole body was focused on that giant bone and my lubed crack. Tom squeezed my butt cheeks together to wrap them around his thrusting dick, and then he pulled them wide apart and rubbed the head all over my slick hole and butt-crevice.

I felt him change his tactics, beginning to concentrate on my asshole. He started to probe at it with the broad head. He held my cheeks apart and jabbed lightly at the slick butt-lips. I gasped and bit my lip and arched my back. All of a sudden, I wanted it bad.

6

I heard my own grunted plea. "Fuck me! Stick your dick up my ass!"

He laughed, but it wasn't the least bit snotty. It was actually pleasant and excited. Then, he pressed forcefully against the rim of my snapping slot. The blunt head pushed, while my tight ass-lips resisted. I snorted in air and focused, pouting out my sphincter, feeling the slippery dickhead rubbing and pressing at it. I felt Tom's fingers surrounding my asshole. They dug at it, stretching it apart. I groaned and bent over, half-squatting. Tom followed me with his dick, pressing inexorably upwards. I felt my hole giving, my tight lips parting. Then something big and hot was sliding up inside me.

"Your dick is up my ass!" I groaned, my tongue hanging out and my body shaking all over.

"It's so tight! So fucking tight! Relax, Danny. I'll wait a minute. Get used to the head in there."

Tom actually crooned as he held his dick poised just inside my trembling sphincter. There was a sharp pain that I felt all the way up into my nipples, but it ebbed and waned within seconds. I think Tom sensed it, and suddenly he was sliding more dick into me. I gasped and he groaned. More dick rode slowly up my ass tunnel.

I grinned from ear to ear, totally focused on the sensation of fullness that overwhelmed my guts. Tom took his time, stabbing an inch deeper, then withdrawing slowly, then working in another inch, and withdrawing. I shook all over, then all at once found myself totally relaxing. That's when his dick slid all the way in, his balls banging against my crack.

"So sweet, so awesome, so fucking good," Tom muttered behind me.

He leaned against my back by then, his large body heavy over me. I had my feet planted wide apart and could hold us both up. He began to fuck my ass slowly, not at all as I would have imagined a big football jock like him doing. It was almost tender. That big rod rode in and out, amazing me that all that fat meat could fit inside me and feel so great at the same time. It didn't hurt, but I could sure feel it as the blunt head rubbed and pressed against my sensitive prostate, while my tight butt lips stretched and ached continually. It was without question the most exciting thing I'd ever done.

Tom's massive arms wrapped around my chest, while his hands dropped down in front to my crotch. He pulled on my dick with one hand and tugged on my nuts with the other.

That made my asshole quiver and snap, which we both appreciated. He rubbed in and out in a steady pumping fuck from behind while he jerked my dick from in front. I leaned into the fence and totally gave in to the feeling of dick stuffing me.

"I'm gonna shoot … up … your … ass!" Tom suddenly blurted out in a high-pitched moan.

The thought of him coming in my ass was too much. He loved my ass so much, he was shooting up it! His fingers on my dick pumped faster as he tensed and thrust into me from behind. He was coming!

My balls roiled. I felt my asshole clamp and spasm. Jizz flew from my dickhead. I barely remained on my feet as both of us jerked like Marionette dolls. His cock spewed up my ass while I sprayed the fence in front of us with spurt after spurt. His massive body surrounded me, his erupting dick pulsing inside me. My head spun. I barely remained on my feet.

Finally, I felt Tom's dick slide from my aching asshole. I moaned out loud, feeling strangely abandoned. Was it over? Were we going back to being unfriendly neighbors?

But then he pulled me up and turned me around. He smiled. He didn't look like a jerk at all anymore.

"We gotta do this again," he laughed then added, "Maybe we can say hi to each other now and then, too."

We both laughed, and that's when I felt his giant meat rubbing against my thigh, rising back up into a stiff boner. My asshole twitched, empty now and throbbing.

Our eyes met. He nodded and winked.

"We have the rest of the day. No use wasting it," I grinned in his face.

"Are you thinking what I'm thinking? Do you want to fuck me now?"

I hadn't been thinking that at all! My asshole felt like a wide-open tunnel, and ached to get stuffed again. But as soon as Tom made that suggestion, my prick reared up like a striking snake. His butt was like two big soccer balls, huge and solid. I'd fantasized many times that I was spreading it open and exploring it, with my fingers and then my aching cock. Was he serious?

Tom laughed, but it wasn't an arrogant laugh. He twisted around in my arms and shoved his naked ass against my crotch, football firm, covered in a soft down of dark hair, the deep crack parted and the pink hole visible.

"There's a condom in my shorts. Put it on, grease your cock, and plough my big jock ass!"

I had died and gone to heaven.

My stiff dick slid up into the tight folds of his football butt hole while he grunted and took it. I hadn't known how exciting that would be, and barely kept from shooting the moment I entered. Taking a deep breath and holding completely still, my near-orgasm gradually subsided as all that snug hole snapped and clamped around my buried meat. Tom wriggled his big white ass and pushed back for more! I fucked him then, in the bushes against the fence just like he'd done me.

We blew our second loads.

I got fucked for the first time that sunny afternoon, and fucked my first ass. And I found out Tom was just quiet and lonely, not a jerk as I'd thought. In the end, that was the best part. We got to be friends.

And we got to fuck each other a hell of a lot.

GARDENER'S SHED
By Wayne Mansfield

It was a drag having to go to college when the hot summer sun beckoned and thoughts of cool waves crashing on white beaches tantalized. Being cooped up in an air-conditioned room was getting me down to the point where I was no longer paying attention to my lecturer, a middle-aged woman named Edith. Instead, my mind was drifting between thoughts of the beach and of the muscular gardener who had just begun raking leaves on the lawn outside the classroom.

At first, my thoughts were innocent. I was envious of him and wished it were I outside in the sun, being active and feeling alive, instead of wasting away in a boring summer class. However, it wasn't too long before I became mesmerized by the man's bulging biceps and triceps, moving under his skin as he dragged the metal prongs of the rake across the leaf-strewn lawn. The tattoo on his right arm seemed to dance of its own accord. Then my eyes were drawn to the gardener's legs, powerful, tanned and hairy. The thighs were thick, like a rugby-player's, and tapered down at the knee only to expand at the calves, which were solid muscle, rounded and disappearing into a pair of thick socks and boots.

"Michael Timms! Are you listening?" Edith barked.

"Yes, Miss," I replied, looking up from my desk by one of the back windows. "I was just thinking about what you were saying."

She could so easily have called my bluff. *Exactly which part were you thinking about?* she could have asked, but she didn't. Instead she continued droning on about Renaissance painters. It was an elective I'd regretted right from the very first lecture. I had no interest in Renaissance painters and had only chosen the unit because it had been the best of a bad lot.

I paid attention for a minute or so since Edith was keeping an eye on me, but it wasn't long before I found my attention wandering again. I stared ahead at the brown batik print from a previous class that had been framed and was hanging above the whiteboard just screaming bad taste. Then I returned my attention to the gardener, whom I'd completely forgotten about.

Whether through good fortune or coincidence, I was just in time to see him remove the navy blue sleeveless shirt he'd been wearing. I glanced at Edith, who was at the whiteboard writing some notes and had her back to me. I could be thankful for that at least. I looked back at the god outside on the lawn unbuttoning his navy blue work shirt. As he got to the last button, I held my breath. When the shirt came off, I could see his sculptured, lightly haired chest, flat stomach and thick, dark snail trail that led down to a pair of shorts barely large enough to be called clothing.

I felt my cock swelling and filling out beneath the tight fabric of my jeans. As I gazed lustily at the near naked vision just meters away through the glass, I subconsciously rested a hand on the large bulge still growing down the side of one leg. I rubbed it slowly but firmly, staring at the gardener as he bent over, picked up a great armful of leaves and deposited them in a nearby wheelbarrow; completely oblivious to the lascivious stares he was producing.

"Michael Timms! I will not ask you again!"

My head spun around, and I blushed. Had I been caught?

"Bitch!" I muttered.

I was eighteen. I didn't have to pay attention if I didn't want to. I was paying for the course, or at least my parents were, and if I didn't want to listen to her dull monologue, what difference was it to her? Three o'clock couldn't come fast enough.

When it did roll around, I was out of class like a flash, a cigarette in my mouth and my hand impatiently playing with the cigarette lighter in my jeans pocket. The second I stepped out of the building, I lit the cigarette and inhaled deeply. The concoction of chemicals in the tobacco may have been deadly, but they sure as hell made me feel better.

I'd smoked two thirds of the cigarette when I saw the gardener out the corner of my eye. He was wheeling the empty barrow back from the incinerator by his shed, still naked but for his shorts and boots.

He looked briefly up at me and smiled a casual, friendly smile. There was nothing in it. He probably smiled at everyone that way. I exhaled, blowing a cloud of dirty, grey smoke into the air and smiled back, suppressing the urge to cough since some smoke had got caught in the back of my throat. Then he disappeared.

I started walking home, but I couldn't get the image of the bronzed gardener and his muscular body out of my head. In the space of two hours I had become desperate for him to notice me. I wanted him to touch me and kiss me. I knew these thoughts and desires would probably remain fantasies, but the chance that one day they might come true would sure make going to college easier.

Instead of going home, I went for a burger and shake at a café just down the road from the college. It was pretty dingy, but it was cheap, and the students liked to congregate there after school. I sat with a group people I barely knew, but they were first years, too, so we were all in the same boat. I was really enjoying myself, making new friends and catching up on all the gossip about the lecturers.

"What about the gardener?" I asked, hardly believing I had been the one to bring him up and so enthusiastically, too.

"Terry?" said one of the girls, chewing on the straw sitting in her spearmint milkshake. "Oh, isn't he gorgeous?"

"I heard he was a fag," said Dominic, the cool guy who still hadn't matured since leaving high school.

"Who cares?" replied Lara, who was sitting next to me. "He's the most attractive thing there."

Dominic blushed and put his arm around the girl chewing the straw.

I sat back in my seat and let the conversation progress without me. *A fag, hey?* I thought to myself. That certainly made things interesting – if it was true. Maybe there was hope for my fantasy happening after all.

I couldn't wait to find out. Even in the air-conditioned café, I could feel waves of heat wafting in through the open door. I was always horny when it was hot. In fact, I found it extremely hard to keep my hand off my cock in the summer. For four or five months, when the temperatures were unrelenting, I wanked myself morning noon and night. If I wasn't wanking, I was having sex. And, if I was in a situation where I couldn't do either, I was thinking about it.

I excused myself from the table, paid for my shake and walked out into the full blast of summer heat. I looked up and down the road deciding what to do, then without having made a conscious decision, I found myself walking back to the college. I looked at my watch. It was five-thirty. The final classes for the day would have just finished, and everyone would be making their way home. I had no idea what time Terry finished, but I guessed there was only one way to find out.

I walked through the corridor of the main building toward the back of the college. I had one purpose in mind, and my heart was beating ten to the dozen. I sure was taking a chance. *What if Dominic had been wrong? What if I ended up with a fat lip, or even worse, what if he reported me?* My pace slowed as these thoughts flashed through my head. Suddenly, I wasn't so sure.

Nevertheless, I kept walking. I had to find out. I couldn't stop thinking about that semi-naked body, that bubble butt, that bulge at the front of his shorts, that smile. And I wasn't so bad either. My body was slim but defined. I had played a lot of sports in high school, and I was in pretty good shape. I was good looking, thanks, I think, to my Italian father. I wasn't as hairy as Terry was, but I had a light covering of hair across the top of my chest and a thick bush growing above my seven and half-inch cock.

I pushed through the door leading to the back of the college, and once again my body was exposed to the heat of the late-summer afternoon. I looked around the empty basketball courts and under the trees at the edge of the college where students liked to eat. Everyone had gone; probably to the nearest swimming pool or to the beach. My eyes then came to rest on the gardener's shed. It was tucked away in a shade covered corner at the far end of the college. There was still smoke coming from the incinerator so that was a good sign. I assumed he wouldn't have gone home and left that burning.

I approached the shed nervously. My heart was pounding and a lump had formed in my throat. Another, however, was rapidly forming in my jeans. I licked my dry lips and raised a hand to knock. Then I stopped. The door was ajar. I poked my head in through the gap, but it was too dim for me to see anything clearly. My eyes hadn't yet adjusted from the bright light outside.

"Can I help you?"

I jumped and spun around.

It was Terry. He was still wearing his shorts and boots, but had put his sleeveless shirt back on. Fortunately, it was still unbuttoned and I could clearly see his well-formed pecs and defined abs, and the dark hair that covered his torso from the base of his neck to the top of his tiny shorts.

I had to think quickly. As I struggled to concoct a valid reason for snooping around his shed, Terry walked into the shed.

"I thought there might be a toilet in here. I have to go." I followed Terry in.

"What's wrong with the student toilets?" he asked.

I gulped. "Er, these were closer."

Terry shot me a strange look then nodded toward the back of the shed.

"Through there."

I thanked him and disappeared into the back room where I was surprised to find not only a toilet but a small shower cubicle as well. I suppose it made sense. He did some pretty dirty things in the course of his day. I hoped he'd do some dirty things with me, too.

I lifted the lid and got my semi-hard cock out. I aimed it at the bowl and waited. I didn't really have to go, but I had to make it look good. Eventually a few drops of golden piss dribbled out, which I shook off before stuffing my cock back into my jeans. As I turned to step out of the toilet, I saw that Terry was now in the back room and in the middle of getting undressed. He had his back to me and had already removed his shirt and shoes and was about to take his shorts off.

I couldn't believe my eyes. I held my breath, hardly daring to breathe in case I broke the spell. As he bent over to pull his shorts off, his milky white ass cheeks parted slightly, allowing me to see the nest of dark hair that grew around his asshole. My cock immediately became as hard as steel, straining against the fabric of my jeans, eager to be freed. As he stepped out of them, first one foot and then the other, the muscles in his buttocks tensed then eased, and I could just make out his low-hanging balls through his legs, swinging each time he moved. Then he pulled off his socks, again allowing me to perv at that inviting hole, ringed with thick black fur, teasing me and tempting me to throw caution to the wind and just bury my face in it.

"You finished in there?" Terry said as he stood up.

I didn't have time to answer before he turned and caught me standing there gawking at him. His eyes dropped immediately to the throbbing cock, clearly defined, in my jeans. A sly smile crossed his lips.

"See something you like, mate?" he asked walking toward me.

I swallowed a thick glob of spit that had collected in the back of my throat and was about to answer, yes, when I felt him rub the back of his hand down the length of my stiff tool.

"Why don't we let the old fella out, hey?"

I nodded, still not believing that this was happening. I looked down and watched his hands unbutton my jeans and pull the zipper down. At the same time, I was drawn to the head of his cock just poking out of the foreskin, red and shiny, revealing more and more of itself as his cock hardened.

Terry pulled my jeans and jocks down, enabling my cock to spring free and almost hitting him in the face. I lifted my feet up, so he could remove them completely, and at the same time, I pulled my sweaty T-shirt off. Now we were both naked.

"Did you lock the door?" I asked.

"Don't worry. It'll be fine."

He leaned in to kiss me, our sweaty bodies coming together as he put his full lips on mine. I closed my eyes and concentrated on the feel of his firm but tender kisses; on his hot breath filling my mouth and brushing the side of my cheek; and on the sensation of our cocks, squashed and rubbing against each other as we kissed.

His lips planted a trail of kisses across my cheek, soft and gentle, before stopping momentarily at the place where my jaw met my ear. The touch of his lips and sensation of his tongue sent volts of electricity coursing through my body. I held his body close to mine, needing something to hang on to in case I passed out in the throes of ecstasy. His torso was solid, and as I ran my hands over his back, I could feel every furrow and rise created by his muscles. I could feel them moving beneath my palms as he moved, taking his lips from my ear to my neck, kissing me, licking me and creating more and more powerful shivers.

He returned briefly to my lips and kissed me again. Then he took hold of my bottom lip between his teeth and gently bit it. I grimaced slightly, but the small taste of pain only excited me more. Then I felt his tongue licking my chin, licking the small patch of hair between my pecs, my navel. I felt his thick, flat tongue then lick my pubic hair, lick it until the whole bush was coated in his saliva.

I ran my hands through the hair on his head, subtly pushing it down so that he would take my cock into his mouth and suck it. My balls were aching, and my cock was begging to be deep throated. I wanted to feel him take my hard cock into his mouth and suck it. I wanted to be in him, to give him something of me. I wanted to empty my full balls into his mouth and have him swallow my load.

As if reading my thoughts, Terry licked the swollen head of my cock. I felt my cock twitch and the muscles around my arse tighten. He licked the head again, keeping his tongue on my cock until he had coated the entire shaft with saliva. Then he took the whole length into his mouth, looking up at me with a definite twinkle in both eyes.

I moaned and writhed against the wall.

"Oh yeah. Swallow my cock. Take it all. Take it all!"

It was impossible for Terry to reply with my cock down the back of his throat, but his panting and the little moans he could let escape let me know he was enjoying himself. Then as he sucked my engorged meat, I felt him stick a finger into my sweaty asshole.

"Ohhhh, fuck yeahhh," I cried. "Finger that sweaty hole. Finger it good."

I began rocking back onto his finger then forward into his mouth. Both of them felt so good. I took my hands off Terry's head and brought one hand up to my nipples and used the other one to balance myself. While he fingered my hungry hole and sucked my cock, I took turns to play with my nipples; tweaking and pulling on them, getting myself even more aroused than I thought possible.

"I'm gonna cum," I shouted.

Terry pulled his finger out of my hole and backed away from my cock, gripping it just below the base to stop me from erupting jism all over him.

"No, not yet. I want to fuck you. I want us to come at the same time."

I was annoyed for a split second, but thought that Terry's idea sounded horny. It would be nice to come at the same time as he did.

"Come here," he said taking me by the hand.

We went out into the main room of the shed where he kept the lawn mower and the tins of paint and kerosene. There were tools everywhere and dirty rags lying around on the bench tops and on the floor.

"Get up there," Terry said, helping me onto the workbench.

As he walked over to a set of shelves on the back wall, I breathed in the oily, earthy smell of the room. It was a masculine, horny smell, and it was embedded in the very bench I was sitting on.

"Never be without some of this," Terry said returning from the shelf with a giant jar of Vaseline. "Never know when you're going to need it."

I leaned back on my elbows, allowing Terry a full view of my hairy, pink asshole.

"That's right,' he said, pushing me back against the wall. "Now let me have a look."

I leaned back as far as I could go, gripping the backs of my knees and pulling them toward me, giving Terry a full view of my twitching hole. He spread my cheeks further apart and rubbed my rosebud with the calloused pad of his thumb. I squirmed beneath its touch and tried my hardest to push myself onto it, wanting more than anything to have any part of him inside me. Terry laughed. Even in the dim light, I could see a sparkle in his eye and wondered what he was up to. Whatever it was I couldn't wait.

He bent down until his nose was nearly touching my love bud. I heard him inhale deeply, breathing in the smell of my sweaty hole. He nuzzled it with his nose, sniffing the whole time, getting the scent of my sweaty crack on the tip of his nose. Then I felt his moist tongue probing it and flicking it, making me shudder. He began to force his tongue in through the puckered muscle, and as I relaxed, he was able to get more and more of it in.

"Mmmmmmm," he moaned, obviously loving every second of eating my arse out.

His slurps and moans filled my ears, and I was once again on the verge of coming. But I didn't want to yet. Terry wanted us to come at the same time, and since he was doing all the work, it was the least I could for him; but I didn't know how much longer I could hold off. His every touch was making me want to explode all over him. I took my fingers off my nipples.

As Terry continued to eat my hole, I stretched forward and grabbed his head. It was already buried in my hairy chute, but I wanted him right up there. I wanted to feel his tongue licking me on the inside. I pulled his face so close to my hungry fuck tunnel that I felt sure he must have been suffocating, and then I began to ride it. I could feel his tongue licking the inside of my hole. It was the deepest anyone had gone inside me, but I wanted it to go deeper.

He pulled away, panting for breath and stood up. He kissed me again, and I could smell the musty stink of my hole on his face. I liked the smell and wondered what his ass smelled like.

Without saying a word, he picked up a screwdriver that was lying next to me and showed it to me. I noticed the handle was thick and had a rounded head. Without speaking, Terry dipped the rounded end into the jar of Vaseline then rubbed it against my quivering pucker. I closed my eyes to revel in the sensation of having the implement so close to penetrating me, though not before I caught Terry glancing up at me.

"Do it," I whispered breathily, needing to feel something more substantial than his tongue inside me.

He pushed the handle of the screwdriver against the puckered entrance to my ass. I could feel the muscles temporarily resist it, but he pushed the tool through, invading me with the plastic handle of his well-used screwdriver. He began thrusting it in and out, and I wriggled on it, barely noticing that he had slipped a second screwdriver handle in. All I knew was that it felt wild. He looked around him, at the collection of tools on the wall, and left the screwdrivers hanging out of my arse to go and get a different tool. He returned with a pair of hedge clippers. They had rubber handles but were not rounded. I gulped as he covered one handle with Vaseline. Although I was a little worried about how thick they were, I was also very excited.

Removing the two screwdrivers, he slipped a couple of fingers in and massaged my hole for a minute or so, giving his rigid meat a couple of tugs as he fingered me. Then, when he thought I was ready, he pressed the end of the hedge clipper handle against my asshole and wriggled it around, inching it further into my eager boy-cunt bit-by-bit. I held my breath as he slowly worked the thick handle in through the band of muscle. The thought of him fucking me with his dirty tools was driving me wild. My hole was becoming so relaxed he could have slipped the whole thing in there, and I wouldn't have cared.

Once the handle was in, he began to gently jiggle it around. It felt enormous inside me. I had taken some pretty big cocks in my time but this was the thickest thing I'd ever had up there. Terry kept looking up at me, smiling and checking that I was still enjoying myself.

"Fuck me," I said finally. "I want to feel you in me."

Terry pulled the hedge clippers carefully out of my hole and put them on the bench next to me. Gripping his monstrous, meaty member with one hand, he slowly fed all eight inches into my welcoming fuck-tunnel.

"Ahhhhh, that's it," I groaned, lying back along the length of the bench.

Terry began to thrust his steel-hard schlong into my well-lubed and lovingly stretched boy-pussy. My anal muscles closed around his pole, riding it and wanting to milk it of every last drop of cream he had. Both of us had been worked up into a state of near-frenzy by our afternoon in his shed, and every time he slid that beautiful organ into me, then out again, I wanted to pull him in even deeper. Every now and again, he removed his whole cock before plunging it in deeper and harder, but even then I wanted more of it.

"How's that?" he asked as his thrusts began to get faster.

"Harder," I begged. "Fuckin' rape my hole. I want that fucking cock so bad."

Terry didn't reply. He didn't have to. I could feel his strong hands grip my hips, and his thrusts becoming harder and more powerful. I gripped my rock hard staff and began jerking it in time with Terry's thrusts.

"That's it," I said again. "Take it. It's yours."

My words seemed to encourage Terry, and soon he was pounding my chute like a madman. The whole bench shook as he rammed his rigid rod up my red-raw fuck tunnel. I had to hold onto the edge of the wooden bench with one hand to stop myself from being fucked right across the bench and over the other side. My other hand worked furiously on my veiny cock, jerking it as roughly as Terry was fucking me. My body was covered in sweat, and I could feel sweat from Terry's brow splashing on my stomach and thighs as he powered into me.

"Oh fuck, I'm gonna cum," he shouted. "I'm gonna flood your hole, man."

I jerked my cock harder and harder, feeling the cream rise and wanting to shoot at exactly the same time as Terry.

"Tell me when," I said, watching Terry's face as it tensed then contorted.

"Ohhhhhh fuckkkk … Here I go!"

He buried his bone as deeply as it would go up my juicy fuck-hole and let a hot spray of thick man juice coat my insides. I could feel his thick meat explode inside me, and it triggered my own eruption of creamy man paste all over my chest and stomach, with sticky ropes of it lying delicately across the wiry hairs of my pubic bush.

Terry fell forward onto me, leaving his cock inside, and rested there for a few minutes while he caught his breath.

"That was so fucking red-hot," he panted.

"You're not wrong," I replied, stroking his hair as his head moved up and down on my chest in rhythm with my breathing. "I have never been fucked like that before."

Terry leaned up and kissed me long and hard. His tongue licked my top lip and then my tongue, exploring my mouth with as much fervor as he had done when he was just starting on me. I could still feel small drops of sweat landing on my face as we kissed, but I didn't mind. They were only there because of our fucking.

"Well, any time you want to go again," he said.

Then he stood back from me. I felt his cock pop out of my throbbing ring, and as I sat up, I could see that it was still semi-hard.

"Want a shower?" he asked as he helped me down off the bench.

"Sure," I agreed, noticing a small pool of cum and sweat on the bench where my arse had been.

I followed him into the tiny bathroom area. My eyes stayed glued to his muscular butt as he walked. He turned on the taps, although only a little warm water was needed just to take the chill off the cold water. Together, we stepped under the cool spray, embracing immediately and kissing again as the water washed the sweat and smell of sex off us.

"Promise we'll do this again," I whispered as he nuzzled my neck.

"Like I said, any time you want. You were hot. Letting me use those tools on your hole really got me horny."

"Got me horny, too."

I grabbed the soap from the small white soap holder on the wall in front of me and began soaping Terry's back. I wondered if tomorrow would be too soon to catch up again.

"Maybe next time we can do something with the lawn-mower," Terry suggested.

I stood behind him aghast, unable to imagine how such a thing was possible, especially since my cock was going to be involved.

He looked over his shoulder and saw the shocked look on my face. "Got you!" he laughed.

THE NOVICE
By Justin Shepherd

After a slow but spectacular journey through the mountains, the train was moving with unusual speed, following the fast-flowing river through a vast expanse of farmland. The river, a travel mate for many rugged miles, now seemed engaged with the train in a race to the coast, some seventy miles away. I would not be seeing the finish line of this race, for as the train rounded a curve, the Benedictine Abbey of St. Anselm, my destination, appeared in the distance. The magnificent elevation of the abbey church, the massive bell tower soaring upward from the main cloister, the ordered assortment of buildings accommodating the monastery's work of education, hospitality and agriculture, the peaceful surroundings and picturesque hilltop venue all combined to suggest a kind of union of heaven and earth. How privileged I felt to be entering such a well-ordered way of life, and how glad I was to be leaving behind the tribulations, anxieties and uncertainties of the past.

Only a handful of passengers disembarked at the town of St. Anselm, and the train lost no time in resuming its journey to the coastal city. It was good to be outdoors and on my feet again, and I decided that I would walk the seven miles to the abbey. It seemed a much better way to make one's approach to such a place than by taxicab. As I climbed the steep ascent, I reflected upon my life's journey and the tortuous route that had brought me here. I was born in a small town, to parents whose little wealth was gained by hard work. I have always been something of an introvert, easily overtaken by feelings of unease at large gatherings. Neither of my parents understood me or spent much time with me, and my only memories of my brother are of his cruelty and belligerence toward me, so that even within my family I felt like an outsider. My imagination provided most of my friends throughout my childhood years, and I would often be absorbed in a paradisiacal, euphoric world of my own devising.

This self-made bliss came to a sudden end with the onset of adolescence, a lonely and desperate struggle, a protracted nightmare from which there was little relief until I entered college at age nineteen. During the fitful passage through my early teen years, my mind was as misshapen as my body, and the new powers welling up within me seemed only a source of more confusion. The endless abuse and hatred I endured at the hands of a large assortment of schoolyard thugs and bullies did much to obliterate what little remained of my childhood fantasy world. Three years of college was a strong antidote to all that, and now at age twenty-one, I had no reservations about committing all of my life's energies and abilities to the Abbey of St. Anselm, whose gates I was now entering.

Three months after my arrival, I was growing accustomed to the rhythms of monastic life as learned in the novitiate, the year-long probationary period that is entered upon admission to the monastery. I cannot say the transition to this life was as easy as I'd expected, and there were many aspects of my former life that I missed, most notably its freedom and spontaneity. Every hour of every day was mapped out, and as a novice I was closely watched, and the tasks I was assigned were often less than desirable. But I was trying hard to fit in, to make a good impression, and to learn the way of life that I had freely chosen and earnestly desired.

What I had not expected was the presence of Brother Matthew McGinley, who entered the abbey at roughly the same time as I, making us classmates in the novitiate. It's difficult to understand the timing of such things. Where had someone like Matt been during my teen years, when I so desperately needed a friend, someone to stand by me, to do things with, to talk to, to grow with; or during my college years, when I finally began to find myself and to experience the joys of friendship, but with the transience and pressures of college life, none of them had lasted more than a couple of years. Now, in monastic life, I was learning to love everyone in a general way, but no one individually. And yet the more time I spent with Matt – and he and I spent much time together as we were both novices – the more I sensed I was falling in love with him. It would be more proper to refer to him as Brother Matthew, but this formality was reserved for certain audiences. To me he was just Matt, even as I was Justin to him.

Matt was a year older than I and had just graduated from Yale. I still had one year left of my undergraduate program, had attended a not very distinguished state university, and had not achieved stellar marks. Matt was the object of much attention and admiration in the abbey, outshining me in every way, so I considered it a great fortune when it became clear that he favored me above all the other suitors for his friendship. Unaccustomed as I was either to great fortune or to close friendship, I was unsure how to respond to Matt, especially in a monastic environment, yet everything about him drew me closer. He had short-cropped black hair that set off his magnificent blue eyes, which melted my heart every time they met mine. He had a radiant smile made all the more beautiful by his perfect white teeth, and his eyes took on a brilliant sparkle with every smile. By Vespers each day he had a five-o'clock-shadow that beautifully accentuated the masculine qualities of his model-like face. His slender body was perfectly proportioned to his athletic build, and whether dressed in his black Benedictine habit or in work clothes, the sight of him unfailingly sent my mind wandering in all sorts of forbidden areas.

Matt's affection toward me did not go unnoticed at the abbey, and the resentment felt by many made itself known in ways that were none too subtle. Every wrong move I made, every annoying tendency I had, the slightest infraction of either the letter or the spirit of the Rule of St. Benedict was instantly complained of to the novice master, who was quick to make each complaint known to me. My earlier years had taught me a certain resilience, so much of this bounced off into space. I was confident in my vocation and encouraged by the many texts I was reading that described the trials and upsets of those who were committed to the religious life. My earlier years had also sharpened my skills at discerning people who were best avoided, or at least not messed with. Chief among these was the third member of our novice class, a certain Brother Peter, an obese, sly man who flaunted his being from New York City at every opportunity. His condescension, his very presence, disgusted me. But there were also professed members of the community, both senior and junior, who seemed to dislike me if for no other reason than Brother Matthew liked me. I was especially wary of Brother Maurus, a surly and abrasive monk whose evil eyes were always upon me, and who went running to the novice master like a tattletale schoolboy with reports of such pettiness that I could scarcely believe it when they were brought to my attention. Fortunately, there were plenty of other monks in the community who inspired me and whose lives provided a model for the kind of monk I hoped one day I would be.

My passion for Matt intensified with the passing of each month, to the point where it was becoming a serious distraction that was beginning to consume me night and day. Only in sleep was my mind released from him, and even then he was probably the subject of any number of dreams. One day in mid-March, during the season of Lent, which I always found long and depressing, Matt and I were assigned to paint the large suite in the guesthouse. The suite was far more luxuriously appointed than the other humble rooms within the guesthouse, and it was reserved for guests who were either very wealthy (and whose wealth was generously shared with the abbey) or distinguished by their achievements or place in society. It gave me a certain thrill to be alone with Matt in this fabled section of the guesthouse, and I savored every minute of it and every word of our lively conversation, which neither St. Benedict nor the novice master would have sanctioned.

My hand was not as steady as Matt's with the roller, and he noticed it. Approaching me from behind, he took hold of my arm as I was painting.

"Try this movement," he said as he gently guided my arm. "Slow and steady, straight up and down. Picture a ruler against the wall, and follow the line perfectly." I surrendered my arm to his, and whether consciously or not, I moved my body closer to his. I could feel his warmth, his closeness, and I felt as if a current of electricity had enlivened every nerve in my body. I stared at the softly-colored wall, its fresh paint glistening in the light of the day. I was too scared to turn my head in any direction, least of all to my right, which would mean meeting Matt's eyes at a range closer by far than ever before. Suddenly, I felt his face next to mine, followed by a kiss to my right cheek. I stopped moving my roller, and pressed my face toward his, feeling the beginnings of the five-o'clock-shadow that I so often noticed at Vespers. Responding to this, Matt drew his left arm around me and slowly stroked my chest as I closed my eyes and continued to caress his face with mine. His hand moved further down my body, coming to rest over my cock, which was now straining against the denim of my jeans. He cupped his hand around my erect piece and gently squeezed, as I slowly turned my head to the right and our lips met. "You know I love you," he whispered. "I've always loved you."

"I can't tell you how much I've wanted you, wanted this," I whispered back, my paint roller returned to the tray, our eyes now looking directly into each others'. "I've tried to keep my mind on other things, but it's no good," I confessed. "There's so much here that puts me on edge. It's only you who's kept me from drowning in it all."

"Same with me," Matt owned. "Sometimes I just don't know what to do. We'll figure something out. God knows where it will take us." The sound of a heavy footprint that we both recognized as Brother Peter's was heard approaching, and we quickly resumed our tasks before he entered the suite. Our first intimate moment was thus brought to an abrupt end, but there would be many more that would last much longer.

I had considerable training in music, and soon after I entered the novitiate, the abbot had appointed me as suborganist under Father Norbert, whose skill as an organist was legendary. There was a fine pipe organ in the abbey church, and one of my duties – one of few that I enjoyed and looked forward to – was playing the organ for *Compline*, the last service of the day, which took place in the late evening. That evening as the monks entered the church for the service, I played a quiet but impassioned improvisation on a favorite Gregorian chant, *Ubi caritas et amor*, *Deus ibi est* – where charity and love abide, there is God. When Matt entered, I felt flushed and instantly added a deep sixteen-foot pedal Bourdon and the two-foot *flute-a-cheminée*, lending a hauntingly full-bodied sound to my subdued yet bewitching prelude on a chant tune that everyone recognized while understanding none of its significance for Matt and me.

As I lay in my bed wide awake that night, I stared at an icon on my wall depicting the face of Christ. His eyes stared at me from the picture, but I sensed more understanding than judgment in his gaze. Comforted by the sight, I repeated the words of Psalm 71 that had been chanted at one of the services in the abbey church that day, "Go not far from me, O God; my God, haste thee to help me."

Three months had passed since the painting of the suite in the guesthouse, and my life was becoming ever more complicated. First profession of vows was only two months away, though I was nowhere near as certain now as I was ten months ago that I would make it to that service. And if I was accepted into first vows, I knew that life among the junior professed would offer nowhere near the opportunities of the novitiate for discrete encounters, for our work assignments as novices often sent us to the furthest reaches of the abbey precincts. Matt and I had entered into what was known in the monastery as a "particular friendship," and while every effort was made to keep these secret, there are in fact no secrets in tightly closed communities such as monasteries. There was plenty of whispering, some of it benign, some of it vicious, all of it menacing. But, we were not deterred and privately rejoiced in this outlet we had found for the deepest longings of our hearts, the truest expression of our humanity, and it must be said, the most forbidden.

The end of June was approaching, and one day Matt and I were assigned to work in the hay loft of the cow barn at the south end of the abbey farmlands. Our job was to move baled hay from the loft on to a flatbed trailer drawn by a tractor, and unload the bales of hay again in an area where feedstock for the dairy cattle was kept. Once in the hayloft, the sweet, musky smell of the hay, the safe enclosure of the loft and the warmth of the summer day formed a potent aphrodisiac for both of us. We drew our bodies close to one another in a tight embrace, and before long we were removing each others' work clothes. In blissful nakedness, we rolled on loose hay that covered the heavily oiled wooden floor, and used baled hay for support for any activity that required it. Our bodies glistened with sweat as we became a tangled union of limbs and other rigid body parts, our hearts pounding a percussive accompaniment to our dance. Suddenly and without a second's warning, the hatch of the loft flew open and our bodies froze in terror. Brother Maurus, looking victorious and imperious in his Napoleonic stance at the entrance to the loft, lost no time in passing sentence on us.

"God have mercy on your souls," he shouted mockingly. "I always knew it! I always knew it, and now I finally have proof. You'll be out of here before dawn tomorrow, and about time, too." With that, he turned tail and pounded down the stairs with none of the silence that he had deployed to ascend them. Still naked, Matt and I watched Brother Maurus charge away from the barn in the direction of the abbey, and we knew that it was all over. We got dressed and strangely enough, carried on with our assigned task, returning to the abbey only when it was completed. I went to my room with a sense of foreboding and found an envelope taped to the door. It was from Father Bernard, the novice master, with an instruction that I should report to him before Vespers that afternoon. I showered and changed into my habit and followed the instruction. I knocked on the door of his office, hiding my fear in the same way I had during the worst of my schooldays.

"Enter," came the none-too-inviting voice from the other side of the door.

"A blessing, Father," I said dutifully.

"*Benedicite*," Father Bernard responded in Latin just as dutifully. "Take a seat," he said coldly. "I'm sure you know why I've asked you here," he said, his tone of voice sounding anything but pastoral. I didn't feel the need to respond, since he was sure I knew. "Do you have anything to say?" he demanded.

"About what?" I asked, possibly recklessly.

"Don't trifle with me, Brother Justin. The report that came to me earlier today is serious. I ask you again, what have you got to say for yourself?"

The question wasn't quite the same, but I wasn't about to quibble with Father Bernard, who was unapproachable at the best of times, and the present moment could hardly be so described. "I don't know what you want me to say, Father. I'm a man, and things happen. I can't explain it, especially not now."

"Well, I'm afraid you won't have too many more chances. I've spoken with the abbot and the prior about this, and they leave the disposition of it in my hands. I've told them I thought it would be best to terminate your candidacy here and ask you to leave immediately. If we knew the identity of the other person who was with you, he'd be facing the same consequences. You can do the right thing and tell me, or do the wrong thing and keep it to yourself."

I paused a moment, feeling as if I'd been violently but mercifully awakened from a bad dream. Collecting myself, I drew the strength to respond.

"I hope I never know what's right and what's wrong as clearly as you do, Father. Is a departure tomorrow morning soon enough for you?"

"That will be fine," he said, completely unaffected by the preamble to my question.

I left the novice master's office and returned to my room, my head spinning like a top. I skipped Vespers and dinner, which was not allowed, but I no longer felt bound by any such rules. I went for a long walk in the woods on the abbey property, trying to piece together the scrambled puzzle, which was my life. I decided to attend *Compline*, if even just to have a last chance to play the abbey organ, which I had come to love. As a prelude, I slowly and quietly played through Henry Purcell's setting of the funeral sentence, "Thou knowest, Lord, the secrets of our heart. Shut not thy merciful ears unto my prayer." I was certain that no one was familiar with the piece, and even if they were, it was doubtful that any of them would have joined the dots. What I was not certain about was whether there were any "merciful ears" to be either shut or opened "unto my prayer," but I played the piece in the belief that there were.

Matt came into the church looking worried and upset. I hadn't seen him since we parted company after the day's work, and I sensed that he was unaware of the outcome of today's events. I tried to enter into the spirit of resignation and reconciliation that characterizes *Compline*, in many ways my favorite service of the daily cycle, but to little avail. At this moment, I wasn't even sure if I believed in God, any God. Late that evening, I told Matt what had happened, being careful not to let anyone see us talking, for I was well aware of how Brother Maurus had construed things, and that version of it would have spread with the speed of lightning throughout the abbey, and I was not inclined to add anything to the story. Matt was clearly shocked by it all, and I wasn't sure what his plan was. I was too busy devising my own in what little time I was given.

"Don't leave without telling me where you're going," he pleaded, the usual look of happiness gone from his face, which was nonetheless beautiful for it.

"I won't," I assured him and went back to my room.

Early the next morning, I was driven to the train station by Friar Damian, a senior member of the community who was often given tasks that no one else wanted. I was not seen off by anyone, having completed the few formalities of departure the evening before. I had slipped a note under Matt's door giving him the address in Portland where I would be for at least the next few weeks. I promised that I would write him, adding a concern that the letter might not reach him if my name was seen on the envelope.

As the train pulled out of St. Anselm station and gathered speed, I rested my head against the window and watched the passing landscape, none of it registering. I felt as if my soul had been torn from my body, that my one chance for happiness and fulfillment in this life had been sacrificed. My newfound faith in love and friendship was as shaken as my much older faith in God, and I wondered if faith itself was anything but a sham.

I stumbled about in Portland taking tenuous but firm steps toward piecing together my life. It was my second day in town, and I was acutely aware of the fact that I didn't know anyone here, apart from the kindly woman who ran the house where I'd taken a room until I could find a job and an apartment. Her warm smile was always a welcome sight, and today upon my return she had more than just a smile for me.

"A phone message for you here, Justin," she said. "Told him I thought you'd be back soon. He said to tell you Matt called, and he's in town. He'll wait for you at the train station."

In the time that it took her to say those words to me, my world turned from shades of gray to a rainbow of brilliant colors. I grasped both of her hands without even thinking of the act.

"When did he call?" I asked excitedly, almost hyperventilating.

"Not half an hour ago."

"Thank you. Thanks a million," I said and raced out the door, leaving the poor woman wondering what in the world was going on.

The station was bustling with the usual crowds of people, but I spotted Matt the instant I entered the concourse, and in seconds we were in each others' arms.

"I couldn't stay there another day," Matt said as we kissed each other tenderly. "I'm so glad I knew where to find you."

"Let's go somewhere where we can sit down," I said, sensing that I was on the brink of tears. "Maybe we can start over again."

"Or at least pick up where we left off," Matt responded.

I'll never fully understand what made me so sure I had a religious vocation, nor will I understand many of the people I met at the abbey. Strangely, I harbor no ill will against any of them, and in fact most of my memories of my ten months of monastic life are good ones. If nothing else, it was a rare experience. And best of all, it's the place where I met Matthew McGinley, known to me as simply Matt. God really does work in mysterious ways.

TEXTED, TEMPTED, TEASED, AND TAPED
By Logan Zachary

"Meet me in the restroom," the text message read.

Didn't Mark work? What was he thinking? I had deadlines. These hospital accounts needed bills sent out before the day was over. My work called to me.

The cell phone vibrated again.

A texted picture of Mark's hard-on straining against his white Calvin Klein's appeared. A wet spot marred the Egyptian cotton.

"Damn," I swore and pushed myself up from the desk and headed to the bathroom.

"Hey Ken, what're you doing for lunch?" Melissa asked.

I glanced at the clock. It was a few minutes after ten. "It's still pretty early."

The phone buzzed again.

"I … I ... I'll be right back." And, I raced to the bathroom.

My hand hit the door, and it swung in. My footfalls echoed in the tiled room. A metal hinge groaned as Mark emerged clad in tight briefs and a white button down shirt.

"Took your sweet time." He ran his hand down his shirt.

"I'm working …"

"Well, get busy on this," Mark grabbed the bulge in his shorts and stepped back. His thumb slipped into the waistband of his shorts and pulled them down, revealing a thick mat of dark curly hair. He backed into the stall, while he motioned for me to follow with his other hand.

My buzzing arousal swelled as I followed him in. I could feel the strain inside of my boxers. Mark's pants hung from the hook on the door as it swung closed. He slipped the bolt and reached for my fly. His fingers pulled back the flap and worked the zipper down.

I swelled to twice my size with the newly found freedom.

Mark's hand found my shaft and caressed down the length. He milked me to full erection and worked lower to my balls. My hands cupped his tight buns as my mouth found his. A slippery wetness covered my cock's tip. I could feel Mark's hand slip and spread it down along my length. A low moan escaped from my mouth, as the restroom door opened.

Mark's hand stopped in mid-stroke.

Footsteps walked past the urinal and headed toward our stall. Mark grabbed his pants and stepped into them. He knelt down and thrust a leg out from under the door as he zipped up his slacks. I followed suit, hoping my engorged flesh would shrink back to normal.

"Watch out where you are stepping, so you don't squish my contact lens," Mark said. "Thanks for helping me look, but I think we need more light in here." He smiled at me and motioned to the door.

Taking my cue, I slid the bolt gently and opened the door. I stepped out and looked up into Frank Miller's eyes. "Do you have a flashlight?" I asked.

He hesitated for a moment. "I have a lighter, would that help?" He fished into his pocket and dug around for a second. He pulled out a lighter and handed it to me.

"Thanks." I took the lighter and flicked it. A flame burst to life. I held it out in front of me and entered the stall. "Does this help?" I asked.

"I need it closer to the floor." Mark rolled his tongue around and licked his lips, then blew me a kiss. "Oh, don't move. I see it." His hand caressed along my inseam and up. "Yup, here it is. Thanks." Mark pinched my butt as he passed behind me and headed to the sink. He ran the water over his fingers and rubbed them together. His reflection winked at me.

"Here's your lighter." I offered it back to Frank, stepping between him and the mirror, so he couldn't see Mark pretending to put his lens in.

Mark blinked his eyes a few times. "I can see; it's a miracle."

I rolled my eyes and headed back to my desk. My chair wasn't even warm, when my cell phone buzzed again. Another text message.

"Meet me in the supply closet."

My fingers spelled out, "I can't," but the phone vibrated again.

"U can & U will."

Another picture appeared. A thick bush of hair poked out over the Calvin Klein waistband. The wet spot doubled in size and revealed the tip of his cock.

I pushed up from my seat, knowing this wouldn't stop until Mark was satisfied. The supply room housed the Xerox machine and all the old patient files. As I entered the small room, the door slammed shut behind me, and the lock clicked into place.

Mark's mouth landed on mine, and his tongue sought out mine. I matched him kiss for kiss, sucking and tonguing, dueling for possession. Mark's hands worked down my body, his fingers fumbled with my belt and worked the zipper. My flesh rose and swelled again with new excitement. What was this effect this man had on me? Love? Lust? Desire? Or plain old horniness?

I humped my pelvis against his and rubbed erection to erection. My mouth was hungry for his. His leg wrapped around my hip and held me trapped against him.

Sweat rolled down my back and between my buttocks before finally being absorbed into my boxers. My arousal slipped out of the fly and brushed against Mark's hand. His fingers curled around me and squeezed. My balls pulled up along side of my shaft and threatened to release. My knees threatened to buckle, but I held back.

Mark turned his head to the side, and my mouth found his ear. My tongue slipped into the opening and explored. My lips pulled his lobe into my mouth and held him trapped. His neck tensed as I licked the salty sweat that ran down his flesh. A moan of pleasure escaped from him, as he threw his head back and savored the feelings. I pushed him back against the copier and held him there. His legs spread and opened to me. I stepped between them and drove my cock against him. His balls rolled against me. My hands grabbed his narrow hips and worked lower on his butt. I lifted him onto the copier and fumbled with his fly. His arousal made the zipper burst open and the button at the waist popped off, flying across the room. I worked his pelvis back and slipped his pants and underwear off his ass. His bare cheeks rested on the Xerox machine, and I longed to press the copy button.

A musky manly scent tickled my nostrils. I inhaled deeply and savored the smell of locker room and sex. My mouth watered in anticipation, as my fingers worked the buttons on his shirt. His sculpted chest emerged; a diamond of fur covered his upper chest and thinned down to a treasure trail. As I lowered my head to follow the road south, the doorknob rattled behind me. I stood bolt upright and fixed my clothing.

Mark struggled to stand and redressed as fast as he could.

"The door's locked." A knock came. "Is someone in there?" Frank's voice asked.

"What is he following us or something?" Mark tucked his shirt into his pants.

"I'm getting something from the files behind the door," I said, "Hang on a sec." I glanced over at Mark and saw his shirt was buttoned wrong. I pointed a finger at him and waved it up and down his body. He turned to the side and struck a pose, modeling for me.

I shook my head and pulled on a button on my shirt and then pointed to his. Mark looked down and shook his head. "He'll never notice." He fastened his belt to cover his lost button.

I shrugged and unlocked the door.

Frank peered in and waited for Mark to step away from the copier. He fumbled a handful of papers at him. "I need these copied before lunch."

My hand covered my crotch. I was sure Frank could see my aroused state and smell the man sweat and sex in the close space. Mark raced past me, and I slowly backed out of the room. My burning face avoided everyone as I stiff-legged my way back to my desk.

Before I could sit down, my cell phone buzzed again. I resisted the urge to take it out of my pocket. A wet spot soaked through my boxers and threatened to stain my slacks. The cell vibrated against my erection. I felt more pre-cum ooze down my shaft. I was so close, I closed my eyes and held my breath.

The phone finally stopped, and I exhaled.

Frank walked by and paused by my desk. "Are you okay? You look a little flustered. Your hair's all messed up, and your clothes look rumpled."

"Thanks for the fashion critique."

"I didn't mean to insult you. I just wanted to see if everything was okay."

"I'm fine." My erection disappeared, and the wet spot stuck to my hairy leg. Frank had that effect on many people.

* * * * *

Mark stopped at my desk on the way to lunch. "I have an idea. Follow me."

We walked through the hospital lobby toward the cafeteria. As we passed the gift shop, Mark ducked under the construction zone yellow tape and motioned for me to follow him to the new chapel.

"Where are you going?" I asked.

"In here." He pointed. "The construction workers are done, and the grand opening is next week. Come on. We'll have the place to ourselves. It's perfect for a nooner."

I ducked under the tape and followed Mark. The hallway zigzagged and opened into a quiet place. Lush plants and small trees lined the area. A rock path, smooth enough for a wheelchair or walker, wound past wooden benches and metal sculptures.

A water fountain bubbled gently over stones and into the small pool. Below, goldfish swam happily around chasing the bubbles and splashing in their new home. Soft music set the atmosphere of the space – new age meets classical with a blend of environmentals.

"The hospital must've spent a pretty penny for this," Mark said, as he pulled me to the wooden bench closest to the fountain.

"Won't someone come in?" I asked, looking around the paradise.

"Nah, we're here all alone, at last."

We sat cheek to cheek, watching the fish dart around in the water. Mark's hand caressed my back. It worked lower and crossed the waistband. Gently, it slid down to the back of my pants and lingered there for a moment.

Slowly, he massaged and explored the small curve above my belt. His fingers slid down between my shirt and waistband. One finger dipped into my crease and ventured lower. He turned to face me, and I rotated enough to look into his eyes. His warm smile revealed even white teeth and an angel's smile. My hands pulled his face to mine, and our noses rubbed against each other. He turned his head one way, and I tilted the other, so our lips brushed against each other. They lingered there for a moment, and slowly, I opened my mouth and pulled his mouth onto mine. Our tongues touched and swirled around each other. He tasted like mint and sex.

His hand slid down deeper into my boxers, his smooth fingers combed through the fur on my buns. He rubbed gently, making static electricity accumulate over my bottom. Blood pounded in my temples and my loins, filling them with each heartbeat. Our bodies swiveled on the bench, each one of us threw a leg over to face each other head on. We scooted forward, pressing our knees together. I could feel the heat radiate off of his body and flow into mine.

"Alone at last," he said, as he broke our kiss.

"And hopefully, no more interruptions."

"Especially Frank." Mark's fingers worked the buttons on my shirt. They played across my chest, and my loins swelled. Working lower, his touch inflamed my flesh. Sweat broke over my body and beaded on my skin.

Mark's teeth caught my lower lip and rolled it. As the last button opened, he pulled my shirt tales out of my pants. The cotton slid over my erection and escaped from my waistband. He pulled open my shirt and ran his fingers over the hair that covered my belly. His finger explored my naval and traced my six pack. They played up to my pecs and circled my nipples. I could feel them rise and swell as he pinched them. He twisted them as if adjusting a dial, sending waves of pleasure over my body.

My hands worked his belt, and his pants spread open with the lost button. My fingers moved to his shirt and soon exposed his perfect chest. Hours in the gym fine tuned each sinewy muscle. His Calvin's waistband came into view, and my gaze followed his treasure trail south. His briefs tented in front of him as he brought my mouth to his. He pushed me back and straddled me. His pelvis drove into me as they dueled. My hands pulled his shirt over his head and tossed it to the floor. I worked his pants down over his slender hips and caught them with my foot. He kicked his shoes off as my feet worked his pants the rest of the way off. Free from them, his hairy legs opened wide, his white briefs strained against the pressure.

A wet spot spread over the white material, made it shear and see-through. The mushroom head of his shaft molded to the cotton and strained to be set free. My erection sprang free from under the boxers. My balls rolled and slipped out one of the leg opening. A cool breeze entered the fly, trying to cool my inflamed flesh. Mark straddled on top of my pelvis. His hairy legs brushed mine and static sparked. The rest of our clothes disappeared, except for our underwear.

Our kisses deepened as we rubbed against each other, hair against hair and sweat made our skin slide easily, back and forth. My cock stuck straight out of my fly, and Mark's Calvin's rode under his balls, our shafts glistened and slid length for length, inch by inch. Pre-cum flowed over our sensitive skin, adding to the sweat.

"Hey, you guys," Frank burst in, racing to our entangled bodies and skidded to a halt. His mouth opened and closed like a fish out of water. His eyes swelled in their sockets as he drank in our aroused states.

Something grew in his pants before our eyes. Mark reached up and unzipped his fly. He quickly worked his magic, and Frank's pants hit the floor in under a second. Frank stepped out of his shoes and pants as if in a trance. Moving closer, Mark pulled on his boxers, and they worked down his legs, as a massive cock swung up and slapped

Frank's belly. His hairy balls dangled low. I couldn't take my eyes off of his erection. It was the biggest and thickest penis I had ever seen. Porn stars would bow in his presence.

Another step closer, and Frank walked out of his underwear.

Mark grasped his erection and guided him onto the bench with us. Frank's balls brushed across my face, and the hair tickled my lips. His cock slid back and forth in Mark's hand.

I arched my neck as my tongue licked one testicle. Frank's whole body went rigid, as he froze in place. My lips pulled one ball into my mouth. My teeth and tongue rolled the orb around and around. A low guttural moan escaped from deep inside him. I tried to swallow and pull the dangling sac in. Frank thrust his pelvis forward and Mark clamped down on his member. Frank threw his head back and bucked against both of us.

My mouth searched for his other ball and tried to take both in, but they were too large. Mark bowed forward and licked the opening of Frank's cock. A gush of creamy pre-cum dripped down his shaft, and across his hairy balls into my mouth. Salty and sweet, mixed with man sweat.

Frank's hips jerked, and his balls sprang out of my mouth and landed on my chin and rolled off over the wiry bristles. His legs relaxed, and his butt landed on my face. My nose drilled into his crack.

I opened my mouth and my tongue sought out a tight opening. The puckered muscle tensed, pinching tightly closed, but my tongue wouldn't be denied access. It drilled in and broke through. Frank's ass opened up, and he rode my tongue, pressing down hard and spreading his cheeks wider. Mark's mouth opened and sucked Frank's length in down to his balls. Our chins rubbed against each other as we ate Frank.

Frank's body didn't know what to do. He rocked back and forth as if in a seizure of pleasure. My hands grabbed his hips and helped rock his body, faster, faster. Once the rhythm was set, my fingers crawled up and tickled his sides. Frank's legs propelled him from our bench, and he seemed to land like a gold medal gymnast.

Mark smiled down at me and crawled up to suck on my erection. He pushed his butt up in the air, like a cat in heat.

Frank saw the invitation and took it. He moved behind Mark's ass, spat into his hand and lubed up his massive dick. He knelt on the wood and pressed his cock against the tight opening. Mark gasped as he pushed inside. His gasp allowed my cock to drive further down his throat.

My hands grasped Mark's head and kept it in place over my dick. As Frank drove into Mark, his arm worked around his narrow hips. His massive fingers combed through his bush and finally found Mark's cock. It curled around like an anaconda seeking his prey and started to jack him off. His pelvis thrusts matched his hands pull.

Mark moaned with pain or pleasure, the vibration descended down my cock and filled my balls. They rattled from side to side and started to rise up to my throbbing shaft. I could hear Frank plow into Mark, and Mark's pleasure flowcd over into me. My ass tightened up, as the spasm burst from deep in my pelvis and exploded out of my dick. A thick wave of hot cream filled Mark's mouth as he swallowed. His butt cheeks clamped down as Frank drove into him one last time.

Frank's orgasm filled Mark and slammed into his prostate. The volcanic eruption triggered off Mark's, setting his to climax with Frank's hand's next stroke.

I felt the splatter of hot cum shoot across my hairy legs and run down the sides. Another spasm of pleasure shot out of my cock and filled Mark's mouth with a second round. My head flopped back on the bench, my body spent.

I could feel Mark's body relax on top of me, and Frank, still inside him, added his weight. All three of us basked in the glow of the moment, our bodies still overly sensitive to any touch or movement. Frank finally removed himself from Mark and looked for his underwear. He stepped into them and bent to find his pants.

Mark sat up smiling, "Best lunch I've ever had. We should've thought of inviting Frank sooner." He rolled off me, and I finally sat up.

Our clothes were scattered across the floor like a tornado had hit. Frank hurried himself as he retrieved the articles and handed them to us.

Mark grabbed his briefs and turned them the right side out. "Frank, what did you want? You burst in here, like you were on fire."

Frank stopped and stared over our heads. "Oh shit."

"His flames of desire burned us all." Mark laughed.

I froze in place and slowly turned in the direction of Frank's stare.

Nothing was in the room.

I glanced back at the fountain, no one had entered. "What is it, Frank?" I finally asked.

Slowly, his arm rose and pointed up to the ceiling.

Mark and I followed his finger. A camera hung down from the ceiling. The red light flashed on and off just below the lens.

Mark stood and bowed. His still semi-hard penis waved with him.

"I don't understand," I said.

"They were filming prayer time in the chapel for an after-lunch meditation today," Frank gasped.

"I'm sure no one even knew about it," Mark said.

The music in the chapel stopped for a moment, and a male voice said, "Today's broadcast will be replayed again at five, six, and ten o'clock. God's blessings."

"It's being sent city wide for the cable access channel," Frank said.

"My mom watches that," Mark said.

My heart sank. "So, does mine."

Mark grabbed my hand and waved. "Hi Mom. Hi Mrs. Andrews. What's for supper?"

MAN TRAP
By Landon Dixon

When my company transferred me to Kansas City, I was none too thrilled. The office was smaller, the pay not much larger, and the job carried way more responsibility. And Kansas City was no New York. The upside, though, was that KC had plenty of fine golf courses, with green fees that didn't require a bank loan.

I've been a golf nut since I was old enough to swing both ways. It's fun, good exercise, and a great way to meet new people and entertain clients. So, I soon joined the Great Plains Golf and Country Club in Mission Hills. And the first day out with the sticks, I knew I'd made a good executive decision. The club superintendent showed me around, showed off his course and his crew, and I was extremely impressed with both. In fact, I'd never seen such a tanned, fit, and good looking grounds crew before in all my life, with the biggest stud on the course being the Assistant Groundskeeper Carlos Sanchez.

Carlos was a tall, muscled thirty-something with short, gleaming, black hair, deep brown eyes, a thin black mustache, and a bronze body. He was clad in a tank top and a pair of faded blue jeans, work boots and a hardhat, when I met and briefly shook hands with him, and his upper body glistened with the sweat of an honest day's work. I became so enthralled with his round, twitching butt cheeks as he strode away that the superintendent had to yell, "Fore!" in my ear to regain my attention.

I played a couple of rounds the following week and really enjoyed the layout. The course was challenging, the clubhouse had a well-stocked bar, the restaurant a talented chef, and to really whet my appetite, there was Carlos. I seemed to see him all over the place, always hard and hot at work, cutting and trimming and digging and watering, dripping with sweat and sensuality.

One time, when I turned the corner on a hidden green, I found Carlos and one of his helpers – a slim, trim straw-blond kid in his early-twenties with melt-in-your-eyes blue eyes – shoveling sand into a trap off the back of a wagon, their golden limbs rippling and glistening with exertion. They were wearing only tight shorts and T-shirts, and when they bent down to chunk sand into their shovels, I grew another club to play with.

Another time, when I was walking up to the tee box on the seventeenth, Carlos and Blondie were there ahead of me, putting on an even better show. Carlos was bare-chested, showering himself with water from a hose, the clear, cool liquid cascading down his smooth, muscular pecs and six-pack abs. Blondie was naked from the waist up, too, sparkling with moisture, his package solidly outlined against his sodden cut-off jeans. I could barely keep my eyes off the hard-body hunks, and they grinned when I sweatily clunked my drive onto the ladies' tee box. I could've really used a squirt from their hose.

A week later, I was sitting in the clubhouse waiting for a client from Independence to show up, when I was paged over the intercom. My client couldn't make it. Well, I wasn't about to let a gorgeous afternoon go to waste in a stuffy office, so I teed off by myself. It was just past noon on a Monday, which meant I had the sun-drenched, emerald-bright course virtually to myself.

On the third hole – a 500-yard par-five with a dogleg left and way too many fairway bunkers – I sailed my second shot into the bush. "Dammit!" I muttered, spanking the island-sized divot I'd excavated with my three-iron.

I trudged down the fairway a hundred yards or so and then took a sharp left into the trees. The vegetation grew denser the further I chased after my Titleist, and I was soon at a frustrated standstill, ready to machete my way back to civilization minus a ball and a stroke. Then I heard something, something other than the nattering birds and the shrubbery springing back to life – someone moaning.

My ears and other appendages instantly pricked up, and I tracked the muffled noise to a clearing in the brush. And, there I beheld something even more exciting than a hole-in-one: Carlos, his jeans down around his ankles and his chest bare, his huge, hard cock in his blond helper's mouth!

Thoughts of balls lost evaporated as I stared, wide-eyed and open-mouthed, at balls found, at the brilliant cock sucking tableau in front of me. The blond kid was kneeling on the ground in his shorts and tee, bobbing his head up and down on Carlos's veiny meat, working the stud's cock with even more intensity than he worked the course. Carlos had his hands on his hips and his head tilted back, lips leaking pleasure as his co-worker sucked him.

I dropped my iron and fumbled my pants open, my shorts, pulled out my favorite wood of all. I started tugging on my cock like Blondie was mouth-tugging on Carlos's.

"Fuck, yeah, Brett!" Carlos groaned, staring down at the young cocksucker now, brown eyes ablaze. Brett was pumping Carlos's dick with one hand, squeezing the guy's clean-shaven balls with the other, wet-vaccing shaft with his lips.

I gave up some wicked cock-strokes to the horny grounds crew, my prick swelling up and out to its full seven inches as I earnestly polished its shaft and head. Then I torqued up the cock-pressure even more when Carlos grabbed Brett's golden head and thrust his hips forward, burying his meat to the base in Brett's mouth. I swirled my sweaty palm and fingers up and down the pulsing length of my prick, as Carlos ruthlessly fucked Brett's mouth, clutching the kid's hair and driving dick down his throat. Work hard, play hardcore, was obviously the motto of this very hands-on stud.

I quickly hit sensory overload, the wind and the sun and the blistering scenery, my practiced, polishing hand, carrying me to the point where I was ready to tee off on the foliage, douse it with my joy. I pressed my balls down and wildly fisted my cock, Carlos churning his rod back and forth in Brett's slobbering mouth, hips flying, ass clenching and unclenching, relentlessly powering the both of us toward ecstasy.

My hand became a blur on my cock, and I stumbled forward with the momentum, snapping a twig in the process. I froze, hand glued to my throbbing prick, Carlos and Brett staring at me staring at them from the bush. The two men made no attempt to cover up their flagrant violation of course etiquette, Carlos's hips moving slowly now, tremendous cock oiling in and out of his boy-toy's mouth.

"H … hi … there," I said sheepishly, holding up a free hand.

They stared at me for a long, tense moment longer, and then Carlos flashed a smile and waved me forward. "How 'bout makin' it a threesome?" he asked. "It's more fun than playin' by yourself, no?"

I jumped out of the leafy hazard and into the stroke-play, double-time shuffling over to the man-loving maintenance men, pants still around my ankles, cock in-hand. And when I was within a club's length of the lusty pair, Carlos reached out and grabbed my shoulder, welcomed me to the off-course action with a long, hard, wet kiss on the lips.

His mouth felt so very good on mine, mustache tickling only a little. He slid a thick, slippery tongue into my open mouth and swirled it around, and my head spun with the overexposed passion of it all. I tongued him back, my hand on his chest, squeezing the slick, cleaved muscle, rolling and pulling on his rubbery, mocha nipples.

We tumbled our tongues together for what seemed like forever under that glaring sun, my body and brain on fire. Our passionate Frenching was only interrupted when I felt a warm hand on my stiff cock, a hot, wet mouth. I glanced down and saw Brett gripping my pole, popping its shiny mushroom head in and out of his sassy mouth.

"Yes," I groaned, watching and deep-body feeling the shaggy-headed kid twirl his pink tongue all around my hardened helmet.

"He's pretty good, huh? Trained him myself," Carlos bragged, squeezing my shoulder and tonguing my ear.

Brett grinned up at me, my cock head between his lips, tugging on my shaft with his left hand, his right working Carlos's greasy rod. He licked the super-sensitive underside of my prick, where shaft meets hood, and my knees buckled. The kid looked adorable bouncing my hard cock up and down on the end of his tongue.

Carlos drew me close, and we entwined our tongues together again, Brett licking and sucking and stroking our cocks. He'd give me the erotic benefit of his lips and tongue and mouth, kissing my slit, licking my shaft, deep-sucking my cock, his cheeks billowing and his humid breath steaming out onto my groin, the heat and the wet and the suction incredible. Then he'd shift cocks, bob his head up and down on Carlos's prick for awhile, taking the muscle stud's gleaming, oversized appendage almost down to the shaven balls before backing off, doing it all over again, his hand pumping my cock.

Back and forth Brett went, one rigid, slimy dick to the other, always sucking and stroking, sending shivers through the both of us. And, when he leaned in and gobbled up my balls, I almost teed off for the sexual second time that sultry afternoon.

"Christ, yes!" I cried, oblivious now as to where I was and who might see. We were hidden from the neighboring fairway by only a thin screen of trees and shrubs, and who knew when someone might come stumbling through in search of an errant ball, like I had. Better yet, though, right then, who the fuck cared!?

Carlos plunged his tongue down my throat, Brett plunged my cock down his throat, and I fought the rising, roiling tide of jizz in my manhandled balls. And just as I was about to flood Brett's mouth with my liquid lust, Carlos suddenly jerked his head back and asked, "How 'bout workin' with Brett?"

I blinked, pulled back from the brink. I smiled shakily at the devastatingly handsome, sweat-sheened stud, not one afraid to get his hands, and mouth, dirty. I gave Carlos's flared nipples a farewell tweak and yanked my cock out of Brett's mouth, dropped to my knees in the warm, good earth.

Brett scooched over, making room for me between his boss's quad-heavy legs. I stared at the man's monster erection, eye-to-eye, Brett kissing and biting my neck, pulling my lips onto his. We kissed and Frenched each other, Carlos towering above us, slick, twitching snake casting a fortuitous shadow over our faces. Finally, I pulled away from Brett's tongue and grasped Carlos's massive tool. His body jerked, and he yelled, "Yeah!"

His cock was heavy and smooth, clean-cut, hood-huge. I pumped the wicked organ, slowly at first, feeling it surge and struggle in my hand, then faster and faster, taking control of it. Brett stuck his tongue in my ear and swirled it around, dove his hand down between my legs and grabbed onto my cock, sending an electric charge coursing all through me.

I pressed Carlos's gorgeous cock up against his hard, flat stomach and lapped at his tightened balls. I juggled them on my tongue, mouthed his sack and tugged on it. Then I brought my tongue up his pinned, pulsating shaft in one, long, hard, wet stroke, repeated it, hard-licking the vulnerable underside of the man's mammoth erection.

He groaned and fumbled with his nipples, body arcing backwards as I pulled his lumber down and swallowed his hood. I bit into his cock head, and his body jumped. Then I clutched his ass and oh-so-slowly inched my lips down his corded shaft, 'til I had a good half of that thunder stick secured in my mouth. I looked up at him, mouthful of his manhood, and he grunted and ran trembling fingers through my hair. I pulled back a bit, started sucking up and down on his cock.

Brett tapped my shoulder, anxious for a piece of the action, and I pulled Carlos dripping wet out of my mouth and stuck him into Brett's. Brett sucked hungrily and expertly on the guy's cock, then turned him back over to me again. We passed Carlos's slickened baton back and forth between the two of us, sucking hard and quick and then sticking the other guy with the joyous task.

Carlos's work-toughened body shook as he watched Brett and me cock-suck him. I could've worshipped that beautiful man's beautiful cock all day, but he had other, even better, ideas. "Get up," he told me, as I was guiding Brett's head up and down on his pole.

I got up, and Carlos pushed me against the rear of his utility buggy parked next to a tree. He pulled me back, kicked my legs apart. "Suck his dick while I fuck him," he ordered his helper. "Time to break this new member in."

Brett scampered in between my legs and grabbed onto my dangling erection, stuffed it into his mouth. I gripped the railing on the back of the buggy, and Carlos dug a condom and a small bottle out of his shorts, then kicked them aside, totally and gloriously naked now except for his work boots. He tore the condom open and rolled it down his prick as far as it would go, then uncapped the bottle and sprayed his cock and my crack with the lube.

I groaned when Carlos fingered my tender asshole, greasing it up with the lube and the sweat off his heaving chest. Then he steered his swollen knob in between my ass cheeks, and I screamed, "Fuck me! Fuck me!" with Brett vacuuming my flaming cock with his mouth.

Carlos laughed, whacked my pale bottom with his lead-heavy dick. I bit my lip, the delicious anticipation driving me wild. Then I dropped my head and stared blindly down at Brett working my cock, feeling Carlos roughly pull my cheeks apart, his bloated cock head probe my pleasure point. The he-man shoved forward, and his hood punched through my pucker and into my anus.

My head swum and my legs shook out-of-control as Carlos gripped my hips with his strong, callused hands and pushed inexorably forward, his pillar of a cock slow-sinking into my chute. I shuddered when body met bum, moaning with that wicked full-up-the-ass feeling. Brett was sucking on a cock now gone numb, Carlos pumping his hips, sliding his hardened meat back and forth inside of me, fucking me as men should always fuck.

"God, that feels good!" I gasped, head up and eyes closed, knuckles white on the railing.

Carlos rocked me to and fro with his plunging cock, Brett sucking me unceasingly. The sun beat harshly down on me, and the wet, smacking sound of Carlos's body smashing against my rippling ass filled my ears, his prick penetrating me to the sexual core, Brett tugging on my cock with his mouth; it was all too fantastically erotically-charged to last for very long.

"I'm going to come!" I yelled, eyes watering and body burning.

"Come in Brett's mouth while I come up your ass!" Carlos growled, hammering me in a frenzy.

Brett squeezed my balls, his lips flying up and down my cock, tongue scouring my shaft, as Carlos plundered my ass with a savage intensity. I went rigid, then exploded. My body danced around on the end of Carlos's cock, and I blasted raw, white-hot semen into Brett's lovely mouth. Carlos hollered his own ecstasy, fingers digging into my damp, heated flesh, cock blazing sperm into my stretched-out ass. He fucked me brutally, emptying his balls inside me, as I shook like a leaf and sprayed what seemed like gallons of jizz down Brett's throat.

I could barely stand when it was all over. Brett milked the last sweet drops of cum out of my wasted dick, and Carlos gingerly unplugged his cock from my battered, buttered asshole, leaving me achingly empty. It was only when we'd moved onto the next hole –

Brett's – that Carlos admitted he'd followed my golf ball into the bush and set up the man-trap.

NATURE BOYS
By Wayne Mansfield

"So he doesn't know about us then?" Dale asked as they drove over to Toby's house to pick him up.

"No, but I think he has the hots for me," replied Simon. "He's supposed to have a girlfriend, too."

"Well that doesn't mean anything," Dale replied.

"True." Simon agreed. "But, I suppose we'll find out one way or another this weekend. He'll definitely find out about us."

Later that afternoon, during a lull in the conversation, Simon looked up at his rearview mirror and noticed Toby, who was sitting in the back seat, staring blankly out the window.

"What's wrong?" Simon asked. "You look a bit preoccupied."

"Nothing," he replied, "just thinking about Julia."

"Aawww what are you thinking about her for?" Dale chimed in. "We're going camping, mate. Forget about her and get into the spirit of it."

Toby knew that Dale was right, but it was a bit hard to get into the spirit of it when there was something weighing heavily on your mind. Nevertheless, he made up his mind to have a good time, besides he didn't want to ruin everyone else's weekend with his problems.

Outside the sun was beating down. There was a heat haze in every direction, and up ahead the surface of the bitumen road was shimmering. Inside Simon's beaten up 1978 Holden station wagon it was forty degrees Celsius in the shade. Despite only wearing shorts and having all the windows down, none of the men could get comfortable on the sticky vinyl seats.

"Shit, Simon," Toby began, "you should invest in some air conditioning. It's bloody boiling in here."

"We're nearly there, Precious," Simon replied with a hint of annoyance. They were all hot, but there wasn't anything anyone could do about it. No use complaining. "Then we can all go for a swim."

Simon was thirty-two years old. He was the oldest of the three friends. He'd been working at MacGregor's Garage for nearly five years and was the senior mechanic. He had thick, curly hair, naturally sun-bleached from surfing, and a dark blond goatee. His body was well-defined, and his chest was covered in coarse, light-brown hair.

Dale worked in retail selling men's clothing. He was about 165 centimeters tall, had dark brown hair and a relatively smooth body apart from a small patch of hair in the center of his chest and a light ring of hair around each nipple. He was clean shaven and while his body was not as defined as Simon's, it was in pretty good shape for someone who shunned all forms of exercise apart from sex and walking.

Toby was a new addition to Simon and Dale's circle of friends. He was twenty-five, around 180 centimeters tall and spent a lot of time at the gym. He had a stocky, defined physique and was quite hirsute, so even though he shaved every day, he always seemed to have whiskers, and because his hair was black and he had olive skin, he was often mistaken for being Greek or Italian, although he wasn't. He was a fifth generation Australian and proud of it. He'd just started work at MacGregor's and seemed to have taken quite a shine to Simon. He could sense something in Simon that he was only just beginning to acknowledge in himself, and there was a certain comfort in that. He'd always done what was expected of him, what his family wanted him to do, rather than pursue what he wanted for himself, but finally he felt that he was on the verge of a turning point in his life.

"It's around here somewhere," Simon said finally. "There's the main camping ground, but we don't want that. There's another one that Dale and I found by accident the last time we were down here."

"Yeah, it was much better," Dale added. "Not another soul for miles around. We had the river and the trees to ourselves. Fantastic!"

Toby was excited about going camping for the first time. Even though he'd grown up in the country, he'd never been before, nor had he ever been this far south. The Karri trees truly amazed him the way they towered overhead, creating a sense of grandeur in the green wilderness. Bracken ferns and other small shrubs competed for space beneath the sparse canopy of the Karries, and every now and again, there were small patches of red and gold wild flowers and delicate white spider orchids.

"God, it's beautiful down here," Toby remarked. "Wouldn't it be great to spend your whole life living in a place like this?"

The other two didn't reply. They were too busy looking for the turn off, which was not much more than a small dirt track, probably overgrown with ferns. "Here it is!" Simon announced suddenly.

"Great," Toby replied, wiping his sweaty brow for the millionth time. "I'm melting back here."

The track was rougher than they remembered. It was a good thing the old Holden had good shock absorbers. But all three of them could put up with a bit of bouncing since they knew the beautiful Blackwood River was just up ahead through the trees.

As Simon pulled into the small clearing, Toby and Dale undid their seat belts. The car had barely stopped before both passengers were out of the vehicle and running toward the river.

"Is it okay to go in?" Toby asked, slowing down as he approached the tranquil waters. "No nasty surprises swimming around?"

"Not yet," replied Dale, peeling off his damp footy shorts and diving in.

Toby followed suit, stripping off his shorts and running, with a wild whoop, into the Blackwood.

"Hey! Thanks for waiting for me," Simon shouted.

He came running toward the river, stopping every couple of steps to lower his shorts further toward his feet until he was finally able to take them off altogether.

"Room for one more?" he asked as he launched himself into the air, bringing his knees up to his chest and landing in the water with an almighty splash that swamped both the other guys.

After fooling around and splashing great sheets of water over each other, the guys settled down to enjoy the serenity of their surroundings.

"Wanna back scrub?" Dale asked Simon.

"Sure," he answered. "Always in the mood for one of those."

Dale waded to the river bank and ran up to the car, fossicked around in the back for a couple of minutes and returned to the water with a bar of soap and a piece of sea sponge. Dipping the soap and the sponge in the water he began washing Simon's back, scrubbing it with the sea sponge and working up a thick, foamy lather.

"Ahhhh that feels great," said Simon, closing his eyes and leaning his head back. "It's just what I need after such a long drive."

"How about you, Toby?" Dale called out as his hand guided the sponge up and down Simon's back. "Want a back scrub?"

Toby, who'd been duck-diving and swimming about further out in the river, looked up. He was about to say yes when he caught sight of Dale's hard-on. It made him feel instantly uncomfortable, and he looked away.

"No thanks, mate," he replied casually. "I'm happy swimming about here."

"Aw come on," Simon said. "You don't know what you're missing. Feels fucking fantastic."

"Yeah, I can see," Toby remarked as Dale and his huge, stiff cock came into view, bouncing around as he worked on Simon's back.

Toby, wanting to distance himself from the scene, dived beneath the surface of the water and swam further upriver. He didn't know why the sight of Dale with an erection had upset him so much, or at least he wasn't willing to acknowledge why, but for the time being, he felt more comfortable with some distance between it and himself.

After spending half an hour in the water, Dale and Simon came out, collected their shorts, and went up to the car. They threw their sweaty, smelly shorts in through the driver's side window, leaving them there until they could be washed at some later time, and set about unpacking the car. Only then did Toby decide to leave the river and help. Since Simon was the more experienced camper, his job was to put up the tent. Toby was given the job of pumping up the air mattresses and Dale was in charge of unpacking the rest of their equipment from the back of the Holden.

"Hey, I might go and look for some firewood," Dale said when he'd finished. "We're going to need something to cook on tonight."

Toby and Simon acknowledged him with a wave and continued with their chores, and in an hour, everything was looking ship-shape. The tent was up and secure; the beds were pumped up and had been put in the tent, along with the pillows and blankets; the firewood had been collected, and a small ring of rocks had been made just in front of the log, which is where they would build the campfire.

That evening after a small but satisfying dinner of fried sausages and salad, followed by tea, made in an old tin kettle, and a couple of cans of Fosters beer, the boys retired early. It had been a big day, and the beer had accentuated their tiredness. They undressed and climbed inside the tent, needing only a pillow for comfort since it was still quite warm outside. One by one they nodded off, although it took Toby a little longer since he wasn't used to sleeping so rough.

The following morning, Toby, who'd been the last one to fall asleep, was the first to wake up. He opened his eyes and looked around him, taking a couple of seconds to realize where he was. Having got his bearings, he looked over at his tent-mates who were still slumbering. Dale had rolled over onto his side and was now facing him, while Simon remained hidden behind him. Toby noticed that Dale's cock was hard and that it was only inches away from where he lay.

He stared at the erect organ for a moment, fascinated by how rigid it was, sticking straight up and twitching every now and again. He then turned his attention to Dale's great, heavy ball sack hanging down over one leg, shaved and with both nuts clearly visible through the thin skin of his scrotum. Surrounding the balls and disappearing between his legs was great thatch of dark, curly hair connecting on either side with his thick pubic bush.

Curiously, he had grown hard, too, and had subconsciously started playing with his own erection then when he realized what he was doing he stopped for a moment. He felt a twinge of guilt. What about Julia? He considered their fractured relationship for a second or two before deciding he didn't care any more. It was over. As Dale had mentioned the previous day, they had gone down south to get away from everything, and aside from that, the sight of Dale's hard cock just inches away had got him so horny that he couldn't help himself. His hand returned to his uncut prick and began jerking it. With firm but slow strokes he massaged his man meat until a small bead of pre-cum appeared at the tip and dribbled onto his leg.

He stared long and hard at Dale's stiff pole, checking every now and again that Dale was still sleeping. It felt so good to be wanking out here in the open, surrounded by nature, but it would be even better if he could just touch it. If only he could feel Dale's cock in his hands. It looked so perfect, straight up and down, not slightly curved upwards as his was, and the head was thick and fleshy, invitingly so.

Toby began to jerk his cock faster and faster. As he thought about touching Dale's penis and even taking it into his mouth, about feeling the pink meaty head in his mouth and feeling the corrugations of the veins running like tentacles up the cock on his lips, he blew. A great fountain of cream streamed out of his cock and covered his hairy belly.

Having ejaculated, he allowed himself a few seconds to enjoy the feeling of satisfaction and relief before being overcome with the panic that someone might wake up and see the small puddles of spoof sprayed across his belly and pubic bush. He looked around for something to wipe it up with, but couldn't see anything he could use, so he did something he'd never done before. He picked small dollops of his cum up with his fingers, sliding it off the hairs, then brought his fingers to his mouth and sucked them clean. Since he was so hairy it was difficult to collect it all, but he managed to clear up most of it, enough to hide the evidence.

It wasn't long after that the others woke up, yawning and stretching, greeting the day and each other before clambering out of the tent. The first order of the day was a swim to freshen up and wash away the last remnants of sleep. Since they were already naked they were able to walk straight from the tent to the river.

"This is the life, isn't it?" Simon said as he lay back and floated on the water. "Just brilliant."

"What are we gonna do today?" Toby asked, washing himself thoroughly with the soap and paying particular attention to his belly. "Got anything planned?"

"Yeah, mate," Simon replied. "Fishing, bushwalking, swimming, relaxing, cooking, eating, drinking. Anything you want."

After a quick breakfast, the adventurous three put their shorts on, some socks and boots and started off through the bush.

"Where are we going?" asked Toby, slightly nervous about getting lost.

"Just for a walk," Dale answered.

"Aren't you worried about getting lost?"

"Can't get lost if we stay close to the river," Simon replied confidently.

Toby nodded, reassured, and followed his friends into the undergrowth.

There was no special purpose for the walk. There was nothing in the area apart from trees, trees and more trees. There was the occasional wild flower and lots of birds, but no animals, at least none that they saw. But walking through the forest was good exercise, climbing over old logs and winding their way through the huge Bracken fern fronds. Then Dale started to sing, badly, shattering the peaceful quiet and making the other two laugh.

"What's wrong with my singing?" he asked, suddenly hit with an unfamiliar feeling of self-consciousness.

"Is that what it was?" Simon laughed.

Dale looked back at Toby and saw that he was laughing, too. He felt his face flush red.

"Wasn't that bad, was it?" he asked Toby.

Toby nodded, so they continued their trek in silence, with only bird song to keep their ears occupied, and for that at least two of them were grateful.

They returned to the campsite two hours later, tired but feeling better for the exercise. While the others sat down and caught their breath, Simon, always "the organizer," got the fishing rods and the thawed bait. He gave the other two a rod each, baited his hook then went down to the edge of the river and cast his line. The thought of eating fresh fish had all of them salivating. There was nothing like fish for lunch, sprinkled with lemon pepper seasoning and eaten with almost-fresh crusty rolls. The only problem was that it could take them a while to catch anything.

They continued to cast their lines for an hour with no luck, not even a nibble. By that time, they were all starving, and Dale had broken open a giant-sized bag of barbecue chips to keep the hunger pangs away, Toby had given up. He'd decided to read a magazine instead, not realizing that if they didn't catch some fish there would be nothing to eat except a bit of salad, some bread rolls and some breakfast cereal.

Eventually Simon managed to catch a freshwater bream, which he set about scaling and cleaning. While Dale continued to try his luck, Simon got out the fry-pan, got the fire going and lightly fried his fish. As the mouth-watering smell of frying fish filled the air, there was a cry from the river, letting everyone know that Dale had caught something as well. Toby rushed over and took the fish, still wriggling, off the hook.

"Well done, man," he said. "Looks delicious."

"Okay then," said Dale as he re-baited his hook. "You can scale and clean it."

Toby looked horrified. "What do you mean? I've never done it before."

"Ask Simon to tell you how," Dale replied, snickering to himself wickedly. "You're gonna have to clean and gut it if you want to eat. That's the way it is out here. You can't sit around while everyone else does the work."

Toby mumbled something and headed off toward the campfire. Dale clicked his teeth. Toby may have been a powerfully built mechanic, but inside he was either a bit of a wimp or just lazy.

The glorious afternoon was spent swimming and relaxing by the cool water of the river. Simon lay on the log near the campfire, sunbathing, and Dale was using his air mattress to float around on the river while chatting to Toby, who was swimming lazily around Dale's air mattress. There was no rush that weekend. There was nothing to do and no one to disturb them. The rest of civilization seemed a million miles away.

For dinner they had fish again. They ate it with the remaining salad, the remaining bread rolls and a baked potato that Dale had cooked in some foil in the coals. It wasn't the most sumptuous meal they'd ever had, but it was filling and nutritious. After dinner, they got into the beer. It was the perfect way to cap off to a relaxing day and a moderately satisfying dinner.

Dale and Simon sat down in front of the log, using it to support their backs while Toby sat opposite them on his beach towel. Simon put his arm around Dale and sighed; both men stared into the flames of the fire. Toby looked at them wide-eyed.

"Are you two ... .erm ... .Are you two, like lovers, or something?" he asked tentatively.

Dale and Simon looked at each other and smiled. "Why, mate?" asked Dale. "You interested?"

The trio had a bit of a chuckle at the small joke, which helped relieve some of the awkwardness Toby was feeling.

"Well are you?" Dale asked again, more seriously this time.

"What? Me?" Toby asked, defensively. He may have been okay with his two mates being gay, but wasn't ready to accept the fact that he was. "No way. I'm going out with Julia. No way, man."

"You don't have to lie to us, Toby. I saw you this morning," Simon confessed, ruining all the work Dale's joke had done to alleviate the awkward situation.

Toby froze. He knew exactly what Simon was going to say.

"You were getting off on Dale's naked body. I saw you looking at his cock. You blew quite a load."

"What do you mean?" Toby asked, thinking that if he played dumb there might still be a chance he could bluff his way out of the sticky situation.

"You were so busy concentrating on old Dale-boy's hard-on that you didn't see me wake up and catch you. But hey, don't worry about it. It means we can all get on a whole lot better."

Toby looked from Simon to Dale, who was keeping silent, then down at the ground in front of him. Finding the situation too confronting, he got up without a word and skulked off into the night.

"What's up with him?" Dale asked.

"Denial," replied Simon, leaning over to kiss his lover. "I'm glad he knows," Simon whispered into Dale's ear, nuzzling it lovingly. "I've been wanting to fuck you for the last twenty-four hours."

"Well, what are you waiting for?" Dale smiled. "I've been waiting to be fucked."

Dale turned over and draped himself over the log while Simon ran into the tent and got some lube. He ran back, cock slapping against his legs and glistening with Satin Smooth Lubrication.

"Ready, baby?" he asked.

"Oh yeah. I was born ready for that cock. Give it to me, babe."

Simon worked his dripping prick into Dale's hairy man-cunt, sliding the whole length in until he had virtually pinned Dale to the wooden log beneath.

"Is that nice?" he asked, grinding his cock into Dale's well-used arse hole.

"You better believe it is," he replied.

"You want more?" Simon asked.

Dale nodded, getting up on his knees and leaning back against Simon, turning his head to meet Simon's soft lips. Simon wrapped his strong arms around Dale's boyish body, pulling him closer as he thrust his cock deeper and deeper inside Dale's fuck tunnel. As their love-making intensified, there was a movement in the bushes behind them, only they were too caught up in each other to notice.

It was Toby. He hadn't gone very far from the campfire, in fact he'd hidden himself behind the first tree he came to, but Dale's moans of sexual pleasure had drawn him back. He approached them silently, transfixed by their love-making, his cock engorged and standing to attention. He stopped just on the other side of the fire, took hold of his erection and began to play with it as he watched the two men gyrating against each other, the muscles in Simon's buttocks rising and falling as he pumped his lover's arse full of cock. Toby had never seen anything so horny in his life. Great strings of clear pre-cum dangled from the end of his knob as he watched the love-making taking place in front of him, as Simon began to fuck Dale harder and faster. Dale dropped forward onto the log and Simon took him by the hips and began to pull him backward to meet his thrusting cock, going deeper into Dale's hairy man hole.

"Fuck me. Fuck me harder. Fuck me with that dirty cock! Oooh yeah. Give me that cock," he could hear Dale saying.

The dirty talk was getting Simon hotter and hotter. He was like a machine, pounding Dale, impaling him on his fleshy prong, getting more and more worked up until he blew right up inside Dale. He continued thrusting after he'd come, making sure that Dale's arse got every last creamy drop of his man juice, then he collapsed on top of Dale. Toby didn't know what to do. He was standing in the fire light with a raging hard on of his own, the show was over, and he was more turned on than he had ever been before.

"What are you doing over there?" asked Simon, noticing Toby, as he pulled his cock out of Dale and lay back against the log. "Come over here."

Toby sheepishly walked toward the men, not knowing what was going to happen next, but sensing that he was going to enjoy it. He felt alive, electric and the sense of anticipation about his first real male-to-male sexual encounter was almost too overwhelming to bear.

"That cock's a lot nicer when it's hard, mate," Dale noted.

Then without asking he put his mouth on it, starting with long, slow sucks at first then swallowing the whole length of it hungrily down his throat. Toby began to groan in ecstasy. It was the first time he'd had another man on his cock, and it felt wonderful; better than any girl had managed before. Then he gasped. Simon, who had gone around behind him, was spreading his toned butt cheeks and licking his arse. His first reaction was one of discomfort. Was it clean? But then he remembered he had gone for a swim only an hour or so before dinner. Satisfied, he gave into the pure pleasure of it, squirming and enjoying the ecstasy of having one man on his cock and the other tongue-fucking his hairy hole.

Toby's big, masculine hands rested on top of Dale's head as he continued to swallow his cock, pushing it rhythmically toward him, forcing Dale to take it further and further down his throat, making him gag twice in the process.

"Ooohhh, that's it," Toby moaned, focusing on Simon's firm, wet tongue trying to force its way inside him.

Toby's whole body seemed like it was burning up. He felt hot, and it wasn't because of the campfire. He removed one hand from Dale's head and used it to caress his hairy chest, tweaking his nipples each in turn. So orgasmic did he feel that he hadn't even noticed Simon stand up and move around to the front. It was a pleasant surprise when he felt Simon's lips upon his own. Simon kissed him passionately, slipping his tongue deep down his throat while Dale took both of the men's cocks into his mouth at the same time, swallowing them down as deep as he could possibly get them, loving the sensation of sucking two cocks.

Toby could feel his cock head rubbing against Simon's, and Dale's tongue massaging them both as he slid his mouth up and down them. He could still smell the rich, earthy mustiness of his arse hole on Simon's face and feel Simon's tongue exploring his mouth. Then he felt the familiar sensation of imminent ejaculation, and his breaths became shorter, faster and deeper.

Dale knew enough to know what was about to happen. He popped Simon's cock out of his mouth and started concentrating on Toby's, wanking it with his hand and sucking it firmly with his mouth. As Simon kissed him, he began to play with Toby's firm nipples, making Toby come like a geyser down Dale's throat. Again and again, he thrust, fucking Dale's face until the intense sensation of orgasm faded enough for him to join the real world again.

"Now it's your turn," Simon said to Dale, kissing his cum-coated lips softly and tenderly.

Dale stepped over to Toby's beach towel and lay down. Simon joined him, squatting down on his erection, taking the whole length up his man cunt, and inviting Toby to squat down on his boyfriend's face.

"You sure?" Toby asked.

Dale just reached up and grabbed Toby's hand, pulling him down toward his face. As Simon began to ride his cock, Dale watched as Toby's hairy man hole got closer and closer to his face, opening slightly as the muscles were stretched apart. Toby was not sure how Dale could be enjoying getting smothered by his butt hole, so was careful not sit down too hard; yet Dale reached up and wrapped an arm around each leg, pulling the novice down until he was being smothered by hairy arse.

Dale loved arses. He got off on the feel of them, the look of them and the smell of them. He loved everything about them, especially hairy ones like Toby's. And the fact his cock was up one hole and he had another hole on his face, meant it wasn't long until he was blowing a jet of cum up inside his boyfriend, flushing his bowels with a river of man cream. Yet even then, as Toby started to get up after hearing Dale moaning in orgasm beneath him, he felt Dale's arms keep his arse pinned to his face.

Toby looked at Simon with an expression of uncertainty, of not knowing what to do.

"He'll let you know," Simon stated knowingly.

When he was ready, Dale pushed him off. Simon got up off his cock and Toby, who had just started to go soft, barred up again when he saw the cum dribbling out of Simon's arse and down Dale's deflating cock.

"You're eager," Dale noted.

"Yeah, got a mind of its own this one," Toby laughed. "Don't know if I'm ready to blow again yet, though."

"Give it time," Simon smiled. "Let's go and wash off."

The three men made their way down to the river and although it was a balmy night, the water temperature had dropped dramatically. None of them could bear to stay in the water any longer than the time it took them to wash their cocks off and clean out their cum-soaked holes.

"Bedtime," Simon yelled as he ran back to the tent to towel himself dry.

The other two followed, wet and shivering slightly, but warming up as soon as they'd dried off. That night they slept together as a threesome, each curled up against the man behind, spooning. Toby felt privileged to be in the middle, feeling Simon's big cock nestled neatly in the crack of his arse, and feeling his cock nestled in the crack of Dale's arse.

The next morning, the trio woke up within minutes of each other. Toby woke up first, followed by Dale. Both had morning erections and didn't want to waste them. Dale reached over and grabbed Toby's cock and Toby reached over and grabbed Dale's. They kissed, sucking each other's lips and tongues, feeling each other's hot breath on their skin. Simon, woken up by the sound of sex, watched from behind, playing with his cock, too, and getting off on being a voyeur, enjoying the visual stimulation of the two men beside him enjoying themselves and listening to the panting and smacking of passionate kisses.

In a short time, Dale came, blowing all over Toby's cock, which set him off, jerking himself off to a shuddering climax using Dale's milky load as lube. Simon blew almost simultaneously, spraying Toby's back with a thick coating of man cum, which he then licked up before kissing each of the men good morning.

As they had done yesterday, the first order of business was a quick dip in the river to clean themselves up and freshen up, followed by breakfast and another swim. Then the time they had all been dreading arrived. It was time to pack the car up and head back to the city, to reality.

"That was a fucking good night last night," Toby said as he helped the other two reload the car.

"You're not wrong," Dale winked. "So what are you going to do about Julia now?"

Toby shrugged his shoulders. "Guess I'm going to tell her what I'd already decided to tell her anyway, that things aren't working out and that I don't love her."

"That's too bad," Simon said. "Though it's better to be honest. If you prefer cock to pussy, better to tell her now. Better for you and better for her."

Toby nodded. "Yeah, you're right. I just hope the three of us can catch up again. I've been thinking about last night ever since I woke up."

Simon and Dale looked up from what they were doing and then at each other.

"We'll see," said Dale. "We'll see."

They checked they had covered the campfire with dirt and that they hadn't left anything behind then piled into the car. As Simon did a U-turn and drove them back out of the forest and onto the main road, it was with a sense of anticipation. And, he was not alone with that eager expectation. None of them could wait to get back to the city and see what would happen between them once they were back in the real world.

BONED BY THE HIGHWAY PATROL
By Jay Starre

If Ross hadn't been such a fuck-up it wouldn't have happened. He compensated for his total lack of responsibility by being easy-going, and naturally his good looks and hot, slim body helped get him by.

"Did you put up the 'closed' sign?" Jasper asked.

"Sure, now gimme that fat dick of yours! I've been cravin' it for hours!"

Jasper was the cook in the small highway diner, while Ross did both the serving and dishwashing on quiet nights like this. The stretch of highway north of Denver was busy in the summers but nearly dead in the late winter.

A blizzard outside had quashed all chance of visitors, and that's when Ross, always horny at only twenty, had propositioned Jasper. The diner cook was only a few years older than the dark-haired waiter, but he was light-years ahead in maturity.

"We're still at work, Ross, so once we blow our loads, you got to get some fucking shit done around here! I want all that pile of dishes cleaned up, and all the tables wiped down good, and … oh yeah!"

Jasper's lecture was cut-off in mid sentence as Ross dropped to his knees, burrowed under the cook's apron with head and hands, tore open his belt, and yanked down on his pants all in one greedy move.

"Sweet! Cock!" Ross panted out just before he gobbled up pink meat with a loud slurp.

Jasper was one of those platinum blonds with nearly translucent skin, white as cream until he heated up, then flushing rose from head to toe. His cock, swelling up instantly in Ross's wet mouth, turned bright pink as did his dangling, hairless nads cupped in one of Ross's hands.

He crammed his crotch into that hot, gurgling face-hole, moaning loudly as a talented tongue swabbed and plump lips massaged. His pants were in a tangle down around his ankles, constricting his movement, but he hardly cared. He reached down and grabbed onto Ross's head, hidden beneath his sauce-stained apron, and held it as the waiter began to bob over his stiffened bone.

Ross was not timid, and he was quick to insinuate a hand up between the blond cook's smooth thighs from in front, digging into the hairless crack and probing for hole. Jasper couldn't open his legs with his tangled clothing at his feet, but he managed to squat slightly to allow that burrowing hand to find his butt-hole.

"Finger that hole while you suck dick, Ross! I might even let you fuck me up the ass if you promise to get something done around here afterwards … sweet … that's it ... dig around in there."

A finger had discovered and assaulted Jasper's asshole. Ross drove deep past a twitching sphincter and twisted, tugging on tight anal lips while jabbing at prostate. Jasper humped downwards on that aggressive finger while hot mouth lathered up his cock and a hand squeezed and tugged on his nut-sack.

The young dude was a firecracker! He'd sucked Jasper off twice before late at night during a similar lull, but that was as far as they'd gone. The waiter had blown his load both times while swallowing cook cock, his hand fisting his boner while he knelt at Jasper's feet.

This time, Jasper noticed Ross wasn't jerking off, both his hands busy working on either the cook's nuts or ass. The slim waiter obviously wanted more this round. That was cool with Jasper. He'd checked out Ross's dick when he'd been jerking off before, and it was one whopper of a tool. Not only was it lengthy, it was thick and solid. Jasper wouldn't mind feeling all that hot sausage riding up his tender hole!

Jasper had been facing the back of the restaurant when Ross approached him. His naked butt, full and firm, faced the front and the door that led out to the dining area. A hand was busy between the pale, round cheeks rooting in hole, visible from that doorway. Ross knelt with his back against a counter, hidden by the cook's stocky body.

"What's going on here? A Food Safety Inspector would fail you on the spot, Blondie."

The voice from behind him sent a shock wave through the cook's heated body. Mouth on his cock suckled greedily, while finger tunneled aggressively in his tender asshole. Those amazing sensations couldn't be ignored, no matter how startled he was by the unexpected arrival of an intruder.

He managed to crane his head around and see who had come into the kitchen so silently. Two emotions warred, one of relief, followed by one of near panic. He'd thought it was their boss, who would have a key to get in the locked front door. The boss was a real asshole and would have probably fired them both on the spot.

It wasn't John. It was a cop – a big one, too, at least six-foot-four and with a giant's frame besides. No donut-eater here! So, panic replaced relief as Jasper realized they were caught in the act by a highway patrolman!

"Uh … sorry ... we're closed," Jasper stammered as he attempted to pull his cock out of Ross's still gobbling mouth and turn to face the cop, hoping his apron would hide his hard-on. As well, his bare ass, a hand shoved between the white cheeks, would no longer be wagging at the giant Patrolman.

"Your sign says 'open' and the door's unlocked. Next time you decide to engage in a little suck and fuck you might want to take care of that."

The voice was barrel-deep but remarkably calm. He obviously had no need to shout or growl, his uniform and his size intimidating enough. Jasper was at a total loss, too stunned to bend over and pull up his pants, while Ross was still kneeling, behind him now and blocked from the Patrolman's view.

Jasper silently cursed the irresponsible waiter. He hadn't bothered to turn that sign around or lock the door! What an idiot!

It got worse. Ross, fool to the end, peeked around the blond cook's waist and grinned at the big patrolman. From on his knees, he blurted out the stupidest thing Jasper had ever heard.

"This ain't illegal is it? If it was, maybe we could get off easy if we let you fuck us both up the ass!"

Jasper groaned and flushed red all over. Totally conscious of his bare ass behind him, his spit-wet cock hidden under his apron, and his tangled pants and underwear around his sneakers, he felt completely vulnerable. And now, that fool of a waiter had just propositioned a highway patrolman and offered him a bribe, too!

Jasper was so hot, he felt as if he was going to faint. The highway patrolman was silent, staring at them out of dark eyes under dark brows under the brim of his officer's cap. His wide mouth was set firmly in a straight, unsmiling line. His large hands were at his waist, holstered gun plainly visible at his belt.

Now what? Both of them arrested? If that happened, he'd make sure he wasn't in the same cell as the brainless waiter!

"Hmmmmm. Now if I'm going to entertain that offer, I should get a look at what's on the menu. Let's see those asses."

Jasper took a deep breath and let it out, shocked, relieved, and uncertain all at the same time. Was the patrolman merely toying with them? He didn't look like someone who joked around all that much.

Ross obviously entertained no such worries. With a foolish grin on his face, he leapt to his feet from behind Jasper, and pulling the cook around with him, he pushed down on Jasper's shoulders, bending him over with his bare ass again waving at the hovering patrolman.

"He's gotta go for your sweet ass, Jasper! It's one amazing butt! Now we won't get arrested," he hissed in the cook's ear.

Maybe the slim waiter wasn't so stupid after all! It was too late by this time for Jasper to do much accept to follow along. They were in big trouble unless they gave up their asses to the cop – if he'd take the bribe.

Jasper's round butt quivered, pale flesh bright pink now, his cock stiffening back up as he felt those dark eyes surveying him from behind. At the same time, Ross yanked down his own pants and kicked them off over his sneakers. Both were bent over the stainless steel counter in front of them as they awaited the patrolman's verdict.

A warm paw seized one of Jasper's smooth ass-cheeks!

He jerked from the unexpected touch, his butt globe jiggling under the firm grasp of patrolman palm. From the corner of his eye, Jasper spotted a second paw seizing Ross's ass.

"Excellent. One round butt, and one compact butt. I think we can overlook any minor infractions the pair of you have managed to incur."

Those massive hands weren't idle as the officer spoke. Long fingers slid into deep cracks and searched out holes. Both cook and waiter squirmed as index fingers found and invaded quivering slots, just like that! Jasper still felt faint. That aggressive finger wormed deep, just like Ross's had. Only now it was a uniformed cop that was rooting around in his ass and about to fuck him! He could hardly believe it was happening.

Not so Ross. "Oh yeah ... officer that feels great! Ummmm ... finger my ass while you fuck Jasper's sweet butt. I want to see your big Patrolman prick ream him out!"

The punk just didn't know when to let up! Would the patrolman get pissed off at Ross's cocky attitude?

Apparently not, by the sound of his next words.

"Yeah? You want to see your buddy get dicked? While you squat over my finger and imagine how my big cop cock will feel when you get it up your tight hole? Fine, then. Get some grease on those holes. Now, Punk."

The nasty words were uttered in the officer's deep voice, surprisingly calm. The finger up Jasper's butt-hole was not so gentle. It twisted, stabbed and stretched. Jasper grunted, bit his lip and shuddered from head to toe. He couldn't help wondering how big the giant cop's cock was!

"How 'bout this tin of lard? Some pig grease for some," Ross just managed to bite off the last few words of his sentence.

"Pig cock? Yeah, boys, lets grease up a pair of pig asses for some pig dick! Gob it on there, punk!"

Ross scooped out a handful of the stuff while Jasper squirmed around the big finger up his butt and grew even more embarrassed as he realized he was about to get greased with lard and fucked up the ass, in his own kitchen! It was unbelievable!

Then it happened. Ross slathered on the lard, his fingers in both their cracks as he writhed around the Patrolman's finger up his own butt and snickered nastily. He didn't seem to be worried or embarrassed in the least.

The finger up Jasper's ass slid out as more fingers, both the patrolman's and Ross's lathered up his crack with gooey grease. The sensation was definitely exciting, especially as a blunt dickhead began to slide in all that grease, rubbing up and down and prodding at his tenderized sphincter.

"Sweet butt, Blondie. All pink and glowing, all greased and slippery. Yeah! Nice little hole too! How's that feel? Want my pig prick in there?"

The voice was still calm and reasonable, regardless of the nasty words, as the patrolman reached around Jasper's waist and pulled him back toward the pressing head of his cock. Jasper moaned, his head down, his butt hole throbbing as a large knob pushed against his quivering anal lips. The patrolman's hand seized Jasper's hard-on and squeezed just as he pushed harder from behind.

"Fuck! Yeah! Ohhhhhhhh ... Give me cock!" Jasper cried out as cock-knob plowed into him.

"You got it, Blondie. And you, waiter boy, watch how your buddy gets fucked good by all this pig dick before you take it up your tight little ass next."

The cock-head pushing into him was huge, and it slid deeper by the second as thick shank followed. Jasper tried to open up his legs but couldn't with his pants tangled at his ankles. He was trapped by the patrolman's powerful arm around his waist and big hand on his dick. All he could do was surrender to that massive heat invading his guts from behind.

Ross leaned in close to whisper in his ear. "Can you believe it? Fucking hot! A cop pounding both our butts! How's it feel up there? It's so fucking huge!"

Jasper was able to form only grunts and gasps as the patrolman slid he dick all the way home, the base of his meat and his big nut sack slapping against Jasper's pink ass crack. The blond cook had never taken such a huge bone up his butt before, and he was feeling every steamy inch of it.

The patrolman took his time then, reaming Jasper's round ass with steady probes. He pumped Jasper's cock at the same time, while fingering a squirming Ross's butt hole, too. Jasper couldn't do much except relax into the patrolman's grasp and take cock up the butt. It was a lot of dick and felt like a massive, burning plunger had invaded him at first. Then slowly it opened him up, and he began to float in the steady thrust and pump.

His cock growing stiffer while his asshole grew looser, orgasm snuck up on him in a rising tide of steamy pleasure. The patrolman behind him felt Jasper's stocky body begin to buck and squirm as the ache in his guts and throb in his cock combined to send him over the brink.

The cop chuckled loudly and shoved his cock in and out in a sudden burst of rapid-fire lunges. "Blow it, Blondie! Give it up for pig cock up your pig-greased asshole! Your buddy is next!"

Jasper groaned as his body turned bright pink all over, and his cock erupted in a spray. The inside of his apron was splattered, while his aching asshole convulsed around the drilling Patrolman dick buried there.

Gasping out his orgasm, Jasper shuddered as that massive meat suddenly yanked out of him, leaving his asshole dripping lard and pulsing pink. For a moment, he felt totally empty and open, his cock lurching as the final spurts of his orgasm were released.

Then, as the patrolman moved away to slide behind the bent-over waiter, the hand around Jasper's dick came away, too. His round butt shaking and his fucked hole leaking, he took a deep breath and wondered what was next.

He found out. The patrolman's hand slid back into his crack and found his greased hole. He thrust three fingers up it!

"Now I'll fuck you, waiter boy, while I finger the cook's nicely fucked hole. Ready for pig prick?"

Ross, who'd been groaning and muttering all along, now practically shouted out his reply. "Fuck yeah! Gimme that pig dick! Fuck me like you fucked Jasper! My tight ass is all yours!"

Jasper moaned as those three fingers strummed his fucked asshole. He took it easily, the big dick up there a few moments earlier having stretched it into a gaping pit. He turned his head and watched as Ross took that giant boner up his compact butt.

The waiter had a high, firm ass that glistened with grease where the patrolman had pawed it. The cock that had just fucked Jasper was enormous! Swollen into a thick pole, it twitched greedily as the cop shoved it up into Ross's squirming crack. Jasper watched as the blunt knob disappeared between smooth white cheeks then listened as Ross yelped and bucked as it pushed into his guts.

Three fingers strobed his own hole, and he empathized with the slim waiter as he was fed massive cop tool inch by inch in a steady goring. Ross's ass rose up to meet the invader, his cock encased in the patrolman's paw.

This time, it seemed the patrolman was determined to get off himself. No slow pump like he'd offered Jasper, but a pummeling drive that had his hips smashing against the squirming waiter's bare ass-cheeks.

Jasper watched with fascination as that purple cock invaded, retreated, then slammed home again, the force of those thrusts lifting Ross up onto his toes.

"Yeah! Fuck! Unnggg! Do me! Like that! Harder! I can take it!"

Ross seemed to have no trouble with that monster meat, even though it looked way too big for his tight ass. Jasper still dripped cum as he sat back on the three fingers working around in his own fucked hole. His dick rose back up, and he realized the sight of that giant cop bone reaming his waiter buddy and those three fingers digging in his own asshole, were bringing him close to a second orgasm!

Ross rode pig dick like a squealing pig himself, jamming his snug ass back over the slamming boner no matter how fast and hard he got it. This seemed to be exactly what the patrolman needed.

"Yeah! Take pig dick up your pig-greased hole! Take pig load up there, too! Here it comes, little piggie!"

Giant bone slammed home as the patrolman unloaded up Ross's squirming ass. He held the waiter in place with one hand around his waist, squeezing the waiter's cock as he primed his hole with spew.

"Oh yeah! Load me up! Oh fuck yeah! I'm coming, too!"

Ross bucked in the patrolman's grasp as Jasper himself shot his second load. It was too hot to see the slim waiter getting stuffed with spurting patrolman bone, while his own asshole ached around the three big patrolman fingers buried knuckle deep inside.

All three gasped and shook as they shot. It took a few moments for the patrolman to catch his breath, but then he was all business. He pulled out of Ross's tenderized butt-hole, stepped back as his fingers slid from Jasper's fucked ass, and zipped up.

"OK boys, now I need a little fuel before I go back out into the blizzard. Some coffee, some ham and eggs, and oh yeah, you might as well add some sausage, too. I do love my pork."

His deep voice contained just a hint of humor as he offered the fucked pair a ghost of a smile. Turning away, he strode out into the dining area as if nothing had happened at all.

Ross grinned from ear to ear. "OK, Jasper. Get cookin' and I'll serve him up. You heard him, pork for the pig!"

Jasper was far too stunned from the last half hour's wild games to argue. He pulled up his pants, ignoring the lard in his crack and turning to his stove. Once the patrolman was served and out of there, then he'd deal with the foolish young waiter.

Maybe he'd fuck that tight ass, just to teach him a lesson, Jasper mused as eggs and ham fried on the stove top.

That sounded good, but he also realized Ross would definitely like it and there would be no lesson in it at all. Oh well, what could he do?

He'd fuck the fool anyway!

SWEATY
By Shane Allison

After days of text message tag, Tim and I were finally able to meet up. Been difficult with his work schedule and his ready-made family waiting at home. He owns his own business. A landscaper whose days start at 6:00 am. Ever since he told me how big his dick was, he's been a consistent hot dream. Especially when I'm naked with nothing but a bottle of lotion. Tim said he got my number off the wall of a fast food bathroom. I may have written it. My number's on so many walls of toilet stalls. It sounded about right considering all the calls I get for blow job service. I make sure that I keep mouthwash and air freshener around. The car can get pretty rank after I've had my share of truckers and hitchhikers.

Thought Tim would be just another bull shitter, wasting my daytime minutes. We decided to meet in the parking lot of the campus football stadium. Drove like a bat out of hell, hoping I wouldn't miss him after we had worked our asses off trying to meet up. I arrived at the lot only minutes before. Tim drove up in a silver pickup that read Timco Landscaping on the door. I saddled up along side. We kept our talk small. Tried to think of a place to go where no one would fuck with us, where we wouldn't be hassled. There was my frequent cruising ground, the Bellamy stalls, but the janitors were around that time of day waxing floors, scrubbing toilets. Besides, I didn't want some dick-blocker moving in on my piece of ass that was rightfully mine. Thought of Caruthers Hall, Montgomery Gym, but didn't want to risk getting caught by some innocent bystander like a campus cop roaming the halls, seeking out the kind of unruliness we were about to commit.

I had to act fast. It was hot as hell that day and sweat was pouring from both our brawns. I let Tim in on the parking garage located on the other side of the campus. The stadium was the only thing in which he was familiar.

"Follow me," I told him.

Tim wasn't what I expected. He sounded older on the phone. Before he told me of his dick size, I was expecting something along the lines of a roasted peanut. I watched Tim from my rearview tail behind. He was still with me, still raring up to fuck. Most dudes chicken shit out of a good time when they think I'm leading them astray through the razor teeth gates of danger, but I only do that with those I don't give a shit for, men whose wallets only hold my interests. Tim pulled in behind. We spiraled up each floor until we got to the fourth one above. Figured we wouldn't be disturbed during that time of day with all the students on summer vacation. There was a campus security office located behind the garage, but I didn't tell Tim. I know how guys like him can get: panicky and scared to the point of not being able to get a hard-on, and I can't do a damn thing with a limp dick.

Tim parked behind me. I watched him get out. I wanted to do it in his truck instead of in my mama's car with the plush, beige seats that were already holding in odors of fast food burgers and BBQ pork skins. I thought being a landscaper with messy kids, his pick-up would be quite the dumping ground.

Tim looked about my age: thirty-four, average height, glasses, with short brown hair. Yeah, he owned his own business, but looked like he didn't have a pot to pee in. Yet, he was a sight damn better looking than those trolls from the 'cades. I unlocked the passenger side door as he drew closer. He was wet with sweat, his clothes soiled with that day's filth.

"So, how's it goin'?" I asked.

"Good, you?"

"Good, good."

I looked around in search of hidden cameras. Had to be sure that we weren't being immortalized in black and white. They've really been on their toes since the Virginia Tech thing.

"I'm glad we're finally able to meet. I thought all we were going do was play text message tag."

"Sorry. I'm just so busy. I had to do six yards today."

"Oh, no. I understand. We all gotta put food on the table." Like I've ever worked to put food on the table for anybody.

"Exactly," he smiled. He had a sweet set of dick- sucking lips.

As I reached in the back for an unlaundered garment, I said, "You mind if I put this on the seat under you?" It was a shirt amongst many I had been meaning to drop off to the cleaners.

"Sure, no problem." Tim lifted his ass out of the seat while I tucked the piece of clothing beneath it.

"Sorry I ..."

"No, it's fine. I understand," he said.

It was better for my shirt to soak up the sweat than my car seats. "Let me roll down the windows, get some air in here." I started to fondle the tent in my jeans.

"Let's see whatchoo got," Tim said with a shit-eating grin on his sweaty, blushed mug.

I drew at my zipper, reached into the copper slit and fished my dick out of the panel of my underwear. Hard-on as it stood ready and anxious for Tim's mouth. I pulled up the armrest that divided us before Tim hunched over and threw himself to my dick. Things were a tight fit with the steering wheel practically in my lap. I swiveled my hips over to avoid further obstruction of his blow job work. His mouth couldn't have felt hotter, his tongue ticklish along the shaft. I hoped we wouldn't be disturbed. It had been weeks since I had been blown.

"Suck it," I told him. "Take it."

I love talking dirty. Especially to the bi-curious breeders who deserve it the most for their sins, for breaking a vow when another man's dick grazes their tonsils. With my hand placed upon his head, fingers rummaging through sweaty almond-brown feathers of hair, I forced his skull down on me, thrusted my stuff in his mouth. His face was a blush of red. Tim only missed a beat when I pulled my jeans down around my ass.

He didn't put up much of a fuss about my showing more skin. Too busy baptizing my dick in spit. He veered up out of my lap with a look of satisfaction – the same look I had when I jacked off every morning, or the face I make when I'm having it pleased through the glory hole of some bathroom stall.

"My turn," I said.

When Tim took his dick out, I was enthralled. When he told me how big he was, I would have never believed it. Not on a white guy. He didn't have a clue that I was a size queen. I'll crawl through a ditch of shit and glass if there's a well-endowed twink-slut at the end of it. With all the dicks I've serviced, I'd never seen anything like that which hung between Tim's knees. I hunched over and started to suck him off. His dick was enough to cause my muscles to burn. A mouthful of sweaty landscaper dick. I felt he was too good for a simple blow job. Up my ass was where his dick was needed.

"I wan'choo to fuck me."

"I don't know. It's too risky out here. We could get caught," he said.

"No ones going t' catch us." Like I was so sure.

"Okay, bu'choo gotta keep a look out."

I opened the glove compartment and took out a small bottle of scented lubricant I bought on sale at a sex toy store. I squeezed some onto Tim's dick.

"Shit's cold," he complained. Took the excess and slathered it up my hole. Hard to believe my butt used to cringe to a dick, now my asshole is the size of a golf ball thanks to all the men that have stretched it.

I worked myself over onto Tim's side, hovering over his lap. I held onto the dashboard for leverage as I glided his dick up inside me. It wasn't long before the car started to smell like artificial strawberries.

"Am I in?"

"All th' way," I said.

I braced the steering wheel and the car door as I rode Tim, bucking about like some deranged cowboy on his bull dick.

"Can I let th' seat back," he asked.

"There should be a thing here on th' side." I felt for it and pushed in with Tim still inside me. The seat maneuvered into a more comfortable position.

"That's good."

I swirled into his lap as he sighed with pleasure.

I was pressed between the windshield and the dash as Tim gave me the nastiest fuck. I was grateful that he had written down my number from the partition of that fast food stall. Tim was worthy enough to earn a place in my cell phone list of booty calls.

Beads of sweat rolled into the cave of my nose. I took the scented grease and squeezed what was left in the tube, on my dick, and started jacking off. It was twice including the work over I gave myself that morning. My dick was hot in my hand, slippery with the stuff. As I beat off, Tim warned me that he was close.

"Not yet," I warned. I wanted to come with him. It's so seldom I get to come with the dudes I get with in situations such as the one Tim and I were in.

"I'm close," he said.

"Not yet, man. Not yet."

I rode him hard and mean.

He let loose orgasmic rebel yells, and I along with him as I shot forth on the dash. I leaned back into the bed of Tim's chest with his dick inside me. I knew my ass would be quite sore that night. I reached for another garment set out to be laundered. We cleaned ourselves up with opposite ends of one of my mama's church dresses.

"I usually have some napkins," I said. We were pouring with sweat. We heard a car coming up to our floor. It was a campus cop. Tim uncorked his dick out of my ass and pushed me back into the driver's seat. We fussed with our clothes, fastening and zipping up jeans.

"Jus' relax," I told him. "Lemme do the talking."

This was the last damn thing I needed. Started to think of people to call that would be able to bail me out. I thought of calling Chris, but he never answers his cell. Then there was Marc, but I haven't spoken to him in years. I thought of Collin, but figured he wouldn't have the bail money being that he's been laid off going on six months now. He parked on the driver's side of me. Tim and I watched nervously as the cop sauntered over.

"How am I going to explain this to my wife," he said.

"Jus' chill."

"Good afternoon," said the cop.

"How you doin'?"

"You two realize the parking garage is closed after five don'choo?"

Was the first I had ever heard of any garage on campus closing after five. There were no signs posted and I had never had a problem before. "No, Sir, I didn't know," I said.

"What are you two doin' up here anyway?"

I had to think of something fast. "He ran out of gas an' I was about t' give him a ride t' a station."

I studied the name tag pinned to the breast pocket of his uniform shirt. Richard Stratton it read. He was sex on legs, muscles tight beneath the polyester. His skin glistened in the summer's humid cruelty.

"I'm gonna write you a warning."

"Come on, man, gimme a break. I to'joo he ran outta gas."

The look he gave me was enough to banish me to the deepest pits I would never be able to crawl back from.

He looked to Tim and said, "You, get lost." Tim got out of the car and walked back to his truck, hauling ass out of the garage.

Stratton waited until Tim was out of sight before laying into me. "Step out of th' car."

Other than hanging around in the garage after hours, I knew he didn't have shit on me, that he was just busting my balls. I mean, shit, they don't even carry guns. Just pepper spray and a baton.

"Putcha hands behind your back."

"Are you serious? Why you arrestin' me?"

"I don't like a smart ass."

I did what he asked.

"Lock yer fingers."

His hands were big and callous.

"Spread 'em," he demanded, kicking my feet apart.

He read me my rights as he cuffed me.

"What about my car?"

"It'll be fine. Watch yer head." Stratton stuffed me in the backseat of his patrol car.

When we got inside, I found it peculiar that there were no other officers around. Station's usually littered with campus po'-po'.

"You the only one here?" I asked.

"It's the summer, an' most of the staff has gone home for t'day."

I've seen situations like these being played out dozens of damn times in movies. The cop takes the perp in back, kicks the shit out of him and trumps up some story about resisting arrest.

"Hey, look, my bad about what I said back there. I'll steer clear of the garage."

I thought of fighting my way out, but I wouldn't have been able to drive with my hands cuffed. "Sir, please." I wrestled with the cuffs, but the more I struggled, the more the steel bit into my wrists. Sweat burned my eyes. I sat begging to be let go. Stratton yanked me to my feet. Thinking for sure he brought me in to use me as a punching bag, I was dumb-founded when he unzipped my jeans and took out my dick. My heart dropped into my boots in disbelief. Stratton took my dick in his hand and began to stroke. I didn't want to put up much of a fuss. This pig could beat my ass, and it would be my word against his. I couldn't stop him due to my binds, and I wasn't sure that I wanted to if I could.

"I didn't bring you here t' hur'choo," he said.

"So, I'm not under arres'?"

"Not if you give me what yer friend was giving you back there."

"You saw us?"

"Me an' my surveillance cameras. If you give me what I want, I'll erase th' footage and le'choo go." I didn't believe any of what he was saying. Cop or not, but what could I do? The shit beat having to call my folks to bail me out again over another embarrassing sexual act committed in public.

"Guess ain't gotta choice. It's either this or jail," I said.

Stratton took my dick into his mouth. His shades grazed against my belly. He undid my jeans and yanked them down.

"What if someone comes in?"

"I'm th' only one here after five."

I gave into Stratton. Drool plummeted to the floor as he went in deep. His lips were a dream.

"Hold up," he said. I hated that he stopped, leaving me erect and wet like that. Stratton walked over to a desk and took out a small bottle and made his way back and dropped trough. His ass was caked with fur. He pressed the cream onto his fingers and slathered it up his asshole. His anus puckered being smeared with goo.

He smeared some of the grease on my dick. He straddled me, holding my sex steady at his anus. He brought his body down. Stratton slid onto me so easily.

"Ya'll think no one's watching, but someone's always watching. Guys bringing their girlfriends here to make out, hustlers sucking off their john's in the stairwell. I get 'em all. Some I bust, while I catch others on tape and keep for my own personal collection."

"So, I'm not the first guy you've brought here?"

"You're th' fifth guy I've fucked this week." Stratton was the best piece of ass. He switched positions to face me. He wanted to look at me when he came. He looked into my eyes as he took me. He squeezed on more grease.

My hands had grown numb from the cuffs, arms sore and burning. Warned him that I was about to come.

I worked his dick fast and hard between us. I let loose a geyser of semen. Stratton came; spunk ran down his fingers, his greased thickness. He wiped himself on my polo. My dick tingled as he eased himself off of me. After he dressed himself, he was courteous enough to clean me up, tucking my spent piece back into my pants. He pulled me to my feet and unlocked the cuffs.

"Take off. If I catchchoo back up there, I'll bust your ass for sure."

I took the elevator up to where my car was left and busted out of the lot.

KERRY IN THE CLOSET
By Stephen Osborne

He was as dumb as a box of rocks, but I didn't really care. Kerry was cute and had the deepest brown eyes I'd ever seen. Cute overrules dumb any day, at least in my book. Also on the plus side, he was a jock. Kerry played baseball for a local team and often could also be found playing football with his buddies out in Garfield Park. I love jocks, so that also helped me to overlook the stupidity.

He also wasn't out. His baseball bat and his football cleats weren't the only things he kept in his closet. I should have seen that as a major warning sign, but I let his looks blind me to the dangers of dating someone dumb and closeted.

Oh, yeah. And he lived in Shelbyville. Shelbyville, for goodness sake. For those of you not in the know, Shelbyville is a dinky little town about forty miles outside of Indianapolis that God forgot about. Still stuck in the 1950s, Shelbyville is one of those towns that you see in movies and think to yourself, "Oh, a place like that really couldn't exist. Not in this day and age." Andy Griffith's Mayberry was positively progressive compared to Shelbyville. Norman Rockwell could have painted loads of scenes of life in Shelbyville, but then even he would have thrown up from the overload of homespun sweetness.

And to top it off, Kerry lived with his grandmother. Dumb, closeted, and living in Shelbyville with his grandmother. The warning signs were all there.

But he was really cute. And a jock. So I fell in love with him.

We traded off weekends. One week he'd come up to Indianapolis and stay with me until Sunday evening, and the next I'd make the trek down to Shelbyville. My first weekend down there started off badly, as I didn't get out of work on time and had to race (well, as much as a Kia will race) down the highway to get there before sunset. I didn't want to have to search for his grandmother's house in the dark. The directions Kerry had given me were sketchy at best, and I was sure I was going to get lost.

Other than having to figure out that "some street with some long name, I can't pronounce it" was actually Monticello Boulevard, I found that Kerry's directions weren't that bad and actually got there a little early. My knock on the door was answered by a slim, dark haired woman who smiled when I asked for Kerry. "He's still out at the park playing baseball," she told me. "They must be going into extra innings, but he should be back soon. Why don't you come in and wait for him?"

She turned out to be Kerry's sister, who was visiting with her new husband, Greg. Kerry had forgotten to tell me that not only would there be house guests for the weekend, but also they'd be sleeping in his room, while Kerry and I would have to make do on the living room floor.

Kerry's sister, Janet, seemed really nice. Husband Greg I wasn't so sure about. He grunted when she introduced me as a friend of Kerry's, not even taking his eyes off the game show on television. Granny May was in the kitchen, and Janet took me to meet her.

Granny May hated me on sight. If Janet or Greg questioned Kerry's sexuality, they didn't show it in the least, but Granny May obviously wondered whether her grandson was really the straight arrow that he claimed to be, and she viewed me as the enemy. I was evil, tempting her kin over to the dark side. Nearly everything she said to me was through clenched teeth, and when she grudgingly offered me a soda while I waited, I pictured her throwing the glass away once I was finished with it. No use to wash it. It had "homo cooties."

Luckily, Kerry made it home before the end of the show Greg was watching. His baseball uniform was a little mud stained, and he was a bit on the sweaty side, but for me he was like a ray of sunshine coming into the room. I nearly gave the whole thing away by rushing over to him and giving him a grope-filled hug, but I remembered in time and settled for a butch, "Hey. How's it going?"

Greg actually took his eyes away from the television long enough to question Kerry about the game. Granny May came into the living room and beamed when she looked at her grandson. She cooed as he told us about the home run he hit late in the game. After several minutes of small talk, he indicated the baseball glove and bat that he still held in his hands and said, "I'm going to put my stuff away in the garage. Steve, you want to come with me? I want to show you my car."

Granny May turned to me and gave me one of those *touch my grandson and I'll kill you* looks. I smiled sweetly at her and followed Kerry out to the garage. Kerry's car was a beat up Volkswagen that had obviously been around when Nixon was still in office, so his excuse to get me alone was a bit lame, but I didn't care. I was glad to get away from his family even for a few minutes.

Kerry stowed his gear in record time and turned to kiss me. The electric shock I got when our tongues met reminded me why I traveled outside of Indianapolis to be with him. When we came up for air, he muttered, "I want to fuck you."

"Here?" I asked. "Now?"

"Yeah. Bend your ass over my car. I want to stick my dick in you."

On the one hand, he looked really hot standing there in his grubby baseball clothes, but his entire family was only a few yards away. "What if someone comes in here?"

"No one ever comes in here but me," he said, gently pushing me back against his VW. "Come on, baby. I'm always horny after a game."

Apparently, I wasn't his first conquest in the garage as he had a secret stash of condoms and lube among the hammers and nails on the workbench. In minutes, I was spread across the hood of his car and he was slamming his cock into me. This was obviously going to be a quickie session as we wasted no time on foreplay. Maybe he wasn't so sure no one would come looking for us after all because once he got inside me the fucking was fast and furious. Kerry just yanked my jeans down to my ankles, pulled his baseball pants down, and got to work. The cool feel of the car hood contrasted nicely with the hot cock pounding my ass. Too soon though I felt him tense. His grip on my hips tightened as he shot his load, filling my ass.

Minutes later, we were seated around the kitchen table with Granny May and Janet. Greg was now watching *WWE Wrestling* and showed no sign of moving away from the television. Janet provided more soda and a slice of cake for each of us, and Kerry went into more detail about the game, but all the time we chatted I felt like there was a neon sign over my head flashing *WE JUST FUCKED OUT IN THE GARAGE*. Granny May seemed to be pretending I wasn't there. The few times she bothered to look my way, she didn't disguise her dislike for me.

Eventually, Janet pulled Greg away from the TV, and they went to Kerry's bedroom for the night. Granny May hovered in the kitchen, reluctant to leave me alone with her precious grandson, but eventually, she got tired enough that she had to get to bed, leaving Kerry and me to ourselves.

We had a pile of pillows and blankets to sleep on, but neither of us was tired. We watched some television with the sound down to a minimum until we were sure everyone else in the house was asleep. The lights went out, and soon we were under the blankets, kissing madly and pulling off each other's clothes.

Even as we were groping each other, the proximity of sleeping family members worried me. As Kerry proceeded to nibble on my neck (which he knew I loved), I whispered, "Should we be doing this? Someone's bound to hear us."

"They're asleep, so as long as we're quiet," Kerry's head disappeared beneath the blanket, and soon I felt his mouth swallowing my cock.

My heart was beating fast, and not just from the sexual excitement. I knew that Granny May suspected something was going on between Kerry and me, and I was pretty sure Janet knew but didn't care. If Greg had any suspicions, he didn't let on. I wasn't sure he was capable of anything other than grunting and watching television. What if Granny May decided to check up on us? What if good old boy Greg had to take a leak in the middle of the night? The bathroom was visible from where we were. Anyone going down the short hall to use the facilities would surely see the two guys having sex in the middle of the living room.

The more Kerry's mouth worked on my rod, the less I worried. Soon I forgot his family even existed and twisted myself around so that I could take his cock into my mouth. We sixty-nined quietly until we both climaxed. Chuckling, Kerry got up to get a cloth from the kitchen so that we could clean up. I watched him as he came back, admiring his athletic movements. In the moonlight coming in from the window, I could see his softening cock flopping around as he walked. He was beautiful.

He hadn't quite made it back to the blankets when we heard the sound of a door opening. Suddenly, his sister was in the hall, making for the bathroom. Kerry quickly dived under the blankets.

Janet paused at the bathroom door. We couldn't see her face, but she must have seen the movement in the living room. "Oh, were you going to use the restroom?"

"No," Kerry said, barely suppressing his giggles. "That's okay. You go ahead."

"If you're sure," she replied. She disappeared into the bathroom, and Kerry and I convulsed in silent laughter.

Greg and Janet left the next afternoon. Apparently, they were just stopping by on their way to a weekend excursion to Six Flags. They invited us along, but Kerry had a baseball game that he didn't want to miss. I certainly didn't want to stay alone with Granny May, so I went with Kerry to watch him from the stands.

I wasn't a huge baseball fan, just a fan of a baseball player. Still, I enjoyed watching the game, especially when Kerry was at bat or out in the field where I could watch him. There were a few other good looking guys on the team (the Shelbyville Hawks, if you can believe it), but they weren't as hot a Kerry. I have to admit the pitcher on the opposing team wasn't bad on the eyes either, but I was a good boyfriend and rooted against him.

The Hawks won 7 to 3. I waited in the stands while Kerry lingered on the field, chatting with his teammates. The small crowd quickly dispersed, and I kept waiting for Kerry to come over and get me, but it seemed he wanted to have conversations with every guy he knew. It finally dawned on me that he was waiting for most of his teammates to leave, so he wouldn't be seen going over to meet me. I probably wasn't butch enough for his crowd, and they might suspect that Kerry pitched for a team other than the Hawks.

He finally sauntered over when there were maybe two cars left in the parking lot. I'd been sitting on bleachers so long my ass was numb. Kerry smiled shyly when he saw me. "Sorry about that. I just don't get much of a chance to talk to the guys."

"You saw them yesterday."

He ignored the ice in my tone. "You ready to go?"

"I don't know. Are you sure you're ready? I think there's one guy left over at the concession stand, cleaning up. He might see you leaving with the skinny fag."

"It's not like that," Kerry insisted. "Let's go get something to eat, and then we'll rent a movie to watch."

Picking out a movie with Kerry was always a chore, since any film he watched had to have things blowing up and cute guys to watch. Anything with an actual plot confused him. We once watched Martin Scorsese's latest picture, and I had to constantly explain to Kerry what was going on. After wandering around the video store for ages, we were unable to agree on a movie. Finally, when Kerry wasn't looking, I went over to the store clerk and asked him to recommend something. "A movie with cute guys and things that explode," I told him. Fuck being in the closet. Even in Shelbyville, one eventually has to come out.

Armed with our movie, we headed back to Granny May's. The house seemed smaller and quieter without Greg and Janet there. Granny May didn't want to watch the movie, so she puttered in the kitchen while Kerry and I settled in the living room. I would have liked to at least have held Kerry's hand while suffering through the film, but every now and then Granny May peeked out to ensure that we were at least several feet apart. Kerry didn't seem to notice the *looks of death* she was shooting my way, but to be fair, he was more engrossed in the movie than I was.

Finally, Granny May decided it was her bedtime. She first went and got out some blankets and pillows and threw them down on the floor in front of the couch.

"What are those for?" Kerry asked with a slight frown.

Her lips were tight. "For him," she said, not wanting to even say my name.

"I thought he could sleep on the floor in my room, so we could talk."

"No," Granny May replied, shaking her head. "That wouldn't be appropriate. He can sleep out here. What would the neighbors say if they found out you two slept in the same room? They might think you were fags or something."

It was a good thing I didn't have a gun on me, or Granny May could have ended up with a couple of unexpected holes in her. Kerry turned red, saying, "No one would know."

"Well, I'd know," Granny May said. With a sniff, she disappeared off into her bedroom.

Kerry winked at me. "Don't worry. We'll just give her some time to fall asleep then we'll sneak into my room."

"Are you sure? If she comes out to use the bathroom she's bound to check to make sure I'm asleep out here."

Scoffing, Kerry replied, "She won't. She sleeps like a log."

I wasn't so sure. I had the feeling old Granny May would be checking up on me, so before I joined Kerry in his bedroom, I arranged a couple of pillows under some of the blankets to create a makeshift me. It didn't look very convincing, but maybe seen through eighty-year-old eyes in the dark it might fool her.

In Kerry's room, we stripped quietly, trying to contain our giggles. We slid into his somewhat narrow bed, and Kerry slid on top of me. Our kisses grew more passionate, and at one point, Kerry emitted a groan of pleasure.

I hissed at him. "You'll wake your grandmother."

He shook his head. "She's a heavy sleeper." He leaned over, so he could grab something under the bed. Apparently, he kept a stash of condoms and lube there, too. Like a Boy Scout, Kerry was always prepared. He got ready while I tried to relax. It seemed like every movement we made caused the bed to squeak loudly, and the sound seemed to echo through the house. Kerry put my legs up on his shoulders and threw the covers up over his shoulders, making a little tent for us to fuck in. Even in the dim lighting, I could see the smile on his face.

"I love fucking you," he said quietly.

I would have answered, but he chose that moment to guide the head of his dick into my ass. I was still a little jittery and the sudden intrusion made me gasp. Kerry chuckled and shushed me. "Relax," he said.

I thought of how good he looked and how hot his cock felt inside me. Finally, I relaxed enough for him to enter me all the way. Slowly, he began to move his hips, thrusting his hard prick into my ass. The bed announced each stroke, the squeaks increasing until they sounded like an alarm going off. Neighbors down the block could probably hear us fucking, so I hoped Kerry was correct in his opinion of Granny May's sleeping habits.

Kerry began slamming into me hard. Drops of sweat fell off his brow and hit my chest. As usual, he began to groan softly when he was ready to climax. I began stroking my own cock and shot a huge load as his grunts grew louder.

"Shit! I'm coming!" he gasped as I felt his cock explode inside me.

Just then, the bedroom door burst open.

Kerry and I froze, my ankles still up around his shoulders. There wasn't a lot of light in the room, but even a blind bat like Granny May could see something was going on. I quickly lowered my legs and Kerry fell on top me just as Granny May snapped out his name.

"Kerry!"

"What?" he asked as innocently as he could.

"What are you doing?"

Kerry always found it hard to think at all, much less quickly. He did, however, come up with an inventive excuse when he replied, "I was doing push-ups in bed. Helps me keep up my strength."

"Where's that friend of yours?" she asked. "I've just looked out in the living room, and he's not there."

He's under your grandson right now, I thought, feeling rather squished.

"I don't know," Kerry said. "Maybe he went out for a walk."

I'm sure that didn't fool her. Who would go out for a walk in Shelbyville at that hour? I couldn't see her standing in the doorway, my head being smothered by Kerry's shoulder, but I could hear her sniff suspiciously.

"I don't like that boy," she stated firmly. "He's putting bad ideas into your head."

I wanted to say, *No, but your grandson has been putting his cock into my ass*, but with Kerry's chest pressing down on my jaw the words would have come out garbled anyway.

"He's all right," Kerry said. "You'll get to like him."

Granny May obviously didn't think so. She huffed loudly, and I heard the bedroom door shutting.

Kerry raised himself up on his elbows and sighed. "That was close."

I couldn't believe my ears. "You think she couldn't see me underneath you with the soles of my feet facing heaven? She knew we were fucking. She just couldn't accuse her dear grandson. It's me she hates, not you. You're her innocent lamb. I'm the big bad wolf."

"She'll grow to like you," Kerry insisted.

He was wrong, of course.

We decided after that to spend our weekends together in Indianapolis. Shelbyville was a little too frosty for our tastes.

A REGULAR BUD
By Ryan Field

Noah's entire adult life had been a narration of discarding other men, casting them off for impractical reasons, pushing them aside for the next promising relationship. Monogamy tended to make him yawn after the first three months usually when the sex became routine. When his last boyfriend, Mike, started to hang a few clothes in the closet after only two weeks of dating, Noah started to lose sleep. How could he ignore that? Clearly, Noah knew it wouldn't be easy to get rid of him if this continued; he could always end it all on the telephone and mail the clothes in a plain brown box. But, he decided to tell Mike that things weren't working out in person and that it was probably for the best if Mike removed all his personal things from the closet. Though Mike didn't take this well, and he lashed out because Noah couldn't give him a solid excuse for ending the relationship, Noah was relieved when he finally heard Mike's car back out of the driveway for good.

Everything else in Noah's life remained stable though. He lived in his dead parents' house, the big stone colonial next door to the free library, in the same small town about thirty miles south of Baltimore where he'd grown up. He had the same job as an international marketing representative for a chemical company since college, with a new company car every two years and free trips around the world. Even his nerdy college roommate, Preston, was still with him.

Noah was an only child, and his parents had been killed in an automobile accident just outside of Baltimore two weeks before his college graduation. When Preston haplessly mentioned he was looking for a place to live back then, within thirty miles of his new teaching job in Baltimore, Noah suggested he rent a room from him, in the house in Martha Falls. And he'd been there ever since. Though the balding Preston was an emaciated man with big ears and thin lips shaped like the letter M, who had been engaged to the same thick ankled school teacher for seven years, and Noah was a handsome, openly gay man with an athletic body and many boyfriends, this peculiar match worked.

Preston was that polite, perpetual boarder who only used the bottom shelf of the refrigerator and spent all of his time tip-toeing around his own bedroom when Noah was home.

Noah didn't travel all the time. He worked at home in a small office on the second floor next to his bedroom. All his work was done with phone calls, computers and fax machines; he went to the corporate offices several times a year for significant sales meetings. The only time he left the house when he wasn't traveling was to go to the market, the gym, or to hook up with guys he'd met on Craig's List – he thought of them as his buds. The old house was immense, and he didn't have to run into Preston if he didn't want to; you could set your watch by that man's routine: up at six, off to school by seven and home again at five thirty. Except for Tuesdays, when he wore his red plaid button down and met his fiancé at the movies. And Preston didn't seem to mind when Noah had the occasional overnight guest, so to speak. Actually, when he did run into one of Noah's buds in the upstairs hall, he'd fold his arms and smile as if he knew a naughty little secret. He'd been living in the same house with Noah for almost nine years, and he knew these guys wouldn't last more than a few weeks, at the most.

But, what Preston didn't know about Noah would have made the few thin strands of hair he had left stand up straight. He never would have suspected that his good looking, dark-haired landlord, whom he'd known since freshmen year in college, had a fetish so unusual, and so kinky, there wasn't even a porn site devoted to it. None of Noah's ex-boyfriends or buds new about his secret either. This was something Noah kept private, and he didn't want to get caught.

Preston's Coke-bottle glasses would have exploded if he'd known that his athletic, masculine roommate had an uncontrollable passion for high heels and cigarettes. Not just any high heels; Noah's had to be white leather pumps, with at least a five inch heel; but the higher the better. Of course, the cigarettes could be any brand; he wasn't too picky about them, and they really were secondary. It was the high heels that made his heart beat faster. And it wasn't that Noah was a transgender who felt trapped in a man's body and he desperately needed to dress up like a woman to feel complete. He'd never been interested in doing drag or becoming a transvestite; he really didn't even like to watch drag shows. Noah loved being a man and wouldn't have changed that for anything. But, when he slipped a pair of white stilettos on his feet, his eyes dilated, his head started to spin and his penis became so hard he could barely walk.

Cigarettes turned him on, too. He'd never been a smoker; not even a social smoker. When he entered a restaurant that allowed smoking, he gritted his teeth and left quickly; when he smelled stale tobacco on someone's clothes he felt nauseous. But put a burning cigarette in his hand, and a pair of white high heels on his feet, and he could orgasm without even touching his own erection. He didn't inhale the smoke; he just puffed. So it wasn't as if he were addicted to nicotine.

Though he kept all this to himself and restricted his high heel and cigarette fetish to private masturbation sessions in his own home, there were times when he needed to wear his high heels and smoke his cigarettes in public. In the middle of the night, while Preston was in his room snoring, Noah would shove a pair of white high heels and a pack of cigarettes into a white plastic grocery bag, slip out the back door, and drive to a truck stop along the interstate. At the truck stop, he'd park in a dark, secluded spot and wait for a horny guy to pull up next to him; and they always did. If he thought the guy was attractive (he didn't have to be a *GQ* model), he'd light up a cigarette, remove all his clothes, put on the high heels and lean over the back seat just long enough to let the guy know he was naked and ready to play. Noah's body was firm and thin and well defined; he shaved all his body hair except for a small dark patch just above his penis. When the other guy saw this open invitation, it was only a matter of minutes before he was sitting in Noah's front passenger seat and running his hands all over Noah's naked ass. If any of these guys didn't like the high heels and the cigarettes, they never mentioned it to Noah, and that's mostly because they couldn't wait to turn him around and bend him over.

But he didn't go to the truck stop very often, and wearing high heels had to be constrained to his home; usually during lunch time, between Monday and Friday, when Preston was at school. Before the 911 terrorist attacks on the World Trade Center, Noah would always take a pair of high heels and a pack of cigarettes with him when he traveled. He grinned for no apparent reason, and he had a semi-erection in his pants when he walked through the airport knowing there was a pair of sexy shoes at the bottom of his suitcase. He'd rush to his hotel room just so he could get naked and walk around a strange room wearing nothing but his favorite heels. However, with heightened security in the airports, the last thing he needed was to have some security guard rummaging through his suitcases and pulling out a pair of white, almond toe pumps in size twelve, extra wide.

When he was working at home, there were some mornings when Noah didn't bother to get dressed. He'd remain in bed long enough to hear Preston's car door slam shut, and then jump out of bed naked and watch Preston drive down the street. Then, even before he took his morning piss, he'd reach into the back corner of his closet and haul out a small black footlocker (he kept the key hidden under a loose floorboard near the closet door); he'd unlock the latch, open the locker and decide which high heels he'd wear that day while he worked in his home office. He had three pairs of white, five inch, almond toe pumps, one pair of red stilettos with pointed toes and six inch heels, and two pairs of black almond toe pumps that were identical to the white ones, but a little worn around the edges. The red stilettos were for when he felt like something a little different; the black pumps looked really good when he had a deep tan in the summertime. Most mornings, Noah chose a pair of the white pumps; they were the ones that made his dick the hardest.

On a morning just like this about a year ago, toward the end of April, Noah watched Preston drive away, and then he stepped into a pair of white pumps. He had an important conference call at nine, with his boss and three of his co-workers that he knew would take at least an hour and a half, if not longer. His boss was one of those obnoxious, overachieving women who wore her hair like Willy Wonka (the Johnny Depp version) and never stopped talking long enough to listen to anyone else. She thought the sales and marketing force needed more future goals to snag more customers; Noah thought she needed to get porked more on a regular basis. While she talked about the foreign markets, Noah stretched his smooth, muscular legs out and admired his white pumps. He smiled and grabbed his shaved balls when she talked about increasing sales figures in the Deep South. Oh, if she could only have seen him sitting there that morning, with one leg dangling off the side of his office chair and a high heel swinging back and forth, she'd have certainly shut her big mouth for at least a minute.

The conference call ended at eleven fifteen, and Noah took a deep breath when he turned the phone off. He stood from his chair, stretched his arms and legs, and then crossed back into the bedroom to get his dildo and cigarettes from the nightstand. His dick became semi-erect when the high heels clicked against the wooden floors; he hadn't jerked off in nearly three days, and his balls were ready to explode. He grabbed the dildo and cigarettes and headed toward the back staircase, which led to the kitchen; his ball sack became tight; but he was so used to walking around in high heels, he didn't even need to hold on to the banister. When Preston wasn't home, Noah preferred jerking off downstairs, in the great room off the kitchen, where it was wide open and there was a wall of mirrors across from a black leather sofa. He liked to see the high heels reflected in the dark mirror, with his legs in the air and a dildo up his ass, while he stroked his dick. The black leather sofa felt soft and easy against his naked back and kept him from sliding down too far.

He usually listened for any unexpected sounds when he was in the main part of the house having a jerk-off session; just to be sure no one would catch him in the act. But, that day he was so involved in getting comfortable in front of the mirrors, he didn't hear the knock on the front door. And, that's probably because a landscape crew was working on the lawn next door, plus, it was a large house with thick plaster walls, and you didn't always hear it in the great room when someone knocked. The noise from the lawn mowers didn't bother Noah (actually he liked the thought of young landscapers working right outside his window while he got off), but they drowned out all other sounds. Of course no one could have portended that Preston's younger brother, who had graduated from college in January, had planned a surprise visit that spring.

So, while Noah's legs were up in the air, and he was slipping a nine inch dildo into his hole with one hand and pulling his dick with the other, Preston's born-again, Christian brother from Montana was lifting the sea grass door mat out front and reaching for the spare key. Noah didn't hear the lock click or clack, and he didn't notice the sound of the front door opening and closing when he lit a cigarette and started to puff. By then, his legs were spread wide, the dildo was all the way up his hole, and he was pumping his cock with power.

When Preston's brother crossed through the long center hallway that led to the kitchen, he walked softly on a red oriental runner. When he reached the doorway, he heard a peculiar slapping noise; and then there was heavy breathing, but he couldn't pigeonhole where it was coming from. He turned the corner and saw that the kitchen was empty; but he smelled burning tobacco. Then he turned to the left and saw a cloud of smoke and Noah's white heels bobbing back and forth in the air. He dropped his black duffle bag on the floor and opened his mouth as broad as it would go.

"Well!"

Noah heard the duffle bag hit the floor; a thud. But it was too late to run and hide by then. He stopped breathing for a moment; the dildo shot out of his ass and hit the coffee table; his legs went down, and he pressed the high heels hard against the bottom of the sofa. He stared at the strange young guy for a few seconds, and then shouted, "Who are you? Why are you in my house?" For all he knew, this guy had come in to rob the place. This was a fine state of affairs, indeed. Now they'd find him shot to death, bone naked with almond toe high heels on his feet.

"Ah, I'm sorry, Bud," the guy said, "I'm Preston's brother, Dave, from Montana. I wanted to surprise him is all." His voice was deep and rugged. He just stood there; his eyes were swelling and his feet were nailed in place. He didn't look anything like Preston. His hair was as dark as Noah's, he had two thick silver earrings in each ear, and he was wearing a pair of tight, low-rise jeans that hugged his slim hips. He reminded Noah of one of those rent boys you see on Santa Monica Blvd. Noah could see that he'd been trying to grow a goatee, but it looked more like dark fuzz. "I tried knocking, but no one answered," he said, "I found the key under the mat out front." He shrugged, and his long arms dangled at his sides.

Noah covered his exposed groin with a gold velvet throw pillow. "Ah well …" His head felt like it would explode; he couldn't seem to form a coherent sentence. His worst nightmare had finally come true. He'd been exposed. But more than that – by his roommate's kid brother.

"Man, I really am sorry; I shouldn't have interrupted," he said. But instead of slowly backing out of the room to give Noah his privacy, Dave dropped his car keys on the kitchen island and crossed into the great room to join him.

"Ah, Dave," Noah said, "Excuse me for being so inhospitable, but isn't this when you are supposed to scream and run out the door with your arms flying in the air? I mean, after all, it's not every day you find your brother's roommate jerking off in a pair of high heels." At first he'd been dumbstruck, but now he was getting pissed off, and sarcasm seemed the best way out.

Dave smiled, and then he sat down in a white club chair not far from the sofa. "I said I was sorry, Bud. And don't worry; it's cool. Preston's told me all about you. You're Noah, and I know you're gay; I don't mind."

Noah's eyes popped, and he clenched the pillow between his legs with one hand; with the other he leaned forward and stamped the cigarette out in a clean ashtray. "Well, maybe I mind. This isn't something I normally share with the public, if you know what I mean; c'mon, Dave." He lifted his right leg and pointed to a high heel.

Dave grinned with such exuberance you could see his upper and lower teeth. "It's kind of hot, Bud, but I won't tell anyone, especially not Preston. So calm your pretty little self down because it's no big deal: Hell, I once nailed this dude from West Virginia who liked to paint his toe nails red, a little blond dude in the dorms, with a sweet little ass. Didn't bother me; he had big lips, and he knew how to suck dick." Dave stretched his legs forward and started rubbing his groin. He kicked off his shoes and pulled down his zipper. He wasn't wearing underwear; a thick, hard dick jumped out of his jeans. He pointed to his cock as if it were a third person in the room, and said, "He likes it kinky, too, Bud."

Noah blinked a couple of times and shook his head. He couldn't believe this kid pulled out his dick, and that it was such a nice dick, too. If this guy was goofy, asexual Preston's younger brother, there must have been a mix up at the hospital. "I think you'd better zip up your pants, Dave. This is not going to happen. I'm not fucking my roommate's kid brother."

"Hey," Dave said, "I'm not a kid. I'm twenty-two and a half years old and only eight years younger than you. And, besides, you're not going to be fucking me; from the way it looks I'm going to be fucking you, Bud." He stood up and dropped his jeans. When he stepped out of them, his solid legs were covered with dark hair. "It's not like I'm a virgin or anything."

"I thought you were a born-again Christian, and extremely religious," Noah said. All those years with Preston as a roommate, and he suddenly realized he knew very little about Preston's background. Just that his family members were conservative, born-again Christians, and his younger brother Dave was very interested in sports, especially football. He'd always pictured Dave to be one of those chunky small town guys who marry their high school sweethearts.

"Not me: my mother and father," Dave said. "I'm into dudes." He pulled off his white tee-shirt. He was naked now except for thin black socks. When he slowly walked toward Noah, his dick started to bounce. He was one of those overly confident, jock-type guys who lope around on the balls of their feet. "I kind of like those high heels; I love it when a hot looking guy has a little kink here or there."

Noah put up his hands. "Stay where you are; I'm serious."

But, Dave continued loping toward the sofa, and though Noah protested, he didn't make a move to leave the room. He could have stood up and walked away, and he could have stopped Dave, but there was something about his eyes that made Noah hold his breath. They were dark and sinister, but at the same time simple and mischievous. Noah's erection was back again now, harder than before, thanks to Dave's wiry, hairy body.

"Damn," Dave said, "Preston told me you were a work-out freak, but I never thought you'd have such a great body." He leaned forward without permission and placed the palms of both hands on Noah's chest muscles and began to squeeze. "Now that's what I call a hard handful of muscle. And you don't have any body hair … freaking hot, Bud."

When he stopped playing with Noah's chest, he spread his legs and leaned back so that his pelvis would move forward, as if he were going to take a piss. His hard dick was now within inches of Noah's face; his balls were so close Noah cold smell them: ripe cheese and watered down vinegar; he probably hadn't showered in a few days because he'd been traveling. Noah's lips were pressed together, but he placed his palms gently on Dave's strong, hairy thighs and took a deep breath. It occurred to him that this was the first time in his life he'd ever been seduced by a younger guy, or that he liked being seduced by a younger guy. Up until then, he'd always been the young one.

Dave lifted one hairy leg up and rested his foot on the sofa so that he could balance his body and press the head of his cock against Noah's cheekbone. His large, dark brown balls started to swing and sway in metered time. Noah closed his eyes, opened his mouth and sucked both hairy balls down his throat at the same time. Heavy, black pubic hair rubbed against his nostrils, and his cheekbones were bulging with testicles; they tasted salty and reminded him of a combination of smoked ham and strong cheese. Dave placed one hand on Noah's head and started to jerk his dirty dick with the other.

By the time Dave's bull sized balls finally fell from Noah's mouth, his lips were swollen and his chin was dripping wet. Then Dave rubbed the head of his cock on Noah's wet chin for a moment and shoved it into Noah's mouth. Dave started to moan; Noah wasn't one of those guys who just moved his head back and forth while the dick slipped in and out. Noah knew how to gobble dick well enough to get any guy off. He closed his eyes and began to suck with great heed; his cheekbones indented, and his tongue gripped the base of Dave's cock that created authentic pressure – so real that Dave's eyes began to roll and his breathing grew heavy. His large hands held the sides of Noah's head, and he began to pump and buck while Noah sucked him off.

Noah was prepared to get him off and swallow the entire blast of seed, but Dave pulled out and said, "I want those high heels hanging over my shoulders, Bud."

Dave stood, so Noah could turn and lie flat on his back. Dave then climbed onto the leather sofa, rested on his knees between Noah's legs and began to run the side of his right hand up and down Noah's hairless ass crack. Noah lifted his right leg up and rested it on the back of the sofa; he turned his ankle, so he could see the white high heel. Dave grabbed Noah's left ankle and lifted the other high heel to his mouth and began to lick the sides of the shoe. "You like that, don't you?" Dave whispered between licks.

Noah sucked his small stomach in and arched his back. "Oh yes," he replied. He'd been dreaming and fantasizing about another guy licking his high heels and his ankles all of his life, though he never thought, not in his wildest dreams, it would come true.

Then Dave pressed his right palm against the back of Noah's left leg, just under the knee, and spread it as wide as it would go. Dave spit on his cock, rubbed the saliva all over his shaft, and started to work the head into Noah's hole. For such a young guy, Noah was amazed at how tender and gentle he was; he knew just when to stop, and then when to go deeper. All eight inches of Dave's football player cock slid into Noah's ass, and he didn't feel so much as an instant of pain. When it was in as far as it would go, and Noah could feel Dave's balls up against his ass, Dave leaned forward and began to buck. He pressed the back of Noah's leg and pushed it forward so that Noah's knee practically touched his shoulder. Noah kept his other leg against the back of the sofa for support, but the high heel was now resting on Dave's wide shoulder. The harder Dave pounded, the more pliable his body became. Noah reached for the back of Dave's neck and pulled his face forward so that he could kiss him. Dave opened his mouth and started sucking Noah's tongue. Both tongues were so hungry and so sloppy Noah's toes started to curl inside the high heels.

Dave raised his head. "Can I spit in your mouth, Bud?"

Noah smiled, opened his mouth and stuck out his tongue. There was something so rough and gauche about the way Dave fucked and moved; his big balls slapped against Noah's ass with no precise rhythm, but the awkwardness had a merit all its own. Dave spit a huge gob into Noah's mouth; Noah swallowed and stuck out his tongue for more. But Dave leaned forward and shoved his tongue into Noah's mouth again. The bucking grew more intense, and Dave began to moan while Noah sucked his tongue. Noah knew he was ready to climax; his hairy legs began to wiggle, and he started to moan with more intensity. So, he pressed his palms against Dave's shoulders and nodded yes.

There were five or six hard slams against Noah's ass, and then he shot his entire fill of cream into Noah's body. When he climaxed, he pressed his lips to Noah's with such force his wiry goatee actually burned Noah's chin. It wasn't the first time a guy had ever blown his load into Noah's hole, but it was the first time any guy had kissed him so passionately while doing it.

Dave opened his eyes and looked down at Noah. "Are you okay?"

Noah nodded, and said, "Don't pull out yet."

Dave slowly leaned backwards, making sure his cock would remain deep inside Noah's body, and rested on his haunches. He smiled and wagged his tongue like a naughty little boy, and then yanked Noah's left foot to his face again and started to lick the high heel. Noah stretched his other leg all the way out and started to jerk off. With Dave's cum soaked cock still up his ass, and Dave licking his high heel, he jerked out a load of juice so powerful it actually landed on his face. There was white cream all over his lips; even a few drops in his hair. While Dave watched, Noah stuck out his tongue and lapped up his own cum. Then he wiped his face with his fingers and licked them clean, too. Dave's eyes grew wide while Noah licked his wet fingers; he smiled and then slapped Noah on the ass.

A moment later, Dave's cock jumped out of Noah's ass, and his body fell forward, pinning Noah to the sofa with all of his weight. Noah wrapped his legs around Dave's waist, crossed his feet at the ankles and rested his high heels on the small of Dave's back.

"My brother is always raving about you when he comes home, it's always 'Noah did this,' or 'Noah did that'; he thinks you are perfect. But I had no idea you'd be anything like this … so fucking hot, Bud," Dave said. He buried his hairy young face in the crook of Noah's neck and started to bite.

"Preston's a good guy," Noah said, "which is why you'd better let me get up and get dressed. I wouldn't want him walking in on us like this." He could feel Dave's cum dripping out of his hole and down his ass crack. "I don't think he'd want to see my legs wrapped around his kid brother's naked body … even if his kid brother is a big strong boy like you."

Dave laughed. "He'd really freak out, Bud."

"Hell, I'd freak out, too," Noah said.

Dave licked his ear a couple of times. "I think it was hot, and the expression on your face when I was licking your shoes was kind of cute."

It occurred to Noah that if Dave hadn't caught him jerking off in high heels, none of this would have happened. "I'm curious. Why are you here? Is it just a visit?"

"Ah well," Dave said, "I decided to move to Baltimore permanently, and I wanted to surprise Preston. I've already got a job with a small ad agency, and I was hoping I could bunk here until I found a place, Bud."

Noah smiled. "You can stay here as long as you want, but I don't think we should tell Preston about any of this."

Dave laughed. "Keep it a secret that I'm fucking your brains out, or that you have a kink for high heels and smoking?"

Noah wrapped his arms around Dave's shoulders and squeezed hard. "Both. Now, be a good boy, and get your hairy legs off me before Preston comes home and catches us like this. With my luck, he'd come home early for the first time in years."

BETRAYAL
By Scott James

"Otto is filthy rich," Jake declared. He tossed back the dregs of his beer. A powerful hulk of a man, he had a shaved head and tattoos. "The old bastard made a fortune in the printing business. It's time we paid him a visit."

The usual crowd packed Duffy's Bar. On the stage, a sinewy Adonis strutted his stuff in a G-string. His bronze skin glistened with sweat.

"What do you have in mind, Jake?" Vinny was a timid little runt with the paleness of an albino. "Are we gonna smack him?"

"Naw, we're gonna serenade him," Jake snapped.

"Sorry," Vinny muttered through nicotine stained teeth. "I just meant are we gonna break into his joint when he's not there, or give him the gears when he is … you know?"

Jake shot him a look that would have shriveled steel while ordering another round. "How the fuck are we gonna get in?" he demanded. "The place is barred up like a fortress and wired with alarms."

Vinny cupped his fresh drink between trembling hands. "You're right, Jake, I'm real sorry. I spoke without thinking."

"You always do, and that's you're fuckin problem. You're a regular pain in the butt."

"Sorry, Jake, it won't happen again. I'm gonna work on that. I truly am."

However, Jake ignored his apology, for he was now ogling the exotic dancer – who had just shed his G-string – with an intensity that obliterated all else. "God is he ever fuckin hung," he murmured lasciviously.

Vinny swiveled around and eyed the dancer with pale eyes that smoldered with jealousy.

"Don't wait up for me," Jake ordered. He swung himself off the stool and headed toward the artist's changing rooms at the back of the stage.

* * * * *

Otto was a stooped matchstick of a man with watery eyes and thin lips. "Ah that feels good, keep goin." He grasped Vinny's head with gnarled fingers.

Vinny was getting tired and his jaw ached. It took Otto a long time to come, and to speed up the process he inched his pinkie into his anus.

"Oh gawd, that's good … good," Otto moaned. He wiggled his bum in appreciation. His saggy old knockers banged against Vinny's chin.

Vinny tapped against the A-spot in perfect tempo with the mouth fucking, but still his stubborn trick refused to go off.

"Rim me Vinny," he gasped. "That'll do it for me … it always does."

It's what Vinny was afraid of and richly dreaded. For he hated to lick the old man's shriveled up bum hole while he gasped and bucked around like an unbroken mare at a high jump.

But pro that he was, he didn't let his personal feelings get in the way of business. The last thing he wanted was for Otto to go limp on him. He soon had his aged client erupting in the few watery spurts that signaled success.

* * * * *

After much discussion about how to best rob the hapless Otto, over countless bottles of beer at Duffy's, they decided on a middle road. This eschewed earlier plans to rough him up and make him pay, or try to break into his house when he wasn't there.

And, this one was so simple they were surprised that they hadn't thought of it before. Namely, that while Vinny gave Otto his weekly blow job, Jake would sneak in through the kitchen window, which was on the ground floor and easily accessible.

The plan worked well, too. "Gotta get a soda, Otto, this is thirsty work." Vinny extricated himself from his client's clutches. Then he opened the window before grabbing a Coke from the refrigerator.

When he returned, Otto was tugging away at his old tool, trying to keep his hard on. "Come on quick, or it'll go soft on me." They were in his living room, the portrait of the stern-faced Helga, his wife of almost fifty years, dominated it.

Soon Otto regained his flagging erection and pumped away in Vinny's mouth for all he was worth. "Bend over the chair; I want to fuck you in the bum." This was such an unexpected departure from his usual repertoire that it took Vinny a moment or two to comply.

"Getting adventuresome now, are we?" He bared his small behind like a sacrifice to some pagan god of old, while keeping an ear cocked for Jake, who he reasoned must be in the house by now.

And, he was, pausing outside the door at that very moment to make sure Vinny had Otto well and truly occupied. Jake set off for the basement. He had scoured every inch of the upstairs and main floor, coming up with nothing at all of value, let alone a fortune in bills. Yet rumor had it that Otto kept most of his cash on the premises, in order to avoid the clutches of the taxman.

* * * * *

"Not a fuckin thing." Jake kicked at a chair with a steel-capped boot. "If that old bastard keeps his money in the house then he's found a way to make it fuckin invisible."

He punched the table top with a massive fist and glowered down at Vinny who nervously nibbled at a donut. "I'm sorry, Jake," he stammered between bites. "I guess we'll just have to knock it out of him."

"I reckon so." Jake had a face like thunder. "But first I'm gonna whip your ass for being such a smart mouth."

"I'm sorry, Jake. I didn't mean nothin by it." Vinny recalled the incident in question. For as Jake ambled past him in Duffy's, with the strutting exotic dancer in tow he had muttered "dancers are sluts," in a voice designed to carry.

"You insulted Brandon," Jake raged. His face was so close to Vinny's that the open pores were clearly visible, along with a good many blackheads. "And after I've given you a licking for it, you're gonna fuckin well clean the shit house floor with a toothbrush, got that?"

"Yes Jake." Vinny fairly quaked at this tower of rage directed at him.

"Problem is," Jake mumbled, as Vinny pulled down his pants and bent across the chair. "I don't take the strop to you enough."

He fetched the razor strop from the bathroom and brought it down across the quivering behind with a loud and fearsome crack.

"Ouch," Vinny screamed out in pain. He tried to suck in his injured ass to protect it from the next stroke.

Thwack … thwack … thwack … thwack … the severe thrashing continued until Vinny pleaded with Jake to stop. His mouth twisted in pain, and his eyes glazed over in ecstasy.

"Stay right where you are." Jake's voice was thick with lust, when he at last threw down the strap. "Whipping your butt has got me hornier than a ten-peckered owl."

Vinny's buttocks were a scourged and bloody mess. He winced in pain as Jake smeared a blob of Vaseline onto his anus before entering it with his bulging cock. "You've got a nice tight little asshole," he groaned hotly. He patted lightly what he had so brutally spanked. "Oh god, I'm not going to last long, you sexy bitch." And he fucked the obliging little orifice with long hard thrusts until he exploded in seismic convulsions.

* * * * *

"He won't be sitting down comfortably for weeks." Jake glanced around at Duffy's terrace with its striped umbrellas thick with bird shit. "I whupped his butt good."

Brandon St. Cloud, whose real name was Vladimar Dimitrievich Khlebnikov, rolled his blue eyes provocatively.

"And if you don't stop playing hard to get," Jake added with hot intent. "I might just do the same thing to you."

Brandon threw his head back and laughed coquettishly. "I haven't been spanked since I was a child," he admitted. He squirmed his bottom around teasingly. "It might be fun."

"Well I'd just put you across my lap to begin with." Jake's cock rose hard at the thought. "And, spank your bare butt with the palm of my hand."

"Mmm … I'm liking the sound of this more and more. But it would have to be a light spanking. I couldn't get up on stage and dance with a welted blistered bum."

"I realize that," Jake muttered hotly. "I would just spank you enough to make you tingle and beg for more."

* * * * *

The guard dog from the junkyard next door had been barking aggressively for hours. It was getting on Vinny's already frazzled nerves, and he felt ready to explode. "Shut the fuck up," he yelled, and slammed the door so hard plaster fell down like a dusty rain shower.

He and Jake had lived in the old house, which Vinny had done his best to keep clean and tidy, for several years.

"I'll need a clean pair of jeans for tonight." Jake stuffed a sandwich into his mouth.

Fuck you, Vinny thought angrily. He tossed a half-smoked cigarette out the kitchen window. The thing was he got off on being treated like a slave. He only asked to be allowed to serve his master in any way possible, while willingly accepting correction for any fault.

However, that all changed with the appearance on the scene of Brandon St. Cloud. He winced as the name conjured up unwelcome images of the sinewy dancer locked in erotic clinches with the burly Jake, his Jake!

It wasn't that Jake hadn't strayed before. In fact, he had had numerous flings during their time together. But none of them had lasted the way that this one had. Vinny knew the reason why – the slutty dancer was playing hard to get – and he grimaced angrily as he ruminated about it.

Night after night, Jake would return home in a lather of frustration, venting all his pent-up horniness on Vinny's quivering butt. He often fucked him without lubrication.

And even Jake's determination to rob poor old Otto, took a back seat to his towering lust for the sexy dancer.

* * * * *

"Lips or hips?" Vinny winked. He and Otto were having a quick drink before beginning their weekly session. He ignored the grim face of the shrewish Helga as it glowered down on them disapprovingly.

If only she could see her husband now. Vinny fastened his thin lips around the old man's firm cock. He drooled down the length of the shaft and worked his own special magic around the head and glans. Otto moaned and would have stumbled if Vinny hadn't grasped the bony buttocks.

"That's lovely … lovely," he moaned. As he drew near orgasm, he rocked so violently Vinny feared he was having a fit.

"You need a massage," he suggested. "Calm you down a bit." Vinny led him to the sofa where he began to soothe and knead the sagging flesh with hands smeared with oil.

* * * * *

"We're gonna hit the old bastard next time you visit," Jake declared. "We've gotta get some cash quick; we're just about busted."

And I know why, Vinny fumed. Jake had been buying the coy Brandon expensive presents. He had found the evidence of this while rifling through Jake's credit card receipts. There had been a cashmere sweater, an initialed signet ring, and a snake's head necklace.

Why that rotten fuckin gold-digger. Vinny was unable to remember the last time Jake had bought a gift for him. So upset was he by his thoughts that he lit another cigarette while there was still one going in the ashtray.

* * * * *

"You have the most beautiful fuckin body." Jake drooled, as Brandon paraded before him in a rhinestone flecked G-string. They were in his tiny dressing room where a sluggish fan whirred ineffectively in the corner. "But, will I ever get to taste its forbidden fruits?"

The truth was that although mightily turned on by Brandon's inaccessibility at first, Jake now grew fed up in his role as spurned wooer. While at the same time, he was still too enamored with the fascinating dancer to call it quits.

"What's the rush?" Brandon cooed. Thoughts of just how many suitors this beautiful young man had tormented Jake. "Remember slow and steady wins the race."

And it was, indeed, a race, to see who would be the first to grasp the prize – Brandon's sexy ass and the joys of his splendid mouth.

"I haven't been exactly unforthcoming with you," he pouted. "Why you enjoy my bottom every night."

"Well that's not exactly what I have in mind." Jake's tone was impatient. He noticed Brandon's peevish expression and added hastily. "But it is a start. No fuckin doubt about that."

"So shall we get started?"

Jake needed no further prompting. He immediately set down his drink on the cluttered dressing table; finding a spot with difficulty between the cold cream and face powder. He sat down on the only chair the room offered.

It was time for Brandon's spanking. As the young man lowered himself across his lap with his toes and hands bearing his weight on the grubby tiled floor, Jake drank in with worshipping eyes the firm round globes with the G-string dividing them.

It was more like a series of love pats than a spanking, first on one tanned cheek then on the other. And the rules – established by Brandon – dictated that no other liberties be taken. Until that is, he agreed to them.

For the first time he submitted to a spanking, Jake had been so excited he had fondled the young man's balls and stroked his muscular thighs.

"Just a dozen light spanks on both bottom cheeks," Brandon decreed. He flexed his toes like a sensuous cat as Jake meted them out. His muscular legs stiffened with excitement.

Jake entertained licentious daydreams about ripping off Brandon's G-String and penetrating his hard-to-get ass with his steely cock. Fucking him within an inch of his life and then making him lick off the cum afterwards. But Jake was in love, and to offend the object of his devotion in this way was unthinkable.

After the spanking was over, Brandon allowed Jake to fondle his bottom for a few minutes. He stroked the firm flesh and murmured endearments. This was a new liberty designed to keep his frustrated suitor happy.

"Just let me stick my fingers in the crack of your ass, and fondle your cock and balls." Jake's voice was thick with longing.

"Maybe tomorrow night." Brandon extricated himself nimbly from Jake's probing hands. "Right now, I have another performance." He twirled around gracefully crying, "My public awaits me."

Jake wanked vigorously with hands that trembled with excitement. He was determined to hold this incorrigible cocktease to his promise and branch out with their sex play.

* * * * *

The following night he did just that. "Now doesn't that feel better?" He had stripped off Brandon's G-string and clasped his cock. "Time for a spanking with a difference."

He tugged away at the dancer's rigid cock while delivering a brisk spanking to his upraised behind.

Spank … spank … spank … spank … spank ... Brandon squirmed with pleasure and fucked Jake's thigh. His neat balls banged against it like battering rams at a stubborn gate. When Jake penetrated the throbbing bunghole with his finger and lightly stroked the A-spot, Brandon squealed in excitement and went off like a missile.

"I want to fuck you properly … in the bum with my cock." He kneaded Brandon's ass with his hands and pressed the head of his cock against it. But the young man resisted. He insisted they had gone far enough for one day.

"Waiting will make it better," he murmured seductively, "when you do finally take me."

Jake responded by spanking the backs of Brandon's thighs, from his bottom down to his knees. He meted out light rhythmic swats that made the dancer squirrely with delight. Next time, Jake promised himself, he was going to suck on the nut-brown nipples and rim the little rosebud of an asshole with his tongue.

* * * * *

Vinny was convinced that once Jake had fucked Brandon his interest would diminish rapidly. It was the challenge and thrill of the chase that was currently holding his interest, a classic case of the forbidden apple.

Meanwhile, he had been taking the brunt of his cheating partner's frustrations, and with growing reluctance had been presenting his ass for an energetic fucking, often repeated far into the night.

"Quit complaining," Jake bellowed, as Vinny patted at his bleeding anus with a tissue. "You'd think you had a virgin ass for fuck's sake." Then he quickly renewed his assault, holding Vinny's buttocks apart to widen the painful bum hole.

"Another peep out of you, and I'll fuckin spank you," he threatened. "And you won't be able to sit down for a month."

It was much later, while he was making Vinny lick the cum off his cock prior to giving him another blow job that he mentioned Otto.

"When you go to see the old bastard tomorrow night, open the fuckin kitchen window like you did before," he instructed. The sagging mattress creaked with the intensity of his response to Vinny's warm probing lips and tongue. "And we'll leave there with cash, fuckin loads of it." Jake intended to beat the old man senseless, unless he divulged the hiding place of his fortune.

But much to his surprise, and considerable disappointment, roughhouse tactics were unnecessary. The following evening, as he crept through Otto's hallway, Vinny intercepted him, his pale eyes bright with excitement. "I found it," he whispered triumphantly, and pointed in the direction of the dining room.

He told Jake, that he'd noticed Otto frequently checking the heating vent, ostensibly to monitor the airflow. But there was something at once so clandestine and compulsive about his actions that he had became suspicious and decided to investigate.

"After you remove the grating, you have to reach in the full length of your arm," he explained to an amazed Jake.

And, there it was a full fucking shelf of money, all neatly stacked in a steel box. "Shit," Jake exclaimed and drove his hands into the bills to look at them closer, to feel their crisp caress. "There must be a half-a-million bucks here … shit."

"We should empty it all into a shopping bag." Vinny thrust a sturdy plastic carry-all in Jake's direction. "And stuff the box with newspaper before putting it back."

"Good thinking." Jake scratched his day old stubble with a dirt-rimmed fingernail. "That way, if the old bastard reaches in to see that it's still there, he'll think that it is." He broke into a bout of maniacal laughter at the thought.

"Better keep it down, Jake," Vinny said; although he'd plied Otto with whiskey laced with sleeping pills, he might still wake up.

"Fuck I almost forgot … we don't want to wake Sleeping Beauty … now do we?"

Vinny watched as Jake strode down the driveway, with the shopping bag full of money clutched fiercely in his hand.

* * * * *

When Vinny returned home later that night, he found that Jake had pulled up stakes and left, taking everything of value with him.

"Why that rotten greedy turd!" He kicked around at the garbage and mess left behind. Jake had absconded with every last cent of Otto's money. He sure hadn't wasted any time.

While he wasn't surprised by this turn of events – in fact, had halfway expected it – there was still a degree of disappointment and rancor that his long-term partner saw fit to treat him in such a shabby fashion. Jake had dumped him for the exotic dancer, and that ugly little fact rankled most of all.

Yet even as Vinny fumed over the injustice, an enigmatic smile played wickedly around the corners of his lips.

* * * * *

"You know I really do appreciate your tipping me off about the robbery." Otto took a hasty sip of a mean looking Scotch. "That way we were able to keep everyone happy … at least for a while."

The portrait of his unsmiling widow no longer hung above the fireplace. In its place was a pleasant watercolor of an inland lake. Otto was making changes and branching out from his former life. Asking Vinny to come and live with him had been one of the major ones. "As a sort of general dogs body and bum boy." He patted the tight behind lovingly to illustrate the point.

"He's a mean bastard, and he'll kick the shit out of you if you don't tell him where the cash is," Vinny had warned. He feared the sadistic Jake would probably beat the poor old bugger to death. Then they'd have a murder charge hanging over their heads. Besides, why should he take that kind of a risk when it was Brandon that Jake pined after?

"There'll never be a better chance to get rid of these." Otto winked conspiratorially. He slapped down a box full of money and created a cloud of dust as he did so. "I made them myself you know?"

"I … what?" Vinny was so amazed he looked comical.

"That's right." Otto nodded proudly. "That was my hobby all those years, printing schoolbooks by day and money at night. I did it for the challenge."

"But didn't you ever get caught?" Vinny had managed to regain his power of speech and looked like a surprised fish gulping down air.

"Good God, I never tried to spend the stuff," Otto hooted delightedly. "It's not that good a quality. Not when you examine it up close."

He held one of the notes beneath a reading lamp and pointed out the various flaws in the watermark and paper quality.

"They'd never past muster with someone who knew what he was doing. But with your friend, I think they'll do just fine."

"Until he gets caught passing them." Vinny slapped his trouser leg with a delighted hand, and laughed more heartily than he had done in years. "Counterfeiting is a bad rap, that's federal." He roared anew at the thought. He would dearly love to see the shocked look on Jake's face and on his paramour's when they were arrested. Too bad, he would have to content himself by just imagining it.

"Here's to you, Otto." They clinked their glasses together in mutual merriment as the trailing fingers of a flaming sun dipped beneath the horizon.

BOYS IN THE BAND
By Jayden Blake

I'd known Caleb Frye for many years. We'd gone to the same high school, but we weren't really friends, not back then. Caleb was one of the upper echelon, a good-looking jock who played basketball and was a star on the swim team and had more girls chasing after him than he could possibly know what to do with, at least at the tender age of seventeen. I, on the other hand, was a total geek, a skinny, bespectacled dork whose only passions were quantum physics and the clarinet.

You'd think I'd have despised him, being so low on the food chain when he was at the top, but Caleb was a decent guy. Everyone liked him, not just the popular kids, but misfits like me as well because he was a genuinely nice person who treated everyone with respect regardless of their social standing.

He was especially nice to me after I soloed in a band concert during sophomore year. It was my first solo – the clarinet piece from Mozart's *Arietta* – and I knew I'd done really well. After the performance, Caleb came right up to me and pumped my hand enthusiastically.

"Man, you were great," he said. "Really outstanding. I'm a musician, too," he confided shyly, "or at least I want to be. I'm taking bass guitar lessons. That's a beautiful instrument," he added, checking out my clarinet.

I was so stunned that Caleb Frye was actually speaking to me that I wasn't sure how to respond. "You want play it?" I said stupidly, thrusting it out at him.

He held it to his mouth and blew experimentally. What came out sounded like a cross between a cow mooing and a balloon leaking air. "You have to control the air flow," I explained, putting my hand over his and nudging his fingers into the proper position to play an A note.

"Like this?" he asked, his brow crinkling in concentration as he blew again. I increased the pressure on his fingers, and what emerged was a shaky but definite A.

"Good!" I enthused and turned my eyes to him. He was regarding me with a peculiar expression, and I realized my fingers were still resting on his, over the valves on the clarinet. Suddenly, I experienced a tingling in my fingertips and a physical thump in my lower abdomen, as if I had been hit.

I snatched my hand away. "I have to go," I blurted. "My folks are waiting." He handed me back my clarinet, and I scampered away, red-faced and vibrating from the waist down.

After that, Caleb went out of his way to talk to me whenever we passed in the halls. Our chats tended to be brief, since he made me uncomfortable as hell. It wasn't just because of who he was (after all, what does a serf say to the crown prince?), but because the memory of my fingers resting over his was enough to bring on a fluttering in my chest and a ruckus in my pants. It was awhile before I realized that there was a word to describe the condition I found myself in whenever Caleb was around – horny. And, I identified a word to describe my own constant condition – gay.

Eventually, we graduated, and I no longer had to deal with the issue of Caleb Frye because I didn't see him any more. I heard he was off at State on an athletic scholarship while I was headed for an Ivy League college and the best engineering program in the country. I aced my classes during my freshman and junior years then horrified my folks by taking a breather to explore the possibilities of a musical career.

Not as a classical musician – my folks would have been one hundred percent behind that – but a rocker. I was hammering out hot boogie woogie on the piano by then, and I got in touch with my old band buddy Dan, who'd been working professionally as a musician during the years I was in college. He was a superb drummer and came on board with Josh Woods on guitar. All we needed was a bass player, so we took out an ad in the Phoenix. We met with five or six guys, none of whom were up to our standards, and then Caleb Frye wandered into one of our auditions.

I recognized him right away, even though his appearance had changed radically since high school. The blond hair he'd always shaved into a regulation jock buzz cut had lengthened into a thick mane that he wore tied back in a tail. He was dressed in black jeans and a white cotton shirt instead of the Levis and oxford shirts he'd habitually worn in high school, and he sported a tiny diamond chip in his left earlobe.

I looked different, too, with my spiky dark hair and goatee, and I was prepared to remind him who I was, but the minute he saw me, his eyes lit up. "Jay!" he said, shaking my hand enthusiastically. "You look great! How've you been?"

He turned out to be quite an excellent bass player, confident, solid and without any of the hesitancy that was always the first sign of an amateur. We hired him on the spot, and he made a great addition to our band. We jelled artistically and within a few months were cranking out some hot music and getting booked on a regular basis.

One weekend, we were lucky enough to snag a lucrative gig at a premium resort upstate. It was a long drive, so we decided to take turns catching some Zs in the back of the retired airport shuttle that served as our band bus.

The bus was crammed with gear, but there was just enough room in the way back for two people to stretch out side by side. Dan and Josh snagged the first shift. After a couple of hours, we switched, and Caleb and I moved into the back.

There was no way I was going to sleep with Caleb Frye lying right beside me, so I curled up on my side, turned my back to him and indulged in a few dirty fantasies about what I wanted to do to his lean, hard body. I hadn't yet had sex with a man, although I'd come to accept that I was gay while I was in college. There had been a few women, but my strongest attractions had always had been to men, starting with that long-ago crush on Caleb Frye.

It didn't take long before my cock was hard as stone and pressing painfully against the zipper of my jeans. I was lying there wondering if there was anything I could do about it when Caleb moved. He shifted toward me, close enough that our bodies were touching, his chest lightly grazing my back. I lay there feeling his breath on the nape of my neck and allowed myself to enjoy the heat bubbling up inside of me.

I thought Caleb was asleep, so when he lifted his hand and placed it on my leg I froze. His hand rested on my thigh for an endless moment. Its weight seemed to sear through my clothes and into my skin, and then the hand began to travel stealthily around to the front of my body, where he laid his palm over my groin.

I didn't know what to do, so I did nothing. His movements had been slow, deliberate, and I knew there was no way they could possibly have been accidental. I fought to remain absolutely still, but when his hand tightened, my cock gave an involuntary twitch.

I was mortified, but Caleb's breathing became thicker, more ragged. He shifted closer, silently so not to attract attention from the front seat, and slipped his hand inside the front of my pants.

I thought I would burst. What he was doing felt so good, his deft fingers milking my cock while his hard member strained against my backside, that I felt ready to explode. The need for release was so intense that I thought I would come in my pants, but then Caleb pulled open the snap on my jeans. He pushed aside the fabric and my cock sprang out, jutting away from my body like a tree limb.

Caleb pressed closer against me, and his breathing became ragged as he slowly, deliberately, began to jerk me off.

It felt so good I wanted to die or, failing that, to pull off my clothes and be naked, to roll over and grind my cock against him, to unzip his pants and feast on what I could feel was an enormous cock. I did none of these things, however. Instead I lay there, silent and still, and concentrated on keeping my breath even while Caleb Frye jerked me off with my band mates just a few feet away.

Before long, I felt a throb deep down in my groin. I knew I was going to come and felt a tendril of panic because I still didn't know what to do.

Then it didn't matter because I blew my wad all over Caleb's hand.

He continued to massage me gently, and I could feel the wet of my cum against my stomach. After a moment, he let go of me and then I felt him mop me with a soft cloth, a handkerchief or bandanna. He cleaned me up the best he could given his limited mobility, zipped and snapped my pants, then drew his body away from me, and during all that, I never moved a muscle or made a single sound.

We'd finished just in time; as a few minutes later, the bus arrived at the resort. When I sat up and looked down at myself, I saw a big cum stain right in the middle of my T-shirt so I reached into my duffle bag for a sweatshirt and casually pulled it on.

Josh had opened the back door, and he and Dan were already unloading the gear. I got out of the bus and pitched in, and after a moment, Caleb climbed out behind me. I never looked at him.

"We're a little late," Dan remarked, checking his watch. "We have to start in less than an hour. Caleb, why don't you go check us in? We get two rooms comp," he added, turning to take the snare drum from Josh.

"Two?" Josh whined. "What happens if somebody scores?"

"Then we'll have to take turns," Dan replied.

"Or use the bus," Caleb offered. "I'm sure it won't be the first time somebody got off in this vehicle." I felt my face grow red and avoided his eyes. As he walked away whistling, though, I sneaked a quick peek after him, to admire how fine his ass looked in his tight jeans.

We hauled our gear inside and set up in record time, finishing with only moments to spare. We used the back room to change clothes and, just as I was putting on my shirt, the door opened and Caleb walked in.

"All set to play?" I asked too brightly, concentrating on my buttons.

He nodded. "Yeah. A little nervous, though."

"Don't be," I replied, picking up my soiled clothes and stuffing them into my bag. "You'll play great. You always do."

"It's not playing that I'm nervous about," he said pointedly.

I hurriedly zipped up my bag and grabbed a folder containing copies of the set list. "See you out there," I called, heading for the door.

"Jay, wait." I turned just as I got to the door and Caleb was right behind me. Too close, I thought, my knees turning to jelly as I looked into his deep blue eyes.

"Yeah?" I said, keeping one hand on the door.

Caleb's brow crinkled. "Nothing, I guess. I mean … I just wanted to say…" he hesitated, then shook his head. "Look," he finally said, "We both know you weren't really asleep, don't we?"

I went still and didn't respond, just stared at him. My face must have given me away, though, because he nodded. "That's what I thought," he said. He hesitated for the briefest moment, then slipped his hand under my chin and kissed me.

If my knees had been jelly before, they turned to water now. I dissolved, and it was only Caleb's hand under my chin that prevented me from sliding all the way down to the floor. His lips were soft yet firm, and I closed my eyes and opened my mouth, then felt his quick intake of breath as his tongue slipped past my lips. It tasted sweet and tart, like a slice of fruit.

"I'm sorry I jumped you like that," Caleb whispered against my lips. "I just couldn't keep my hands off of you for another second."

A tap on the door behind me made me start. "What!" I barked, leaping away just as the door opened.

Dan's face appeared. "You guys almost ready? Five minutes," he reported.

"Just getting the set list," I told him, waving the folder at him.

Dan nodded and turned away. I started after him, but paused when I felt something prod my hand.

Caleb was handing me a white plastic card. "What's this?" I asked him.

"Your key card," he replied, then smiled. "By the way, you and I are sharing a room tonight."

I barely remember playing. I was in such an intense state of arousal that it took every ounce of concentration. As it was, I hit a couple of glaring clams, enough to elicit a comment from Dan.

"Dude, what's going on with you tonight?" he asked me, his brow crinkling. "It's usually you keeping the rest of us on track, not the other way around."

I shrugged. "Just an off night, I guess," I said, but my eyes were glued to Caleb. He was at the bar, sandwiched between two blonde girls. They were hot and gorgeous, and they were hanging all over him. My stomach went cold as I watched the three of them.

As soon as we finished playing, I beat a hasty retreat. Typically, the band would hang around drinking until after close, but I told Dan I felt sick just to get away. It was true, anyways. The blondes were still there, holding Caleb's full attention, and the sight of them was making me nauseous.

I went back to the room, stripped down to my T-shirt and boxers and climbed into bed. I was so exhausted I expected to fall asleep the minute my head hit the pillow, but instead I tossed and turned, imagining Caleb in the bus with those two blondes. I pictured the three of them naked, the two bitches sharing the thick cock that I hadn't gotten the chance to taste for myself.

I hadn't lain there torturing myself for long, maybe twenty minutes, when I heard sounds at the door. A click, a scrape, then a sliver of light appeared. "Jay?"

Caleb. I went hot and prickly all over, but my tongue seemed to be frozen. He came into the room, and I heard the click of the bolt being turned. "You asleep?" he asked.

Again I said nothing. I was terrified, both of what had happened between us and what might happen next, so I lay there and pretended to be asleep again. Coward, an internal voice hissed at me. Caleb didn't turn on the light. He went into the bathroom, and I heard the sound of him relieving himself, the toilet flushing and then water running. He emerged and in the dark there were snaps and rustles as he got ready for bed. My cock swelled as I listened to the sounds he made. He moved between the two double beds and I heard him place something on the nightstand. He stood there for an endless moment, and then the other bed creaked.

My stomach plunged. This was the moment, the one I had dreamed of, and I was letting it slip away. The object of my most lustful thoughts was a mere two feet away, close enough to touch, and I was afraid to make a sound.

I lay there in a state of agonizing indecision. My body was on fire, a physical torment unlike anything I had ever experienced. My flesh ached for Caleb's body, yearned for the relief he would give me like one yearns to plunge into a cool pool on a scorching day.

He shifted, just a slight movement, but it was enough to inflame me to action. I sat up, swinging my legs over the side of the bed. "I'm awake," I announced, and climbed on top of him.

"Thank God," Caleb whispered, and wrapped his arms around me. I felt his mouth search for my lips, and when he found them, we kissed. The heat between us was unmistakable as our tongues twisted and wound together, mating like two snakes.

I kissed him and kissed him, and as I did so I felt him tug the blanket from between us and push it aside. Then I felt what seemed like acres of warm, bare flesh.

Naked! My mind sang and I nearly groaned aloud. Caleb Frye is naked underneath me! I began to thrash and twist my way out of my clothes, wanting nothing more than to hump and grind my nude body against his. My hands were shaking, so I could barely pull my clothes off, but Caleb helped, reaching for my T-shirt and drawing it over my head. He nuzzled my chest, then found my nipples and sucked them, and they contracted to razor sharp points against his tongue. He nudged me over onto my side and reached for my boxers, pulling them down to my ankles. I worked to kick them free as his head moved down to my stomach. Finally, I kicked off my shorts and yanked my arms out of my T-shirt just as Caleb's mouth reached my throbbing cock and, in a single slick movement, sucked it into his mouth and swallowed it down.

I gasped as I was engulfed by the wet warmth of his throat. His mouth was like liquid velvet, his tongue a living thing that swirled around my stiff member. It was the best head I'd ever had, but I didn't want to come ... no, I wanted it to last and last.

"Stop," I groaned even as I pumped my rigid cock in and out of his talented mouth. "Stop, or you're going to make me come."

His response was to increase the suction, his mouth straining as he took me deeper into his throat. His hands reached for my balls, squeezed and massaged them, and when his tongue began to dance over the sensitive spot just beneath the swollen head of my cock, I summoned up a Herculean effort and pulled away.

"I'm sorry," I groaned, my cock seeming to strain toward him even as I held my body back. "It's just ... I want it to last."

"Oh God, don't apologize," Caleb sighed, reaching for my hand. "You're wonderful." He placed my hand on his dick and drew in his breath sharply as I curled my fingers around it. I squeezed it gently, reverently then slid my hand down to fondle his tight, firm balls. I reached again for his cock. I worked it hard, diligently, and soon Caleb's hips were gyrating up and down in time with my motions.

He was groaning, totally into what I was doing to him, helpless under my ministrations. I felt myself swell anew, drunk on the absolute power I had over him. "Jay," he sighed. "I've thought about this so many times. I've wanted you for so long ... if you only knew."

He had? I released his cock and rolled on top of him in a frenzy of heat. Since I'd never been with a man I had no technique to fall back on, so I acted out of blind lust. I pressed my cock against his and began to hump him like a German Shepherd going to town on someone's leg.

The action pinched my cock and rubbed it nearly raw, but it was so goddamn good I didn't care. "Shit," Caleb sighed, meeting me thrust for thrust as we thrashed against each other's bodies. "Shit, that's hot. It hurts, but it's so fucking hot."

Our bodies were slippery with sweat, our cocks slick with pre-cum, when Caleb finally rolled away from me. I could feel the bed rock as he shifted his position, and a moment later, his slick, hard dick was hovering over my lips.

"Suck me," he begged. "Suck my cock, Jay."

My mouth watering, I opened it wide. He had a long, thick cock, and as he pushed it past my lips, I welcomed the taste of it, the salty drops of fluid that lubricated my tongue, and most of all, the scent of maleness and sex that emanated from the dense hair between his legs.

I feasted on his cock, delighting in the scent and the feel and the taste, and wished I could spend the rest of my life sucking this man's delicious cock. I never knew it could be so erotic and satisfying, sucking cock, and I felt I would never get enough.

He rose up on his knees and straddled my face, pressing his cock deeper into my throat. I felt the silken brush of his hair across my thighs, and I realized that Caleb's head was back between my legs. My cock was like stone as he kissed it then caressed it with his tongue. His ministrations were slow this time, painfully, wonderfully lazy and gentle as he fondled me, cupping and squeezing my balls while continuing to glide his own hard dick in and out of my mouth. He gave my cock a long, luxuriant lick, then turned his attention to my balls, rolling them gently with his tongue while he explored around them with his fingers. He stroked the area behind my balls lightly, then traced a sensuous path to my anus and slipped one finger inside.

No one had ever done that to me before, and I gasped, heaving up with my entire body. Caleb went still for a moment then slowly, experimentally, pushed his finger deeper inside of me. I moaned out loud. His finger in my ass was absolutely the best thing I'd ever felt, and I spread my legs as far as I could to give him the deepest access.

Caleb drew his cock out of my mouth and slid further between my legs, using his elbows to push them even further apart. His dick bumped against my chest as I felt his hands on my ass, separating my cheeks. His mouth closed over my anus, making a perfect seal, and I felt his tongue slip inside of me.

I went crazy, humping and rocking against his face. He ate my ass as if it were a pussy, nibbling and sucking and swirling his long tongue. His cock was hard as rock, bumping and against my chest, but I couldn't attend to it just then. I was too totally into what he was doing to me. I couldn't imagine what I must look like, both legs locked around his chest, arms spread wide and gripping the mattress on either side of me, my ass spread wide for his hungry mouth.

He ate me for a good, long time, then pulled away. I cried out, bereft, but his hands were on me again, rolling me onto my stomach, urging me up onto my knees.

He was going to fuck me. Somehow my mind hadn't gone in this direction, but here it was. Caleb Frye was going to fuck me in the ass, and I was going to let him do it.

I felt him reach past me, then heard a clatter from the nightstand as something fell to the floor. Caleb swore under his breath as he fumbled around in the dark.

A click, and a moment later the room was filled with dim light. I found myself staring at my own reflection in the mirror on the back of the closet door, up on my knees with my ass raised high to receive Caleb's cock. "Oh God," I choked, "look at us."

Caleb turned to face the mirror, and I was struck by how beautiful he was. His hair had slipped loose from its ponytail and was hanging around his shoulders, blond strands glimmering in the soft light. "Yes," he said dreamily. "Look at us." He stroked my buttocks as he reached for the night stand, and I saw what it was he'd placed there earlier: a tube of lubricant and a strip of condoms.

I felt a hum begin deep in my belly as I watched Caleb unroll a condom over his stiff cock, then smear it with a generous squirt of lube. He slipped his cock between my ass cheeks. It felt cold and slippery.

Caleb paused and looked up at me in the mirror. "I really want this," he said, "Do you?"

I felt a rush of something – love? – and moved back against him ever so lightly. "I'll take that as a yes," he whispered, and I closed my eyes as he began to work his cock inside of me.

When he entered me, my body jerked and tightened. It hurt – a lot – but Caleb went slow, progressing little by little until his cock was fully encased by my ass. "Are you all right?" he whispered.

"It hurts," I muttered, my face buried into the pillow.

"Try to relax," Caleb said, "and it will stop hurting." He began to gyrate back and forth, tiny minute movements. I felt him press against something inside of me, something sensitive that sent electric jolts through me.

I moaned, suddenly realizing that Caleb was right, it had stopped hurting. I could hear his breath catch, then come faster as he pulled out of me, then pressed deeper inside. My own body began to move back and forth.

"Sweet Jesus," he groaned. I opened my eyes to look at him in the mirror. His eyes were glazed and his mouth agape, his head thrown back in an expression of absolute ecstasy. His hips were moving back and forth in a marvelous dance of flexing muscle. His cock plunged into me with long fluid strokes, and my cock swelled tighter at the sight of him.

It was bouncing rampantly, begging for attention. I raised one hand to reach for it then had to steady myself as a particularly firm thrust from Caleb nearly knocked me flat.

He saw, and paused his thrusting for a moment. "Jesus, don't stop," I begged him. He was searching for something on the bed and when he turned back I saw his hand was coated with a light film of lubricant.

He reached around me to grip my cock and began fucking me again, this time accompanying each thrust with a long, wonderful tug. Faster and faster he moved, jerking me off as he fucked me, and before long I felt that hot tension in the pit of my groin that meant I was going to come.

When my cock went off, it shot a thick rope of sperm across the bed underneath me. One ... two ... three spurts. Caleb's movements became frantic, and I knew from his groans that he was coming, too, shooting his load deep in my ass.

I dropped forward and Caleb collapsed on top of me. We lay there for a few moments, our limbs sweaty and loosely entwined. The room reeked of semen and sex, and I could feel the moistness of my own cum on the bed sheets.

After a while, I opened my eyes and found Caleb regarding me tenderly in the mirror. "That was the first time I've ever done that," I admitted.

Caleb lifted one hand to my shoulder and slid it down the length of my bare back until his fingers were resting lightly between the cheeks of my ass. "I'm guessing it won't be the last," he whispered.

He kissed me, and I could feel the smile on his lips. No, it wouldn't be the last. As his arms encircled me, I knew that Caleb Frye and I were in for a long, wondrous ride together.

PARK LIFE
By Wayne Mansfield

The night was dark. A thick blanket of summer rain-cloud obscured the starry skies and blocked the light of a full moon. A line of street lamps stood like sentinels, casting small circles of light on the drying grass by the road. Down a small bank, toward the twin lakes at the heart of the public park, there was a large grove of trees and shrubs, surrounded by an inner ring of irises and an outer ring of pansies. This area was shrouded in darkness.

Every now and again, a wild duck let out a series of quacks before settling again on one of the lakes. The only other sound to break the silence of the night was that of a stiff summer breeze racing through the leaves of the many trees that grew around the edge of the park and in small pockets within its boundaries. The light of the public toilet was on, but the building was empty. Any activity there had long since ceased. It was too dangerous to enter the small building at night. The police often raided it and so did drunken thugs on their way home from a night at the nearby Highgate Pub.

By day, the park was a Mecca for married couples who would picnic by the twin ornamental lakes and watch their children play on the playground equipment or chase ducks. Single men and women took their dogs for walks, doing endless laps around the two lakes while talking on their mobile phones or listening to music on tiny earphones. Just about every Saturday, there would be one or two wedding parties being photographed amidst the lush foliage of the bushes and colorful floral displays, which made an ideal backdrop for such a memorable occasion.

At night, however, it was an entirely different world.

At the center of the grove, behind the flowers and shrubs, there was a clearing of about three or four meters square in area. The thing was if you didn't know about it, you would never find it. You had to maneuver your way through the flowers at a particular point to find the hidden entrance.

That night, since it was so dark, the small clearing had been busy, though it was now well after one o'clock in the morning, and most of the men who usually frequented the area had gone home. After a succession of twosomes and threesomes, the small, secluded area was now silent, although two shadowy figures remained. One of the men, moaning almost inaudibly, was leaning on a branch, his shirt in one hand and his pants down around his ankles. A second figure stood behind him, slowly thrusting his thick, hard cock in and out of the other guy's already well-fucked ass.

"Fuck me harder," Neil whispered, reaching around with one hand to pull one of his cheeks apart. "Shoot your load right up inside me. I wanna feel you fill me, man."

The second guy didn't reply but did as he'd been asked, eagerly slamming his rock-hard ramrod as far up Neil's fuck-hole as he could, twisting his hips to get his veiny cock further inside. The strong aroma of sweaty man-sex surrounded them, filling their nostrils as their whispered moans of delight escaped parted lips to drift away on the breeze and into the night. As the second guy's thighs slapped against Neil's buttocks, he kept one eye and both ears on the surrounding parkland. There was a sense of danger about fucking a complete stranger in the middle of a public park and that was the half the thrill, but there was still a need for caution. The park was just on the outskirts of the city center, and the cops knew all about it.

"I'm gonna blow!" the second guy grunted suddenly, his thrusts becoming faster and more urgent.

"Hang on!" said Neil, who had been stroking his meat casually up to that point, wanting to prolong the experience. "I'm not ready yet."

"Can't help it. Gotta … come… Oh fuck! Here it comes! Here it comessssss."

Neil steadied himself on the branch as the guy behind him filled his ass with a thick load of creamy man-juice. As the stranger pounded the last few drops of cum out of his swollen knob, Neil could feel his own dribbling cock slapping against his stomach though there was nothing he could do to relieve the tension. He wasn't even close to coming, and the guy behind him was pulling out.

"That was fucking hot!" the second guy said as he flicked a stray glob of cum off his fingers, pulled his pants up and began doing up his belt.

"Hello, boys," said a voice from behind them.

"Shit!" gasped the second guy turning toward the dazzling beam of torchlight coming toward them along the narrow path. "The cops!"

In a blind panic, he pushed past Neil and clambered through the tangle of branches and foliage toward the irises, sustaining several cuts as he ran. Visions of police stations and of his wife's face after being told the reason for his arrest flooded his mind. A few cuts and bruises were nothing compared to the humiliation and trauma of having to face his wife from behind a set of prison bars.

"You! Stay there!" shouted Mike, the first officer to make his way into the clearing.

"Should I go after the other one?" said Tyler, his partner.

"Nah. Too late now. Probably halfway across the park."

Neil felt a rush of adrenalin surge though his body, making his heart race and his breathing quicken. Reacting automatically now, he went to pull his jeans up, but Mike wasn't going to let him.

"Leave 'em down," he said, shining his torch into Neil's startled face. "What's your name?"

"N-n-eil," he stuttered, his cock shriveling instantly to the size of a large broad bean.

The officers positioned themselves so that Neil had one of them on either side, one blocking the main entrance and the other blocking the newly created exit.

"So what were you doing in here?" Mike asked in a deep, authoritative voice.

"You know what I was doing," Neil replied, trying to sound defiant but failing miserably.

"Wise guy, huh?" Mike growled. "What's that in your hand? Drop it!"

"It's just my shirt," Neil explained.

"Drop it!" Mike said again, his tone defying the young man in front of him to disobey. "And, put your hands on your head!"

Neil dropped the shirt.

He may have been twenty-eight, well-built and handsome, but none of that was going to help him now. He'd been busted. Too afraid not to, he did as he was ordered and placed his hands on top of his clippered head; his lean, muscular torso looking even thinner as he stretched his arms upwards.

"Step out of your pants and spread those legs!" Mike ordered him as he stepped closer to the trembling young man.

Neil stepped out of his pants, kicked them out of the way and then spread his legs. He had never felt so vulnerable in his life. He was totally naked, and he could feel the cool night air on his dangling cock and balls.

"Check him!" Mike ordered the officer standing in the shadows opposite.

Neil looked over his shoulder at the approaching officer and although it was difficult to see in the torchlight, he could see enough to know that Tyler was tall – well over six-feet. His short-sleeved shirt revealed thick, muscular forearms, lightly haired, and there was a tattoo on the arm that he could see. As Tyler moved closer, he noticed that the officer had a blond moustache and that his hair had been similarly clippered – a number two cut if he wasn't mistaken.

"Turn around!" barked Mike. All Neil knew about Mike was that he had dark hair, was clean shaven and was slightly pudgy around the middle. Like his partner, Mike was in his late thirties or early forties. "Don't move unless I tell ya!"

Neil's head immediately spun around to face the barely lit branches in front of him, concentrating on a moth dancing in the beam of light to try and take his mind of his current predicament. He shuddered when Tyler finally touched him on the shoulders, pushing them forward so that Neil had to bend forward.

He heard the officer's knee click as he squatted down and saw by the faint scraps of torch light on the bushes in front of him that they were checking out his ass.

"Pull 'em apart," Mike demanded as he too squatted down for a better look.

Tyler did as he'd been ordered. Neil could feel his hole being opened and a thick, hairy finger being pushed just inside the sphincter. He grimaced slightly, gasping, as the finger slid in and came back out again.

"Anything?" Mike asked.

"Sure is. Look at this. Definitely been fucked tonight," replied Tyler, holding up a finger coated in the sticky, slightly brown, traces of semen, which had been blasted into Neil's hole not five minutes earlier.

Tyler wiped his finger clean on the back of Neil's leg and stuck his nose in the crease of Neil's taut butt cheeks. He inhaled deeply, savoring the smell of fresh sex. Despite himself, Neil could feel himself getting hard. The sound of the cop sniffing around his lightly-haired fuck-tunnel was too horny to ignore, and knowing the other officer was watching just multiplied the thrill.

"Looks ripe and juicy from where I'm standin'," Mike smirked, noticing how the pink skin of the boy's arse glistened in the torchlight. "How does it taste?"

Although Neil had been confused by the way things had been going, not knowing whether they were gonna haul his ass down to the nearest station or not, he soon forgot his confusion. The officer behind him had spent more than enough time inspecting his naked ass to have seen the evidence. Yet he lingered there. Neil sensed what might happen next and wanted to turn around to see what was happening, but he dare not risk getting the other cop angry. He was already in a shit load of trouble, though he suspected his luck might be about to change for the better.

Then, just when he thought he couldn't bare the suspense any longer, he felt Tyler's tongue on the puckered skin of his freshly fucked fuck-hole. He wanted so badly to thrust his arse into the officer's face, inviting the uniformed cop to eat his insatiable ass out, but he held back. He didn't want to spoil the moment by being too eager. But he didn't have long to wait before he got what he wanted. Tyler grabbed Neil's firm buttocks and pulled them roughly apart, thrusting his tongue straight up into Wayne's tasty hole, his thick moustache pressing into the sensitive skin at the top of his pucker. Neil moaned and began to gently gyrate.

"Eat the little slut out real good!" Mike growled. "The bitch obviously likes it!"

Tyler didn't need to be told. He was already rock-hard inside his dark blue trousers. Eating out this boy's freshly creamed hole, with the strong aroma of cum and ass juices filling his twitching nostrils, was driving him crazy. He probed Neil's cum-soaked boy cunt with all the fervor of a sex maniac. He couldn't get enough. He pushed his face so far into the crack that he could barely breathe. His lips sucked and kissed the pink, lightly-haired hole, while his tongue continued to fuck it, stabbing into the slimy pucker as far in as he could get it.

Mike reached under his gun belt and undid the belt on his trousers, removing them and his jocks completely before hanging them over a nearby branch.

"Out of my way," he grunted, pushing his partner aside. He wasn't a man to waste time with words.

With his huge, dribbling nine-incher waving stiffly about in front of him, he stepped up behind Neil, found the spit-soaked boy-pussy and slipped a hairy finger in.

"Mmmm," he commented, adjusting his gun belt with the other hand. "Nice tight hole."

Neil felt Officer Mike's huge knob-head press against his asshole. He sighed and closed his eyes, concentrating on how large and fleshy the head of the officer's cock felt against him. He pushed back onto it, desperate to have something more fulfilling than a tongue inside him.

"Horny little slut, aren't ya?" Mike snarled. "Well ya should like this then."

And with that he pushed the swollen head of his thick, veiny nine-incher past the boy's sphincter, slowly sliding his engorged shaft right the way up the boy's fuck-tunnel. Neil cried out. The puckers of his ass were now stretched to ripping point. Mike clasped his big, thick-fingered hand across his mouth.

"Shut the fuck up!" he ordered as he began thrusting into Neil's ass. "The more noise you make, the harder I go!"

Behind Mike's powerful hand, Neil moaned in a combination of pleasure and pain. He grimaced and clenched his teeth as the monster cock invaded his bowels; Mike's thick patch of wiry pubic hair rubbing on the skin at the top of his ass each time he plunged in. He closed his eyes tighter and began to concentrate on relaxing his anal muscles to better accommodate Mike's enormous organ but was distracted by the twitching of his own steel-hard cock and the man's large, pendulous balls slapping against the inside of his thighs, gently at first, then more violently as the fucking became more intense.

Tyler, who had dropped his pants, too, was standing with one hand on his cock and the other wrapped around the torch, aimed squarely at his buddy's swollen prong as it slid out of Neil's well-stretched hole. But watching wasn't enough. Tyler wanted to get in on the action. Like his boss, he whipped off his pants then scrambled under the branch until he was facing Neil. He shone his torch into Neil's face, seeing his eyes closed tight and the hand of his partner across the boy's mouth. He smiled and then dropped to his knees. He placed his torch on the ground then turned his attention to the cock wobbling just inches in front of him. He took the fleshy wand into his mouth and swallowed it right down the back of his throat. How sweet that young meat tasted, though it was difficult to get any kind of rhythm going with his buddy, Mike, pounding the poor boy's fuck-hole like crazy. Nevertheless, he did his best to slide his mouth up and down Neil's dribbling tool as best he could.

Mike was still going strong at the rear, ramming his raging rod right up inside Neil. His huge cock was coated in the boy's ass juice and the cream of the stranger who had fled as they arrived. The thought of using another man's cum as lube made fucking Neil all the more thrilling. It was dirty, and Mike was one dirty fucker. He couldn't have cared if ten men had dropped their load inside the boy. The more the better as far as he was concerned.

Mike placed another hand in the small of Neil's back, making the boy arch his back more and enabling him to get just that bit further inside. Of course, it made things a bit more difficult for Tyler. With the boy bent even further forward there was not as much room for his head. Still, he did the best he could, sucking the juicy man-pole with relish and loving the feel of the boy's fleshy cock head at the back of his throat. The anticipation of tasting a load of fresh boy juice made any discomfort bearable.

Neil, steadying himself with one arm, reached down with the other and grabbed the back of Tyler's head, pulling it further onto his cock. He was beyond caring what happened to him now. The twin pleasures of having Mike's huge schlong ramming his ass and an expert mouth on his own cock eradicated any fear or nervousness. All he could think about was how soft and smooth Tyler's lips felt on his engorged cock and how warm and velvety the inside of the officer's mouth felt. Every cell in his body seemed charged with electricity, even his nipples were tingling as the two officers used his body for their pleasure.

After ten long minutes of rampant fucking, Mike grabbed Neil by the hair, pulling his head back as far as it would go. Neil cried out in pain and surprise.

"Shut you're fuckin' mouth," Mike grunted as the veins at the side of his head began to throb and pulse. "I'm gonna fucking' fill your guts."

Mike began pounding Neil's fuck-tunnel like a pile driver, slamming his cock into him with such a force that it almost knocked Tyler over.

"Take my fucking load, bitch!" he snarled through gritted teeth. "Yeah, fuckin' yeah!"

Despite the searing pain of having his hair pulled so violently and the ache that was creeping into his neck, Neil found himself on the verge of coming. The sensation of Tyler's expert cock-sucking mouth on his cock, Mike's thick salami raping his fuck-hole and the pain of getting his hair pulled soon had his cock blowing a stream of creamy ball-juice down the cop's hungry mouth. It took Tyler by surprise, but he gulped the boy's load down hungrily, sucking at Neil's piss slit like a voracious animal.

Mike's steel-hard stabber erupted at the same time, and a thick spray of man goo flooded Neil's well-used hole, filling it almost to capacity since it had been a long time for Mike. He grunted, roughly pulling Neil's hips toward him as the last few drop of pearly-white cop-cream dribbled out of his piss-slit and into the boy's anus. He shuddered then slowly withdrew his slippery cock from the boy. As the head popped out a large drop of his cum dribbled out, too, hovering on the hairs at the base of the boy's ass before dropping to the ground.

"Get around here!" he barked, knowing that Tyler, who was still sucking the last drops of cream from Neil's cock, would relish what was to come.

Tyler released the boy's cock, which was still hard enough to slap back against the Neil's furry belly and scrambled on his knees to where Mike stood.

Mike grabbed his colleague by the hair and shoved his face in between the boy's butt cheeks.

"Now fuckin' eat it!" he barked at Tyler.

Tyler, knowing that the boy's ass was filled with his buddy's spunk, lapped hungrily at the small trickle of cream dribbling out. He wished he'd been allowed to suck Mike's cock clean, but he knew he couldn't have everything his own way. Besides, there had been many other nights on patrol together where they had only had each other and Mike had given him everything. He also knew there would be many more nights.

"Now get down on this cock, boy, and suck it good!" he said, taking up position in front of Neil.

Neil bent down and took the Sergeant's cock into his mouth, not caring that it had been up his ass. He sucked it with all the love a slave had for his master. He so much wanted to please the copper who had been so rough with him. Meanwhile, as Neil went down on the slimy cock, his throbbing boy-hole opened up and released a dribble of Mike's cum into Tyler's open and waiting mouth.

"Make sure you swallow the whole load, Tyler!" ordered Mike while Neil sucked his cock clean.

Tyler was going to take everything the boy's hole had anyway. With an open mouth positioned right beneath the glistening sphincter, Tyler waited for more of Mike's cum to dribble out, and when it did it, tasted like nectar from the Gods. As the thick, ropey threads of man cream welled up at the very edge of Neil's pucker then spilled over the edge to fall through the air, Tyler starting pulling his cock fervently, his balls tightening as the second installment of second-hand cum reached his outstretched tongue. The twin sensations of his hand cranking his engorged fuck-stick and the funky taste of asshole and his boss' cream were all too much. It wasn't long before he was blowing great geysers of cum all over his bare legs and the leafy ground beneath. As the first spurt erupted, Tyler nuzzled the boy's ass, sucking at it like a baby on the breast, draining the boy's ass of every drop of cum whether it was from Mike or the stranger who had fucked him earlier.

"Ya finished back there?" Mike barked as Neil continued to lick and suck the Sergeant's still swollen man pole.

"Sure am, Sarg. Just finishing up," Tyler gasped, flicking a string of his own nut juice off his hand before climbing to his feet.

Mike pushed Neil's head off his cock, ducked under the branch and stepped over to where Tyler was waiting.

"You have a good time, babe?" he asked in a tone more tender than any he had used that night.

"Sure did," Tyler whispered, bringing a hand up to stroke the bristles on Mike's cheek.

Neil stood up, struggling to stay upright after having been bent over and abused for so long, just in time to see Mike and Tyler kiss. Their cocks, still stiff, rubbed together as Mike's lips touched the cum-smeared lips of his partner. He sucked Tyler's top lip first, savoring the softness of the lip coated with his cum then he tasted the bottom lip, sucking every last trace of his own sperm off it. Then their tongues locked, searching and tasting in the darkness, illuminated by only the faint traces of moonlight that filtered in through the leafy canopy.

Neil pulled on his pants and managed to find his shirt after scrambling around in the darkness for a few minutes, then stood there watching the two lovers. Part of him was telling him to run, to get away while the going was good; to flee while the two officers were entwined in each others arms and while their lips were locked together. But part of him wanted to stay, refusing to believe that the wildest night of his entire life had ended. Maybe if he stayed, there would be more fun to be had.

Finally, the decision was made for him. The very second he'd decided to leave, Mike broke away from the kiss and turned.

"Where are you goin', punk?" he asked, noticing a movement in the shadows next to him.

"Er, nowhere..." Neil replied.

"Well, get over here then!" barked Mike.

Neil did as he was asked, joining them in a hot three-way tongue-kiss; the taste of sweat and cum thick on their lips and on their breath. He could feel himself getting hard again as he gripped the two policemen's cocks, drawing them together with his own, and wondered how much more he could take. He figured that only time would tell.

NO RUBBER GLOVES, NO LOVE
By Shane Allison

After weeks of driving around in the stifling capitol city humidity without air-conditioning, filling out every application I could get my mitts on, Nathan was the one who finally saved my ass from another week of standing in endless unemployment lines. When I got home, armed with several applications from fast-food joints to gas stations, and Ma told me that someone from Po' Folks called. I had forgotten all about them really. I had applied for a prep cook position two weeks ago. Thought if I didn't hear back within the week, then they weren't interested. I had to get my ass in gear. My monthly note on my truck was due, and those mother fuckers don't give an inch when it comes down to money.

I returned the call only to be told that the manager had left for that day, and that I could call the next morning between seven and eleven. Daddy calls Po' Folks the hog trough. He spends the whole time gawking and pointing at the fat, gospel singing women who top their plates with fried chicken, rice, candied yams, fish, steak, ham and more fried chicken, not understanding the concept of a buffet.

The next day, I didn't bother to suit up for job hunts, but called the manager back at Po'Folks. I told him who I was, that I was returning his call.

"Can you come in today, around eleven, for an interview? he asked.

"Yeah, sure," I said, using my best white boy's voice.

"When you come, jus' ring th' doorbell out front."

When I told Ma about the interview, I thought her ass was going to keel over with a heart attack. She acted like I had just won the lottery or some shit. "Thank ya, Jesus!" she kept hollering. "See what God'll do fuh you?"

"Dog, iss only an interview. Ain' got th' job yet."

"You go'n get it watch an' see. If iss in th' Lord's plan, you go'n get it"

The way she went on, it told me where her mind was, that even though I attended a prestigious graduate school in New York, I wasn't shit if I wasn't working on somebody's job. Didn't matter to her weather I was digging ditches or bussing tables for shit bucks an hour. But because I hadn't worked in almost a year, I ended up developing her small-minded mentality. After returning home from The Apple, I took a job doing retail grunt work only to end up getting my ass axed because I lied about having a criminal record. I was fired for not letting them in on the indecent exposure charge that happened ages ago when I was a dumb twenty-five-year-old. Two petty theft charges on my sheet, and they let me go for showing my dick to some undercover cop in the park. I didn't cry over it. Job was starting to bore me anyway.

I was only going to stay long enough to get my laptop off layaway. Needless to say, it went back in stock, 'cause I couldn't afford the monthly payments. Thought if the job at Po' Folks worked out, I could save up enough to buy it flat out.

The day of my interview, I grabbed a pair of pants off the hanger that were brand new, the tag still on, and my favorite rust-colored, stain resistant Oxford. I finished my duds off with my Elizabeth Taylor tie, which had landed me a ton of jobs during my teen years. Guess you could say it was my good luck charm.

"I sho' hope you get it," Ma said, as she followed me out the door. When I arrived, there were two other cars parked. Po' Folks didn't open until eleven for the lunch crowd.

I had about a week of restaurant experience working at a grill and bar called the Colorado Rooster Club, but when I got burned by a mozzarella cheese stick, I knew it was time for me to go.

I rang the doorbell. This bald, red-bone of a brotha answered. He reminded me of a guy I used to be obsessed with in high school.

"G' mornin'," he said, as he held the door ajar to let me in. I returned the hospitality with a good morning of my own.

"You Terrance?" he asked, as we came together with a firm hand shake.

"U'm Nathan."

I searched it for any sign of a wedding ring. There wasn't one meaning this daddy was on the market.

"I'm Nathan."

Po' Folks smelled faintly of southern fixings. Nathan escorted me to the rear where the office and the kitchen lay. It was sullen, yet clean with every pot and pan, every spoon, fork and steak knife in its place.

"'On' know if they tol'joo, but U'm th' head dishwasha."

"Mkay," I said. Nathan sifted through a stack of papers and pulled out my application. It was spotted with a few grease stains.

"It say here you applied fuh a busboy position."

"Yes."

"Did Mr. Shulte tell ya they all been filled?"

"He wutton th' one I talked to. They tol' me he had gone home fuh t'day."

"You know who tol'ja dat?" Nathan asked.

"Th' hos'. 'On' know 'is name."

"Pro'ly Matt."

"Sorry," I said.

"No, it's no problem. I had one o' my guys quit on me yestaday. Wou'joo be interested in a dishwasha position?"

"Yeah, 'on' care."

"You uh be workin' wit me."

I should hope so, I thought. I'd always preferred being in the back where I didn't have to deal with the little eccentricities of customers. I figured how hard could it be, right?

"Then th' job yours if you wone it," said Nathan.

"When you won't me t' start?"

"Can ya come in tomorra, 'round six? I can show ya 'round an' introduce ya t' th' res' o' th' kitchen staff."

"I'll be here."

Working nights meant I would miss all my favorite TV shows, but I always say you gotta give up something to get something. Besides, it wasn't like the shit was a life sentence. The plan was too stay long enough to get my laptop and get a better paying job, and then it was *sayonara*.

Nathan gave me some paper work to fill out. I was checking boxes and signing forms as he informed me of the kitchen dress code.

"Jeans an' sneakas, some dat'll preven'choo from fallin' back here. What size shirt you wear?" Nathan asked.

I was a bit embarrassed to say.

"3x."

"I thank th' highes' we got iza 2x," he said as he rummaged through a tattered box of shirts sitting on the floor.

It would be a tight fit, but I said, "Yeah, dat should be fine."

Nathan tossed me the shirt and made out a name tag.

"Welcome t' Po' Folks," he said.

I got to the car and called Ma to tell her about my newfound employment. "Hey, I got th' job."

I held my cell away from my ear as she hollered with glee. Even if it was a measly part-time dishwashing gig, it was a job nonetheless. It meant I would have money to buy shit that I wanted. I could finally exhale, dry my hands from worry.

When I got home, after Ma showered me with perfume hugs, I went through all my slips of paper used to write down all this shit I wanted to buy. I called it my "Shit I Want to Buy Once I Get a Job List." CDs of new bands, newly released DVDs, and a number of books. I was glad I didn't have to work some insane fucking morning shift like on my last job where I had to be to work at 7:00 am just to vacuum fitting rooms and empty trashcans.

I was a mess my first day with twenty ton butterflies fluttering around in my gut. The shirt Nathan issued, barely gave me breathing room. Ma tried to get me to eat something before going to work, but I was too nervous for food. I had the shits because of it. Didn't think I would make it on time 'cause my nerves kept me on the toilet. I drank Pepto like booze to soothe the savagery in my belly. All was calm by the time I got to Po' Folks. The lot was full with schools of cars. When I walked inside, the all-you-can-eat style restaurant was bustling with folks stacking their plates to the ceiling fans with large portions of soul food, people eating as if it was Jesus's last supper.

My tee was so tight that it kept riding up over my belly and showing the crack of my ass, and who wants to see that while their eating banana pudding? I kept pulling it down, but it still would not give in. I looked for my time card, but one had not been made up. Nathan and I had discussed every rule and regulation, every paper was given my *John Hancock*, but we had not talked about time cards. When I walked hesitantly into the kitchen, it was no longer quiet, but thunderous with clanging steel, fussy with cooks, prep cooks, waiters and waitresses. Everyone was so occupied with their jobs, they didn't notice that I had walked in. 'Cept for Nathan who was at the helm of the dishwasher manhandling soiled glassware. His apron was stained with who knows what. He was pouring with perspiration from the washer's steam. He looked on me with a sort of wide-eyed relief.

"Gimme a han'," he yelled over the kitchen commotion.

I stepped over a hole in the floor that was filled with food and stagnant water. "Ain' see my time card up front," I hollered over the kitchen noises.

"I'll gitchoo one once this dinner crowd done died down. Grab some gloves and run the silverware for me." Nathan was nice, not a tyrant about asking. There was an extra pair of rubber gloves under the dishwasher in between boxes of Cascade. I slipped my hand into the mitts of yellow rubber feeling as if I was about to go in for some major surgical procedure. When I put them on, I thought of prostate exams, of shoving a single rubber finger up Nathan's butt for personal pleasure. I was just as fast as Nathan. It was that type of job that required speed more than accuracy. There was no time for staff introductions. We all exchanged names as we passed in and out of the kitchen.

"When you done wit th' silvaware, put 'em in one of deeze racks an' stack 'em agains' th' wall fuh th' wait staff t' take out on th' floor," said Nathan. "Then, when you done wit those, help me wit deeze plates an' glasses."

The faster we scraped and hauled dishes through the machine, the wait staff would burst in with more stacks. I didn't think we would ever get through it, but with Nathan by my side, I knew there was nothing we couldn't handle.

"One thang t' remember. Make sure you wearin' gloves." Nathan showed me the battle scars from ends of forks and the heinous edges of knives.

"Dis kitchen done seen a lotta accidents. See Don ova there? He damn near cut haff 'is han' off in th' ham slica."

After I was done with the utensils, I started helping Nathan. I took two loads of dishes onto me, wiping them clean of food that didn't quite make it in the stomachs of the glutinous hogs out front.

"An' if you breaka plate, it comes oucha ass," he said, fussing with his half of dirty dishware. "U'm playin', man," he smiled. "Jus' be careful."

Things were starting to slow down. Fewer dishes and silverware were being dropped off. Sweat was drying from both our brows as we moved to a steadier, less back-breaking pace. We were quite the dynamic duo as we did away with dish after cruddy dish. As the dinner rush faded, the kitchen staff also began to thin until Nathan and I were the only two left at the restaurant.

"You did a good job for ya firs' night," he said as we organized the last remaining batches of silverware.

"Yeah, but I dropped a shit loada plates."

"Don't worry 'bout it. All us was new once."

We both looked a mess. My tight new T-shirt was no longer new.

"So, U'm workin' tomorra?"

"Th' schedule's in th' office. I need t' git you a time card, too," said Nathan.

I tailed behind him, watching his ass taut in jeans. We studied the work schedule pinned to a bulletin board. "Dis where they keep it fuh th' kitchen staff. Dere's a copy up front too behin' th' register, so when you off an' you wanna see when you workin', jus' check up front. Looks like Mr.Shulte gotchoo down fuh five t' close tomorra. You a be wit me fuh 'bout a week t' show ya th' ropes, then Shulte'll cutchoo loose on ya own."

"What about th' weekends?" I asked.

"I thank it'll jus' be me an' you on th' weekens. Tomorra's Carver's Night, so we go'n have t' git it togetha."

My back was killing me due to the long hours of standing without a break.

"You all 'ight?" Nathan asked.

"As soon as I get home and soak deeze dogs of mine in some Epson Salt I will be."

"I saw how you was hol'in ya side. Here, sit 'own." Nathan pulled out a chair.

"Iss okay. I jus' need t' go home an' take a bath."

"If you thought t'night was bad, wait 'til tomorra. Thank about bein' slammed all day wit th' occasional busload who come in wit growlin' guts. You go'n have plenty nights of so' backs an' achin'feet, so git use t' it."

I sat down not knowing what the hell to expect. Nathan was still wearing his gloves as he kneaded tense muscle.

"U'm goin' t' school t' be a masseuse."

I was surprised to find that Nathan actually had plans outside of the hog trough. "How long ya been into that?" I asked.

"'Bout two years. Dis my las' year. I have classes Saturday mornins." His hands worked wonders on my shoulders. They were strong and too damn good to be tossing dishes. I sat there and imagined my ass cupped in that dirty, yolk-yellow rubber.

"Dat feels good."

"My bad." He was about to take off the gloves, but I protested, telling him to leave them on. "So, what's ya story?" Nathan asked.

"My story?"

"You from Tallahassee? Do ya go t' school?" You gotta girlfrien'?"

I was always careful about divulging my personal life at work. 'Fore you know it, everybody's in your Kool-Aid and don't know the flavor.

"U'm from Tally, born an' raised, I go t' FSU. So what's your story?"

"Born in Fort Myers, lived in Orlando fuh five years where I managed a Big Boy Burger, then moved t' Tallahassee back in 2001. What about a girlfrien'?" asked Nathan. His question tumbled out of his mouth like chewed food. You would think he was asking me about the size of my dick.

"You ask everybody dat on they firs' day?"

"Jus' curious," he said, "ain' tryin' t' be rude."

"Howjoo know anyway?" I asked.

"I knew as soon ajoo opened ya mouth."

They all say that when I trust them enough to step out of that walk-in closet of mine.

"Yo' parent's know?" he queried, being a long shot away from the only guy to ask that question.

"Jus' close friends of mine." I stopped the conversation before Nathan could squeeze out more of my secrets. My dick was beating crazy in my jeans smudged with buffet stains from the nightly grind. I stood up out of his grip. "It's gettin' late," I told him.

"When ya come in tomorra, ya time card'll be here," he said, sticking it in a vacant pocket with the others. Nathan and I said good-night and dispersed in the lot to our respected cars.

I took the truck route home, a short cut to avoid the cops scavenging the streets for those under the influence. I could still feel the phantom grip from Nathan's mitts on my shoulders. My dick was finally starting to soften. Days flew and weeks had tumbled head long into months, and there I was still on the J-O-B. Three months was usually my limit. I would quit for some reason or another. Not enough hours, manager was a bitch, employees were kicking up shit eight fucking hours a day, but my position at Po' Folks seemed to be working out. I bought everything on my Shit I Want to Buy List and was finally able to get my laptop, bought it flat out just as I planned. It looked nice sitting on my desk. No more waiting in line at the library. I could check my e-mail ten times every minute if I wanted without having to endure hour-long waits.

I was finally cut loose to work the night shift by myself during the week. I became just as fast as Nathan. I was breaking fewer and fewer plates. I had yet to cut myself. Knock on wood. Nathan and I worked together during the slam-packed weekends. When Mr. Shulte announced that they would start serving breakfast, I picked up a few breakfast shifts. Those mornings were a bitch, but I got used to getting up at 5:00 am.

The kitchen staff started teasing us about being boyfriend and boyfriend because they couldn't see one without the other. Even on our off days, we would hang out for drinks at local watering holes.

One night after an exhausting Saturday night shift, Mr. Shulte asked me to stay behind and help Nathan move some boxes of frozen broiled chicken into the kitchen's freezer. We were the only two he trusted. I was organizing the boxes in a column of six when I suddenly felt a slap across my behind.

"Oh, hell naw," I laughed, chasing Nathan around the kitchen.

"You know you like dat shit." It was true. I liked that it was him. I yanked my pants down around my ass and mooned him.

"Watch it. They got cameras in here," he warned.

"Shit, I forgot. See wha'choo made me do."

"I'll erase th' tape befo' we leave," Nathan said.

The ice from the freezer had turned into water, trundling off the rubber fingers of Nathan's gloves. As I started to pull up and buckle my britches, Nathan yanked at the waistline of denim with brute force.

"Leave them shit's down," he said. Nathan reached in with a single gloved hand, past my briefs and started groping my butt. He pushed me over the kitchen's island, pulling my clothes down around my thighs, exposing my ass to a draft from the freezer. He tugged at my Po' Folk's T-shirt, choking me as he spanked. I felt him toying with me, moving damp fingers along my trench. My blood ran hot, cum swirled in my balls, my dick awoke out of its limp slumber as he eased a single yellow, rubbery digit up inside. It slid in easily.

I braced the table's edge, the aftermath of meat and chopped onions infiltrating my senses as Nathan filled and pushed within. One gloved finger turned into two exploring my anus. I could feel webs of cold pre-cum sticking against my inner thigh. Nathan folded me over, the lower part of my back jabbing into the table. My dick was erect and sticky thanks to Nathan's efforts.

"Git up on th' table," he said. I did what was told of me. Nathan pulled off my shoes, my britches cinched around my ankles. He tugged me sweetly at the edge, inserting his previous fingers back up inside me, manhandling me with filthy rubber. With his digits planted, he leaned in and took my dick into his warm, slick mouth. I ran my fingers threw his peppered hair of black and white as he blew and fingered me. I gripped both ends of the island. I could feel myself approaching that climactic end. Nathan was relentless as he did me in with those talented hands of rubber, those lips around muscle and foreskin.

"U'm gonna …U'mma …"

Nathan pulled me out and began jacking me off with a gloved mitt. I shot then oozed semen lavaling down the gloves. He shook my juices into the garbage nearby, leaving me to get dressed. I pulled on my clothes, tucking my sloppy dick into underwear. Nathan and I resumed with the boxes of frozen, charbroiled poultry, not saying much in the lot before leaving for home.

"You work tomorrow?" I asked.

"Six t' close. You?"

"Yep," I said.

I drove home with the delight of Nathan's spit drying on my penis. We had twelve hours before we were back at it, shoving plates and glasses through the steaming mouth of a dishwasher.

The next morning I awoke with Nathan on the brain. I was taking my morning piss with a toothbrush protruding out of my mouth, when the phone rang.

"Terrence!" Ma yelled from the living-room.

"Huh?"

"Phone fuh you."

I shook my dick free of pee, and unfurled a few tufts of toilet paper wiping urine from the lip of the commode. I spat out the lather of toothpaste into the sink and grabbed the phone.

"I got it," I told Ma waiting on the other end for me to retrieve my call.

"Hello?"

"Hey, did Shulte call you?" It was Nathan.

"Not dat I know of why?"

"He jus' called wontin' me t' come in at eleven."

"Why?" I asked.

"'On' know. You sure heen call you?"

"Hol' on," I said.

I flipped through the names in my caller ID. The number from Po' Folks was listed.

"Th' numba from work on my calla ID."

"Ask ya ma if he called," said Nathan.

"Hol' on."

"Ma!" I hollered.

"Wha'choo callin' me like that fuh, boy?"

"Did somebody from work call here?"

159

"Yeah, some man named Mr. Shulte. He said he wants you to come in."

"That's all he said?" I asked.

"Yeah, why?"

"U'm jus' askin." Ma closed my room door and returned to her cleaning.

"My ma said he called earlia askin' th'same thing. I wonda what he want."

"Guess we'll find out when we git dere," Nathan said.

When I got to Po' Folks, Nathan was standing out front to be let in. Shulte answered our call with a sober glance unlike the chipper good morning or how ya doin' he usually expressed. We followed him through the empty, southern eatery to the office.

"Before I get started, is there anything you two want to tell me, anything ya'll want to come clean about?"

Nathan and I looked at each other puzzled, not having a clue as to what was up.

I thought maybe I was in hot shit for the soda I took from the refrigerator in the lounge or the baked chicken I took home that Nathan said would only get thrown out anyway.

"No, sir," Nathan replied.

"No, sir, sorry." I said.

Shulte reclined steady into his desk chair.

"I came in this morning to go over last night's earnings and the surveillance videos."

As soon as he said video, I thought of Nathan and me in the kitchen. The back of my throat grew parched realizing the quicksand of shit we were in.

"I stopped at the part where you were bent over the table, Terrence, with your ass in the air," he said. Shulte held up two envelopes and said, "This is your severance pay. You're both are terminated effective immediately. Ya'll are lucky I don't have your asses arrested and charged with lewdness."

We took our pay and took that walk of shame out of the hog trough. I laid into Nathan once we got out to the parking lot. "You didn't fuckin' erase th' tape!"

"It was a mistake, fuck, man, I forgot."

"He got us on tape wi'cha han' up my ass, an' all you can say iz you forgot?"

"Wha'choo want me t' do, go back an' wrestle th' tape out 'is hand?" he asked.

"He still might call th' cops on our asses," I said.

"Man, fuck dis job. I was go'n quit anyway."

"You know how long it took me t' git dis shit? Drivin' in th' heat from one Now Hiring sign t' th' nex'?" I asked.

"Chill. I gotta frien' dat work fuh th' state. He say he can pro'ly hook me up. I'll ask 'im if he knows of anymore positions dats open."

"Now I caint lis' dis shit unda employment history on my job applications," I said.

"C'mon, we can go talk t' 'im now," Nathan laughed.

"If we 'on' git dis job, iss ya ass," I told him.

"Dis ain' no time t' be thinkin' 'bout sex."

A MARRIED CONSTRUCTION WORKER'S HOT MOUTH
By Shane Allison

My dick kicked in my jeans beneath the steering wheel as I sat at the light, PJ Harvey blared from the speakers. The light took forever to turn. Try our new Asian salad, read the Mc Donald's sign from across the street. It wasn't salad I was hungry for. You see, I just had to get my dick sucked. Beatin' off only goes so far, you know? I pulled into the lot and parked between a Monte Carlo and a Silverado. I hadn't been out here in two weeks. I didn't want to run into that asshole I came to blows with the last time I was here. We walked away with scratches, me with a pair of broken glasses. It could have been a lot worse. Son of a bitch could've shot me; the two of us could have ended up in the emergency room with gun shots in our guts just 'cause I wouldn't suck his dick.

I'm scared about coming here during the day, that someone's going to spot me in this Bible-beating town, this capital city of southern Baptists. But I got my needs, you know?

The bell above the door chimed as I walked in. There was no one behind the counter. I heard girl giggles. They didn't bother to check and see me. For all they knew, I could've been a curious twelve-year-old. I ducked into the arcade. The place smelled of semen. There was one other guy standing around, studying gay porn with titles like *Slurpin' Jizz*, *Black Nutz Juice*, and *Black and White Twinks in Lust* incased behind locked, plate glass. It was Powder. I got nicknames for them all. I crown him this 'cause he's pale and bald resembling Sean Patrick Flanery from the movie of the same name. He's everywhere milling around here for men. I sucked his dick once. It was nothing special. I cruised down the hall of gentle lighting strung high to blanket shadows that reeked of poppers, searching for others that were out looking for an afternoon pleasure. Booth Three was occupied. I jiggled the knob only to find that it was locked. A cold, glow of light seeped from beneath the slit of the door. Booth Six was cracked just enough to watch some construction worker type jacking off to straight porn. His dick wasn't much, but suckable. When I moved in to get a better view, he looked to me like I was a stranger he had never seen before, but never missed a beat so to speak as he shut himself inside, but I didn't give a shit, 'cause there was someone in Booth Nine, which is infamous for its glory hole action. These are the nastier stalls of the arcade. Spit and cum in pools glazing the walls. Cubby little whore holes that reek of piss and shit. No one booth ever smelling worse than the other.

I crept into Nine, which had no knob. Most of them are shot to shit like this. Some don't lock while others are equipped with bad machines that steal your money. They say this place is owned by the Russian mafia. I believe it.

I shut myself in and peeked through. It was an older dude. Well-dressed in black slacks and a white shirt to match. His dick wasn't out. I took a seat and unzipped. Pulled my dick past the copper teeth of my jeans. Didn't take long for things to rise. He stared through gloriously at me, watching me play with foreskin, diddle my nuts. He summoned me with his fingers, and I knew the signal. I pushed my jeans down low on the totem poll of my body. Pulled my shirt up out the way, worked my dick through that tennis ball-sized cut out. The booth smelled of ass, but I never did mind the little things. He touched me. His fingers were pings of cold. I was tuned to the footsteps outside my stall, one of many that didn't lock according to the sign posted.

THIS DOOR IS BROKEN.

THIS BOOTH IS OUT OF ORDER. IF YOU USE THIS BOOTH, IT'S YOUR OWN FAULT WHEN YOU GET STUCK, AND NO, WE WON'T HELP YOU OUT WHEN YOU REALIZE YOU'RE STUCK BECAUSE THE BOOTH DOESN'T OPEN.

He opened my door, letting out the fornication. It was Powder. He saw that I was busy, up to no good with my ass exposed, dick planted past some old fucker's lips. Powder watched me, which I didn't mind 'cause he's cute. I waved him in to join me, but he just smiled like he does and shut the door, leaving me to my own devices. That geezer's mouth was wet and warm on me. I can't tell you how long it'd been since I'd been blown. The last guy that had me sucked at sucking. He beat my dick up pretty good with those teeth he was giving. He left me scabbed up for days. It was weeks before I could jack off. Had to use the Vaseline for other things.

That silver daddy sucked and slurped, licking dick head, a tongue wrapped around the shaft. Only ten minutes in, and I was about to come, but I wasn't ready yet. There was more fun to be had, and I was getting bored with this man's mouth. I pulled out. The dirty bastard lapped at the glory hole, hungry for more of me. I made myself decent. I wanted a new stud muffin. I wanted that dusty stranger closed off from me in booth three. I pressed my ear to his door to listen in on fake screams from porn bitches begging for it.

"Ah, yeah," this and "fuck my ass" that. Powder lingered in the dark, watching me. He must have thought me such a slut, but I didn't care because behind these walls of caked on cum, I'm a dick-sucking whore and I don't care who knows. I jiggled his knob again. His pants were down this time, shirt up over that pot belly grown with black fur. His dick was thicker. He looked up at me, didn't shut me out, but waved me in. I stepped over this worker's boots, squeezing into his booth. It smelled of dirt and sweat. I plucked out my dick, damn near wet with spit from that silver daddy. Porn star pussy gleamed in our eyes. We took things slow. I veered my candy toward his mug. The adult actress getting her phat black ass pounded turned me on, but not enough.

"Turn it to gay porn," I whispered. He did what I wanted flipping the channels with his one free hand.

"That's good," I told him. He stopped to a scene of a marine getting butt-fucked by a dirty blond in army garb. I couldn't get any hornier than I was that afternoon. Dicks slithering in and out of the tan-lined asses of hung, Hungarian boys has always been my forte.

"Suck me," I told him. I wanted to feed this dirty worker. When he turned his hat backwards, I knew I was in for it. He took deep whiffs from his bottle of poppers. He offered me some, but I refused. I don't know what they get out of it. The stuff only gives me a headache. He's better at it than the dude across the way. I notice the biggest wedding band on his hand, those nails cluttered with grit. It made my heart flutter knowing I had down low lips around my dick. The arcades are no mystery to these sorts. If I had a dime every time I faced-fucked some wifey's husband, my student loans would be paid in full. I pushed off my sneaks, stepped out of my loose fits. I was naked with a worker's rough mitts on my hips, moustache harmonious lips around my stuff.

"More spit," I told him. Construction workers are so nasty. He rolled his mouth around, hand going up and down.

"Wanna fuck me?" he asked.

I usually don't in a place like this, a space this size. It's curtains for us if we're caught according to the signs:

ANYONE SUSPECTED OF DOING ANYTHING OTHER THAN PREVIEWING THE MOVIES (STANDING AROUND, TALKING, SEXUAL ACTIVITIES,) WILL BE REPORTED TO THE POLICE AND BANNED.

All that shit about fucking in the booths, going on about health risks and final warnings. I hated it when he stopped blowing me. He turned himself off into the corner of the booth, lifting his shirt cured with sweat, smudged with dirt.

"Fuck me," he said.

"I don't have any rubbers," I told him.

"They sell some up front," he said in his country twang.

"Hol' up." I buckled my soaked dick into jeans. I unlocked the door, silver porno glow spirited out into the hall of men that had gathered outside our booth. That filthy worker locked himself in behind me. I stepped up to the counter eyeing the fishbowl of condoms and the miniature tubes of lubricant.

"How much are the?" I pointed. Kim was working. Thankfully. She's cool with me. She's got a gay brother.

"They're on the house," she smiled. I took one of each.

"Thanks, babe." Kim knew I was about to get some ass. I returned to the back. That daddy from earlier was gone. Powder was lingering about with the others, waiting for the next piece of arcade trade. I knocked nicely. The worker let me in. He was keeping his dick stiff as he watched some barely legal blonde get fucked on top of a pinball machine. I stepped over him and locked ourselves in. I dropped trou and tore the prophylactic from the cellophane and rolled it on. He assumed the position; his ass point blank. I took the lube and slathered on the stuff, smeared the rest up his blue-collar butt. He took me and led me to his bull's eye. I slid in between him so easily. I held onto his shoulders like reigns and pushed. I worked his ass like there was no tomorrow. Porn mingled with the sounds he made as I fucked the pimpled ass of some wife's husband. We heard the feet of men rustling outside our door, hungry to get in on our action. The muscles in my thighs started to burn, sweat forming. Who knew fucking could be such hard work, so we switched positions. I sat in the chair, he straddled me. I glided him in; the chair squeaked to our weight. My glasses fogged from perspiration. When the movie was up, when his money had run out, he fished more out of the breast pocket of his shirt and slid his hard-working dough into the mouth of the money slot. The worker switched it back to regularly scheduled smut. "Fuck me, eat my pussy" it went on.

"Come for me," he said. This carpenter's butt was a dream. I could have sworn the chair was going to snap to the floor. I was ready, drawing to climax. I clawed at his back, pulled his mane of dirty hair as I pumped semen in the rubber, up his butt. My legs damn near collapsed from under me. He sat up off me and shot off onto the monitor. I rolled the rubber off my dick onto the floor. He went on about how hot it was, how good I can fuck like I haven't heard that before. I tucked my sloppy dick back into pants. We opened the door to a gang of cruisers dispersing into the dimlitness of the arcade. It had grown late as we went in separate directions of the parking lot, never exchanging names, remaining the same. Anonymous.

JAM SESSION
By Rob Rosen

"Later, dude," I yelled to Jon, my roommate, as I hurried out the door for my band's weekly jam session.

"Later," he yelled back from the couch in the living room.

Normally, the band, a bunch of guys with musical aspirations but not enough talent, or money, to make a living out of it, got together at Nate's house. Since he had the biggest garage, that was our home base, except for tonight, as Nate's garage had suddenly developed a mouse infestation. So, as I usually did, I was on my way over there, but to pick him up and drive the two of us over to Steve's, who at least had an attic that was vermin-free.

"Yo," Nate said to me, hopping in the car, before adding, "What, no coffee?"

I grinned. "I don't always drink coffee before a jam session."

"Um," he replied. "Yeah, you do. In fact, every day is planned out the same, from your morning piss right on up to your evening paper. Your whole life is set in stone, dude. So, where's the coffee?"

A red flush crept up my neck. My friends knew me all too well. "The line at Starbucks was way long. I thought I'd pick you up first and head over there next."

"Good idea," he concurred, a silly smile spreading across his impossibly handsome face. "And you can pay for mine, while you're at it."

I patted my jacket pocket, and replied, "If it helps with your lousy playing, then by all means." It was then I realized that my pocket was somehow empty. "Fuck," I quickly added.

Nate looked over at me. "Hey, my drumming's not that bad."

"No," I replied. "I must've forgotten my wallet at home, hence the fuck."

He laughed, and chided, "Not like you, dude. You sure you're not just being your usual cheap self?"

I was already heading back home when I told him, "Just for that, you're only getting a tall non-fat latté. No cream. No sugar. No cookie."

A minute later, we were parked in my driveway and running into my house.

Though my wallet wasn't the only thing we found when we entered.

Jon, still on the couch in the living room, was now naked, a raging boner slicked up and pointing at Nate and me as we stood there staring at it in stunned shock.

"Oh," Jon said, scrunching his legs together and trying as best he could to cover himself up.

"Oh," I echoed, quickly diverting my eyes.

And, "Oh," Nate said, tripling the motion; only his Oh came out in one long, deep, jagged breathe, tinted and edged with something other than surprise.

Still looking away, I said, "I, um, forgot my wallet. I'll just get it and, um, we'll let you get back to …" I finished my train of thought by pointing in the general direction of his crotch, still laden with a fierce hard-on, the tip of which was clearly visible, pink and fat and wet as it was.

I ran to my room, found my wallet on the bed, and ran back into the living room only to find our drummer a few feet closer to the couch, his arms akimbo and a strange look plastered across his face – lust, if I wasn't mistaken – which was something I'd never witnessed before; on him, I mean.

"Found it," I announced, nervously, waiving my wallet in the air. "Ready, Nate?"

Nate looked at me and grinned. "What's the hurry?"

Confused, I replied, "The band's waiting. And Jon here seems to have things well in, uh, hand."

Jon looked up at Nate and then over at me and, equally as confusing, said, "Actually, I could use some help." He lifted his hands away and settled his legs back down. His cock was still rigid, seven thick inches of soft supple skin and coursing blood. We'd lived together for well over two years, and I rarely ever saw him shirtless. Now, all of a sudden, I was getting the grand unveiling.

Then, to add to my consternation, Nate flipped open his cell, hit a few buttons, and said, "Hey Steve, we're having some car trouble. We'll be there as soon as possible."

I looked at him in bewildered alarm, and asked, "What's going on?"

He merely shrugged, and replied, "Guy said he needs some help."

"Help, please," Jon cried out from the couch, again reaching for his swollen prick.

"See," Nate said, moving in even closer.

In the year since I'd met Nate, I never even suspected he was gay. Now, out of the blue, I had a horny roommate to contend with and, judging from the tenting in his jeans, an equally horny and seemingly gay drummer. Since neither was making a move to exit the scene, I acquiesced. Who, after all, was I to look a gift horse, or two, in the mouth? "Well," I said, "seeing as you said please."

I walked over to the couch and stared down at my lean, somewhat hirsute, and vastly adorable roommate. Nate followed close behind. "I should come over here more often," he quipped.

Jon put his hands behind his head and smiled up at us. "Come wherever you like, just make sure that I do, too."

Nate took the hint and began to shuck off his clothes, yanking his T-shirt over his head, kicking off his sneakers, and sliding down his jeans. Our drummer, it seemed, preferred going commando. A thick slab of arching cock began a gradual rise right before my very eyes, nestled as it was within a trimmed blond bush that trailed up and down his body in ever darkening shades. "Your turn," he told me.

I gulped and followed suit, mildly embarrassed at getting naked in front of two friends who were sporting impressive boners that were pointing up and over at me. Then, soon enough, Nate and I stood there bare-assed, except for our socks, above Jon, who was now slowly stroking his rod as he stared appreciatively at the two of us. "Buffet is served, dig in," he offered.

Good timing because boy was I ever hungry. I sunk to my knees to the side of Jon's muscular chest as Nate did the same by my roomie's narrow waist. My hands instinctively reached out and caressed the soft brown down that spread across Jon's torso, running rings around his eraser-tipped nipples, which I took in my hands to pull and tweak on. Nate, of course, grabbed for Jon's fat rod in one hand and his heavy nutsac in the other, until we were both working his body in unison, causing my roommate to moan and squirm as we grabbed and groped at him.

Nate upped the ante by lifting Jon's legs and spreading them apart, causing his pink puckered hole to come into view. "You take the meat," he told me, "and I'll take the middle."

I did as I was told and craned my neck downwards, until my mouth was just above the tip of Jon's wide, helmeted head, already slick with salty pre-cum. I took a deep whiff of his sweaty crotch and then gladly chowed down, engulfing his prick in one eager swoop. Nate, just as happy with his serving, delved into Jon's ass, rimming and reaming it out. I stared down while he munched, he stared up as I swallowed; two eyes locked, watching, waiting for what was to come next – or who.

"Your roommate's ass tastes great, dude," he told me.

"His cock's pretty nifty, too," I said, sucking and slurping on the beast.

Nate let his tongue travel up Jon's crack, gliding over his two heavy, hairy balls, until his mouth was in front of my own. I popped the prick out and let my friend have a go at it. Back and forth it went. In an out of two wet mouths. Then we both sucked up and down the shaft, and alternated between making out with it and then each other. And all the while, Jon bucked his ass off the couch and his dick down our waiting throats.

Eventually, he rasped. "Now, who's gonna fuck me?"

"Funny," Nate said, running his tongue around Jon's leaking head. "I was just going to ask the same question."

Again, I looked deep into Nate's eyes, sparkling blue beneath the overhead lights, then I looked up Jon's lean body and into his blinking peepers, green as shimmering emeralds, and the answer was plainly obvious. "On your knees, Jon," I commanded.

"No prob, dude," he readily agreed, hopping off the couch and onto the carpeted floor. His beautiful ass stared back up at us, alabaster white with a sprinkling of light brown hairs that ran down the crack.

I jumped up to retrieve some lube and a couple of rubbers. When I returned, Nate had already spread Jon's cheeks apart and was slowly, gently probing his hole with two spit-slick fingers, opening my roommate up and getting him ready for the onslaught.

Then both men were on all fours, and I was working a lubed finger inside of Nate's shute, in and up and back, feeling the muscled interior of his perfect butt. When he was good and wet and ready, I said, "Now it's time for a real jam session."

I handed Nate a rubber, which he deftly slid over his thick prick. Then I did the same with my own, and watched, intently, as my drummer boy crouched down just above my roommate's upturned ass, placing the head of his fat prick against Jon's winking hole. Gradually, he slid it on home. Jon sucked in his breath, tensed, and then soon enough allowed the intrusion, until Nate had completely penetrated him, his balls lapping up against two pink cheeks.

Then it was my turn.

I lubed up my friends hairy hole and then slicked up my rubbered-cock before getting it into position. Nate waited, his arms wrapped around Jon's waist; and then, one, two, lickety-split, my dick was gliding inside, sending a thousand volts of adrenalin through my crotch and up my spine. Nate's ass sucked me in like a Hoover, until the three of us were pressed up tight against one another and we each filled the room with the sounds of steady, joyful groans – beautiful music to anyone's ears, to be certain.

Pretty quickly, Nate and I got into a good rhythm, him pulling his cock out of Jon's ass, slowly, evenly, and me doing the same; then him ramming it back on in, and me plowing it to his hilt. Each time three grunts, milliseconds apart, escaped from three panting mouths. When Nate sped up, I did the same; when he slowed down, catching his breath, so did I. We were like one giant, naked, sweaty machine, pumping and grinding away on my living room carpet.

Then the pistons went into high gear.

Nate began to pummel my roomie's rump, which, in turn, caused the middle man's ass to jack at my pulsing cock. And when I could feel the telltale hardening of a prostate and my balls began their gradual rise, I knew the inevitable was drawing near. When Jon moaned a, "Close, dudes," I let go with both guns, rocketing, rocketing, rocketing my cock up Nate's tight hole.

Jon shot first, trembling beneath the both of us as he sighed long and low and deep. Nate followed close behind, and with a final ram he arched his back upwards, allowing me to suck and slurp on his neck. And another sigh went out, ricocheting throughout the room. Nate's ass clenched around my cock as he came, and then I too shot a mighty load, filling up the rubber with ounce after sticky, white ounce of hot, molten cum. It was then that the man-sandwich collapsed in on itself, sending the three of us down to the floor in a glorious pile of sticky flesh.

Sweat-soaked and near exhausted, I eased out of Nate just as he eased out of Jon. We didn't, however, have long to bask in the after-sex glow; the band was waiting, and probably not patiently. Jon stood up and watched, again from the couch, as the two of us toweled off, a smile stretched wide from one side of his adorable face to the other.

"Later, dude," I eventually told him, for the second time that night, as Nate and I closed the door behind us and headed back to my car.

"Well," Nate said as he put his seatbelt on, "that was an unexpected detour."

I smiled, knowing that what he had said wasn't entirely true. It was then I realized I'd left my wallet in the living room. "Um, I'll be right back," I announced, hopping back out and running back in.

Jon was on the couch, his pretty peter flaccid this time around, and he was waiving my wallet at me. "Forget something?" he asked.

I smiled. "Yep."

I leaned down and retrieved my wallet, and then gave him a deep, wonderful, soul kiss on his soft waiting lips. "Next time, let's make it a duet. Without a drummer."

His prick began a steady rise. "Next time, huh?"

I smiled and headed for the door, yelling over my shoulder at him as I closed it behind me, "Practice makes perfect, dude. Practice makes perfect."

MIKE THE MARRIED MAN
By Ryan Field

One autumn a few years back, there was a young man who began to wonder if his life was heading in the right direction, but he was having such a damn good time with his married lover, he decided not to think about it – too much.

He was only twenty-two years old at the time, a recent college graduate with a degree in business, but still working as a waiter in a small rural town in eastern Pennsylvania. He was slim and lanky and muscle-toned, with a shock of dark brown hair that screened his forehead; thick tresses that always appeared slightly wind blown. Dark eyelashes framed his deep blue eyes. If you didn't really know him you'd say he had an unadventurous style of dress veering precariously close to parochial school uniform.

Give him a break though. Most guys his age, with his small town background, would have settled for marrying their high school sweethearts and ignoring their innate, primal urges. It's only a phase I'm going through, they would have told themselves; just get married, have a few kids, and you'll stop thinking about this married guy sooner or later.

It never occurred to Nate to say that even once. He just couldn't help the way he felt about Mike, is all.

But, on the night he began to question where his life was going and the magnitude of sleeping around with a married man finally hit him, he was meeting Mike at the rest stop on the interstate. This was his first and only lover; a man who could curl his toes and make his eyes roll to the back of his head. It was a cool, damp night in late October, and the rest stop was crowded with hungry drivers: men looking for other men on the down-low.

All styles and makes of cars, from minivans to BMWs, were parked on an angle in the parking spaces that circled the grey brick public rest rooms. Off to the right, beyond the automobile section, large trucks with motors running endlessly lined a manmade wooded area where truckers could park and sleep in their air conditioned cabs. Some stood outside, leaning against their rigs puffing one cigarette after the other, while the local tranny would sashay by in red stilettos and a black mini skirt waiting for one of them to say something like, "Hey baby, you got a light." But it was a safe place, too; for some reason, there were never any cops after ten at night.

For about nine months, Nate had been meeting Mike at the rest stop every Saturday night at ten. He was an ex-Marine-turned-farmer, same age as Nate, who looked really hot in baggy jeans and always wore black steel toe half boots; he was a crew cut, ex-high-school-jock type of guy who still played baseball with his buddies in the spring. Mike never spoke much, but whatever he said was always a compliment, and he treated Nate like a fragile wine goblet that might crack with the wrong move. He also didn't bother explaining, or hiding, his gold wedding band, and Nate understood there would be no fantasy of ever having a real relationship. Mike liked fucking good looking young guys, and Nate liked getting fucked by straight guys who drank beer and wore baseball caps.

When Nate pulled alongside Mike's beat up Chevy sedan that night, it suddenly occurred to him he got a sinking feeling in his stomach lately when he saw Mike. But still exciting, too, and Nate needed dick. So he got out of his Honda and slipped into the backseat, where Mike was finishing another bottle of beer. Nate gently placed his palm on Mike's large bicep and leaned forward to kiss the stubble on his cheek. "Hey, Baby," Mike said, as he chugged down what was left in the beer bottle and then belched.

It all went as predicted – no talking while Nate systematically removed all his clothes and Mike watched with a fierce look in his eyes as though he hadn't been fed in months. The exhibitionist in Nate liked this part the most; Mike's glaring, his need to pounce on Nate's smooth body with force. When Nate's clothes (even his socks) were on the front seat, Mike spread his strong legs, and Nate slowly unfastened Mike's jeans and pulled down the zipper. He fumbled for a moment, until he reached through Mike's loose boxer shorts for his thick, hard cock. He leaned over and gently slipped it into his warm mouth while Mike moaned and felt up Nate's bare ass with his coarse hand. It was a good dick to suck: really hard, extra thick and always tasted tangy and salty because Mike hadn't showered since the early morning.

That night, as usual, Nate sucked and slurped the big thing until his jaw hurt, and when it was just about ready to shoot a load, Mike pulled out and slipped on a lubricated condom. He stretched his big legs, and Nate slowly climbed up on his lap. He pressed his hands on Mike's chest for support, straddled the thick, familiar dick and then lowered himself onto it until he could feel the hard denim fabric of Mike's jeans brush against his smooth ass. While Mike's hands were firmly positioned on his waist, Nate arched his back, folded his hands at the back of his neck and began to ride. A couple of guys passing by on foot stopped to watch the show. Though a bit creepy (and never mentioned aloud) both Mike and Nate silently enjoyed putting on a show for the other guys who circled the rest stop on foot; they even slowed down to let the guys watch Mike's cock slowly going in and out of Nate's hole.

Mike enjoyed Nate on his lap, but he preferred to climax on top. So eventually, Nate slid off the dick, went flat on his back and put his legs over Mike's shoulders.

Mike, who could fuck like a bull, banged away to the finish while Nate moaned and begged for more, jerking his own cock so they'd both come at the same time.

When the fucking was over, Mike's eyebrows creased as he tossed the used condom out the back window and shoved his cock back into his jeans. Nate slowly bent over the front seat to gather his clothes, so Mike could gently slap his bare ass. With a turned down mouth Mike said, as he always did, "Thanks, baby, gotta go home now. The wife keeps tabs." But for some strange reason, Nate didn't reply, "See you next week," as he usually did. And he didn't bend over to gently kiss Mike's crotch good-bye either. Actually, Nate didn't even bother to get dressed. He just grabbed his shoes and clothes in a heap, pressed them against his stomach and got out of the car totally naked while five guys watched in the shadows to see what would happen next.

Mike's eyes popped, and he climbed up to the front seat and lowered the window. "What are you doing?"

"I'm changing my life," Nate answered. His face was red and his fists were clenched as he tossed his clothes into the front passenger side of his car and casually walked around to the driver's side, still naked. There were red marks on his smooth ass, revealing paw marks that he'd just been nailed by Mike.

Mike opened the car door and jumped out, ignoring the small audience of voyeurs in the darkness. He reached Nate's car and blocked the driver's door. "What's wrong?"

"Mike, I'm standing here totally naked with a bunch of guys watching me, at least let me get into the car," said Nate.

"Not until you tell me what's going on," said Mike. He wrapped his strong arms around Nate's body, resting his large hands on Nate's ass.

Nate sighed. In Mike's arms he'd always been safe. He reached up, wrapped his arms around Mike's wide neck and rested his cheek against Mike's chest. He spread his legs and arched his back, hoping Mike would start to squeeze and feel up his ass again.

"Will I see you again next weekend?" Mike asked. He began to play with Nate's ass cheeks as though he were kneading bread dough. "C'mon baby, talk to me."

Nate frowned. "No. You probably won't see me again. I'm moving to New York; been thinking about it for a while. And, I don't want this to be dramatic; we both knew it would end sooner or later. You're never going to leave your wife, and I'm tired of cheating with you."

Mike began to lick his ear lobe; he slid his large hands down Nate's back and started to massage Nate's ass. "C'mon baby, please say you'll be here again next weekend; you know you need me as much as I need you ... we need each other," Mike whispered.

Nate leaned forward and rested his weight on Mike's large chest. He knew this all went deeper than just sex; there was a bond between the two men. "Ah well ..." he said. But he also knew deep down he had to get out of this harmful relationship, but when he was with Mike he simply could not say no. And, it wasn't as if he were moving to New York within the week. Probably more like six months. So, he nodded yes, raised his head to look Mike in the eyes, and promised he'd return the following Saturday night against his better judgment. When he pictured Mike's wife in his mind's eye, he saw a pretty young woman with soft eyes and a nice even smile. He didn't want to wreck someone's happy home life, but he couldn't get enough of Mike.

Mike kissed him on the mouth, stuck his tongue all the way down Nate's throat, and then he slapped him on the ass again. "Then I'll see you next week, but an hour later than usual, Baby."

Nate frowned. "Why an hour later?"

"Because it's Halloween, and I have to help the wife hand out candy to the kids," Mike said. His voice was low and soft, almost as if he were asking a difficult question. He didn't want to piss Nate off again.

Nate opened the car door and sat down behind the wheel naked. "That's right: I nearly forgot all about Halloween. Let's make it two hours later than usual: midnight. I have a costume party to go to, and I'm actually wearing a costume for the first time since I was a little kid."

Mike's eyes became animated and he smiled. "What kind of costume?"

"It's a surprise," Nate said, "and you'll either love it, or you'll hate it. But I'm not saying anything else." Then he shut the car door, turned on the engine and lowered the window half way.

"Don't you think you should put on your pants now?" Mike asked. He looked around the rest stop. There were still two or three guys lurking in the bushes, waiting to see what Mike and Nate would do next.

"I'll put them on when I get on the highway," Nate said, "I kind of like driving around naked, especially after I just got nailed by a hot looking guy who wears old baseball caps."

Mike laughed and rubbed his jaw, and then he leaned closer to the window with a more serious expression on his face. "Are we good now? Are you okay?"

"We're good," Nate said.

"And I'll see you next week?" Mike asked.

"Yes, you'll see me next week."

But, the following week Nate had serious second thoughts about meeting Mike in his outrageous Halloween costume. For the first time in his adult life, he'd gone to a costume party in full drag. Not the funny-campy kind of drag, with chunky women's shoes, big balloon tits and a cheap wig, either. Nate had decided that as long as he was going to do this once in his life, he may as well do it right. He spent a small fortune on the blonde Tina Turner style wig; his six-inch stilettos in black leather were almost as much as his monthly car payment. A good friend who was a hairdresser helped him with his make up, accessories, and long red fingernails. When he finally slipped a black Lycra mini dress over his slim body, he looked into a full-length mirror and nearly choked. Though he had to wear a tight, uncomfortable jock strap to keep his dick down, and dressing as a woman wasn't something he knew he'd to again for a long time, he immediately felt dangerous and exhilarated when he noticed how round his ass looked and how long and sexy his legs were in high heels (he'd shaved them smooth; he didn't need panty hose). The fake sponge tits he'd borrowed looked so real he had to squeeze them to prove they weren't. It was almost as if he'd stepped outside of his own body to be a completely different person. But he wasn't sure how Mike would react to all this.

It helped that people at the costume party didn't recognize him at first; even if you knew him well you had to look twice to be sure it was really conservative Nate who usually wore nothing but white button down shirts and beige slacks. A few strange men either stared at his ass and whistled, or felt it up a couple of times. One cute young guy, who was dressed as The Professor from *Gilligan's Island*, actually put his hand up Nate's dress and started to pinch and squeeze his ass. Nate got an instant erection beneath the tight jock strap, and if he hadn't been meeting Mike later that night he would have opened his legs and let the guy lift his dress all the way up.

When he left the party and headed toward the rest stop to meet Mike, he had to force himself to keep from biting his lower lip, so he wouldn't ruin his lip gloss. And those high heels were murder with a clutch; he kept getting the high heel caught on the floor mat whenever he switched gears.

Mike was there, in the usual parking spot, waiting for him that night. When Nate pulled up alongside the old Chevy sedan and turned off his headlights, Mike looked over because he recognized the car.

But, then when he saw who was driving his mouth opened wide and his eyes started to bulge. Nate slowly stepped out of the car and smoothed his mini skirt down; a couple of guys in the shadows who were only interested in other guys looked the other way when they saw a woman get out of the car. He carefully loped toward Mike's car, amazed at how well he gotten the hang of walking around in high heels in such a short amount of time.

Mike literally jumped out of the car. "Baby? Is that really you?" He was smiling now; his hands were in his pockets and he was bouncing around on the balls of his big feet.

Nate smiled. "It's me alright." Then he looked down at the pavement. "Are you upset? Is this over the top?"

Mike reached out and pressed his palm on the small of Nate's back. "Baby! You look so freaking hot I wanna get down on my knees and lick those legs from the ankle all the way up to your ass." His eyes were still wide; he kept looking Nate up and down, as if he were ready to make an expensive purchase.

Nate laughed. "You are one kinky sonofabitch, man."

"And that's why you like me so much," he said. He pressed harder on the small of Nate's back and pulled him closer. He reached around with his other hand and started to squeeze Nate's ass. "Get into the back seat. I wanna get me some of that hot ass, Baby." He was laughing now, acting out cliché lines from a bad porno movie.

When they were in the back seat, Nate sat next to him and reached for his crotch. He carefully unzipped Mike's jeans, so he wouldn't break one of his long red fingernails, while Mike opened his legs and closed his eyes. He pulled Mike's cock from the opening and softly ran the red fingernails all over the shaft. When he pulled out Mike's big balls and scratched them, the big cock jumped and jerked on its own. Mike spread his legs even wider so that Nate could open his mouth and wrap his ruby red lips around the dick head.

"Yeah, Baby," Mike moaned, with his deep voice, "Suck me off, Baby."

Nate stuck out his tongue and licked Mike's cock from the bottom of the shaft to the tip of the head. And then he wrapped his red lips around the head and went down all the way to Mike's big balls. He sucked so hard his cheekbones indented. Mike leaned forward a little, so he could put one of his hands up Nate's dress and stroke the inside of his thighs. But just when Nate was ready to start bobbing his head and get into some serious cock sucking, there was a loud thump on the back window. Nate looked up, with a mouth full of dick, and saw a wide-faced woman with short, greasy brown hair making a fist at the window. Here eyes were wild, and she started to pound on the glass.

"Oh shit," Mike shouted. He punched the back of the front seat. His hand was still up Nate's dress.

The dick slipped out of Nate's mouth. "Who the fuck is that?"

"Oh shit, it's my wife," Mike shouted.

The wife started to scream, "So this is what you're doing on Saturday nights, you piece of shit? You're out screwing around with whores, common gutter whores, while I'm home all alone night after night. I'll cut your fucking dick off now, you piece of shit. This is the last straw. Get the fuck out of that car! And get that fucking whore out of that car!" She started to pound on the window again; good thing Mike always locked the doors.

"She thinks I'm really a woman," Nate whispered, while Mike shoved his dick back into his pants.

"Could you pretend you really are?" Mike asked, and then shrugged his shoulders.

Nate looked at the fat, screaming shrew outside the car. She was wearing a gray sweat suit, no make up, her hair was limp and greasy, and she was pounding the glass with the shortest little hands Nate had ever seen. And then he looked at Mike. He was rubbing his temples and breathing heavy. Nate smiled. "I guess it's a good thing she caught us on Halloween. She can think I'm a woman, if that's what you want; it's cool, Mike."

Though his wife was still banging on the window, Mike stared at him and said, "Thank you, you're really the best, Baby."

Nate smoothed out his dress and shook his head. "Now, you're going to get out first and hold her down. And then I'm going to slip out the other door and run to my car. Will I see you again?" Someone else might have just left and given the whole affair up for good after being caught in the act like that; but Nate had to ask.

Mike pounded the back of the front seat again, as if he'd just made the most important decision of his life. "Meet me here on Friday night after work ... around six. I'll be here waiting, and we can talk ... okay?"

Nate nodded.

Mike opened the car door and stepped out. The wife tried to push past him; her arms were stretched out, and she was lunging for Nate's throat. She kept screaming things like, "You piece of shit ... get that whore out of your car," but Mike grabbed her by the arms, so Nate could make a run for his car.

Nate jumped out the other door, and headed toward the driver's side of his car. Oh, the wife wanted to bitch slap him, he knew. She would have pulled him down to the pavement if she could have. Mike had to hold the cow back with all his strength; she kept screaming, "You fucking whore ... slutty fucking cunt ... I'll kick the shit out of you, you dirty whore!"

Nate didn't respond though. Even when he backed out of the parking space and she kicked the back door of his car with her dirty sneaker, he flipped a piece of blond wig away from his cheek and kept his eyes focused straight ahead. First, he knew he wasn't a whore; not with Mike. And second, he was actually relieved they'd finally been caught.

ONE NIGHT IN SPINWICK
A Novella By DesertMac

One

You all knew guys like me back in high school: The social misfit, pretty much blending into the background. I was quiet most of the time because I knew that most of the crap that came out of my mouth when I did talk was just plain annoying to people. This had been reinforced constantly over my eighteen years – pretty much anytime I talked to more than one person at a time – with snide retorts and rolled eyes that were meant for me to see. So I had a self-imposed gag order that was, unfortunately, forgotten whenever I got fucked up.

"People skills" are what they call it and are what I didn't have. So, I mostly just tried to keep my mouth shut. Being socially inept and only having lived about a year here in LaPorte, southeast of Houston, I didn't have what you'd call a full social calendar. I was decent enough looking. My body was trim and fairly fit, though I played no sports. I was just average; hard to picture just because it's actually hard to picture anyone so average, isn't it?

And, it wasn't as if I were a total outcast or nothing; nobody was hateful toward me in general. They all knew my name and all; they just didn't notice me much when I wasn't irritating them. I did everything I could to fit in and be an upstanding citizen of Kelly's Cue, the game room/pool hall that was the center of our universe. I grew my shaggy brown hair as long as my folks would allow, a little past my collar, and smoked pot and did other drugs every chance I got. At least I had some money to spend, and that gets you included in some things, and you can bribe your way into other things. I played a pretty decent game of foosball, too.

I had been gradually realizing something was wrong with me. And, that something was I had a thing for boys. I had tried like hell to ignore it but found that impossible. The more I tried to ignore it, the stronger the urges got.

I fought, debated, and reasoned with myself all through my seventeenth year – having nightly raw, steamy fantasies about guys the whole time. By the time I was eighteen, I was just starting to accept and feel okay about how guys turned me on, when one night in Spinwick changed my life in ways I couldn't possibly have anticipated. It was early in that momentous summer of 1977, a steam bath of a Texas summer night in the suburbs of the polluted boomtown, close to the Houston Ship Channel and Galveston Bay, where LaPorte, Pasadena and Deer Park all come together.

I'd been hangin' at Kelly's on a really slow evening playing foosball with a kid called Skunk when my best friend, Jimmy Small, came in and told me there was a party at Kevin Landry's house. Now Kevin Landry was what you call white trash. Jimmy called him a thug. Yeah, probably a majority of us would be considered white trash or lower middle class at best, even though we mostly lived in brand new houses. Where else would you see bumper stickers all over town that said, "Oilfield Trash And Proud Of It!" even on Cadillacs and the like? It was a point of pride for the locals. But Kevin and his clan walked the walk and talked the talk. The cool thing about his family though was that you could get away with *anything* at their house.

It was hopelessly trashed out from raising the six wild, delinquent sons of drunk parents who had given up long ago. Plus, with the occasional wife or girlfriend of this or that brother, and their spawn, you couldn't really find anything that hadn't already been damaged – except their stereos, and GOD HELP YOU if you fucked with their usually battling stereos! His parents always passed out around eight on Valium and beer and couldn't be roused by anything less than a category three hurricane until 5:00 am.

Kevin was near the top of my pantheon of guys I fantasized about regularly. He could easily have been number one if I'd been around him more. He was wired, violent, hot headed and sexy as hell, which scared me enough to steer clear of him most of the time but kept me intrigued and salivating over him for some of those same reasons.

He'd been in jail more than once, just as all of his older brothers had. The one I'd never seen was doing fifteen years in

Huntsville State Penitentiary for aggravated armed robbery. The "aggravated" part was that the clerk resisted, so he pistol whipped him so badly that the guy had to have reconstructive surgery. One of his brothers had cut off another brother's ear in a fight one time, and they'd had it sewn back on. That was the kind of family they were. But if anyone outside the family fucked with any one of them, he had to deal with *all* of "The Landry Boys," as they were known to the law and others. The thing is all of them were so fucking gorgeous that I just couldn't help the boners I got and had to hide when I was around them. If they hadn't been such a menace to society and had any talent among them, they could have all been models or actors or something.

Kevin, at eighteen had short, curly, nearly platinum blond hair streaked with gold and a hint of copper, silvery gray eyes and stood about six-one, I guess. I just compared him to my five-eleven. He had dark lashes and eyebrows streaked with that platinum blond for a dazzling effect that really turned me on. His skin was perpetually tanned a translucent bronze that can't be adequately described. He was slender and wiry – but not skinny – with broad shoulders and muscular tattooed arms. He was a hound dog from hell, *always* talking pussy, all the time, nonstop. The only things he ever talked about besides pussy were drugs, cars, rock music and fighting, in no particular order.

The most surprising thing about Kevin was that he had just graduated high school, as every one of his brothers had dropped out, including the younger one, sixteen-year-old Peter, who was, of course, also gorgeous – well, beautiful. I say "beautiful" because he wasn't much like his brothers. Where they were all tall, with platinum hair and light features like Kevin, he was shorter and had brown hair and eyes. Where his brothers were all similarly hyper-masculine, hot headed and prone to violence, Peter was nearly the opposite, soft spoken, quiet and kind – and a talented artist. And contrary to what you'd expect from their contempt for any sign of weakness, and the way they fought with each other, they were all very protective of him and never picked on him.

So anyway, their house was kind of a hangout, and I'd been there several times. It was over in Spinwick, the only older housing division in the middle of long expanses of flood plane cow pastures, with a few trailers, but mostly wood frame houses up on cement blocks, like Kevin's.

We showed up at Kevin's around ten, but there wasn't really much of a party going on, compared to the blow-outs some guys had. There was booze and pot, and Billy West had sold most everyone a Quaalude or two, but it was just about fifteen guys, sitting around the living room talking over the stereo. Kevin and his next oldest brother Stan were jousting to be the center of attention. Mark and Peter, the other two brothers living at home at that time, weren't there that night.

Stan was even more gorgeous than Kevin, and all of Kevin's friends were easily drawn to the sexy, shirtless twenty-year-old on the rare occasion he'd treat the *youngsters* as if they were somebody worth talking to. He only did so when he was bored and wanted to drive Kevin insane by taking away his friends for the moment, obviously getting great satisfaction at how easy it was to do. I know I had to force myself to not stare at his incredibly sexy torso and his bulging Levis. This kind of competition was what Kevin dealt with every day of his life at home, and everyone sitting there was acutely aware that it could erupt in a serious fight at any given moment.

Billy sold me, Jimmy and Aaron a Quaalude each, and I bought his last one for Donald, as thanks for the ride over. We set about to party, and mine began to hit as I drank some gross gin and coke. I started talking too loud and being stupid, getting a few of those annoyed looks and curt comments from others, coming dangerously close to really pissing Kevin off at one point – so I shut my mouth.

I hung back on the edge of the group and just watched everyone for a while. Jimmy and I weren't included in the bong passing circle, and just as well, as I didn't need it. But things like that would get to me anyway. It just rubbed it in that we weren't part of the "in" group, ya know?

The conversation had degenerated to the see-who-can-'dis'-the-other-best stage, everyone roaring with laughter as they traded insults with each other. At times like that, I was glad to be invisible.

Two

I slipped out to go pee, staggering into the bathroom at the far end of the long house, feeling no pain, kinda floating. I was just about through when Kevin came in and pushed his way in beside me.

"Move over, pussy," he mumbled drunkenly, shouldering me to one side.

That stung, until I realized he would likely have said it to anyone standing there. The very last of my piss stream was interrupted, and I strained to get it back while trying to think of a comeback that wouldn't piss him off. I could think of nothing.

"Why you always go talkin' shit, Bobby, pissin' people off?" He threw me an annoyed glance while he fumbled with his jean buttons.

I knew there was no way I'd be able to finish that last bit of pee if he pulled out his dick in front of me. I could never pee in front of anyone I thought was hot. But not wanting Kevin Landry mad at me was of paramount concern, so I tried to smooth it over.

"Aw man, Kevin, I'm sorry I'm so fuckin' stupid sometimes. I just open my mouth 'n stupid shit comes out, ya know? I didn't mean anything by it, dude."

He had pulled his dick out by the time I finished saying that, and I stared at it. I was so fucked up I wasn't aware I was staring. He was starting to respond to what I said and surprised me by putting his arm around my shoulders, looking down to watch his own piss stream starting.

"Shit, man, y'know, ya always seem to say the wrong thing, bruh. How you come up with the shit you do all the time, I don't …" he trailed off as he looked up and saw me staring at his dick. I could tell in my peripheral vision that he looked at my face. That made me snap that I was staring, and I quickly trained my eyes on my own dick, which was just hanging there, starting to fill out a little. I'm pretty sure a smile appeared on his face, but couldn't be positive of that. I blushed so deeply I could see it in my arms.

His dick was fat, really fat. I'd never seen such a fat dick, and I was pretty good at checking out dicks in locker rooms and urinals without getting caught. The second I felt mine start filling out, I shook it and stuffed it back into my pants before it could embarrass me. Kevin still had his arm around my shoulders and didn't let me move away when I started to back up.

"Hang on, bruh, I need ya to help hold me up while I finish." He sounded more fucked up than he had a moment ago. I didn't argue with him, as I didn't want to piss him off any more. I was scared shitless that he'd caught me staring at his dick. I began praying he wouldn't beat the shit out of me and tell everyone I was a fag. I knew he hated fags 'cause he called anyone he didn't like a fag. I was extremely careful that not even a hint of "gayness" ever be associated with me, even in joking. I wanted to leave as quickly as possible, but I was dependent on Donald for a ride.

Kevin must have peed a gallon, while I stared up at the cracked and peeling paint on the wall in front of me. Oddly out of place was an eight-by-ten framed, faded and water stained print of a Rockwell, *Saturday Evening Post* cover of two boys taking a bubble bath. Was there ever a time when this family even vaguely resembled Norman Rockwell's imagery? I seriously doubted it. This wasn't Rockwell's America; this was the nitty gritty dirt base of the real America.

He still had his right arm around my shoulders, and when I heard the last dribbles fall in the water I looked down to see him grasp the counter edge with his left hand and sway. "Oh man, I'm so fucked up, I can't *even* maintain. Why don't ya shake it for me, bruh?"

"Huh?" I looked at him as if he was insane.

He drew my eyes down to his dick as he looked at it. "C'mon, Bobby, help a brother out, man. Shake it for me." He made it sound purely utilitarian, a simple favor, as if there could be no recriminations from it, as he wobbled around just a little too dramatically.

It had filled out some since I'd been looking up at the wall. It was even fatter and was now hanging about five inches over his zipper. I stared at the eighth wonder hanging out his fly and tried to come up with an eloquent response to his request.

"Fuck you, Kevin!" was the best I could do.

He pleaded with me, "Come on, Bobby, don't be a shit, maaan. I'd do it for you if you was this fucked up, bruh." He drew his head back and looked askance at me, "What, you don't like me or somethin'? You don't wanna be my bruh? Well *fuck* you then, bitch!" He started to slowly remove his arm from my shoulder, acting all indignant.

My mind was moving slow. It took a moment for what he said to soak in. When I finally processed it, I panicked. The last thing in the world I wanted was to have Kevin Landry as an enemy. I would rather eat ground glass than make him hate me. He got way too much pleasure out of terrorizing anyone he considered an enemy.

I looked up into his gray eyes as he towered over me. "What? NO, man! I've always liked you, Kevin!" I was frantic to correct this, momentarily forgetting what he was asking me to do. "Why would you think I don't like you?"

He smiled at how his ploy worked – me totally uncomprehending – and put his arm back around my shoulder, draping it around my neck and pulling me closer into his side, "Well ya wouldn't help a brother out, 'n ya told me to fuck off. I'd say that pretty much says ya don't like me. I mean, what's a brother t' think?" He smiled the whole time, while I absorbed the body heat from his armpit on my shoulder.

"No dude, it's not like that at all! I just thought you were fuckin' with me, you know." I glanced down at his dick, which was now filled out significantly, but not hard. It was beautiful hanging out his fly, all meaty, beefy, big and bouncy. I wanted to touch it so badly. The erection I'd been fighting in my jeans went ahead and finished embarrassing me by stretching it's full six and three eighths inches-with-the-ruler-on-top, with me praying he didn't notice it.

"So ya do like me then?" It was more like a challenge than a question. I nodded, and he glanced down at his dick and back up to me. "Well then, go ahead 'n shake it for me, bruh. I'm sooo fucked up." He rolled his head a little to illustrate his plight.

He looked into my eyes, and I thought I saw some kind of spark in there behind the glassy stare. It seemed like he was wanting to instigate some kind of sex with me, but I couldn't be sure. The thought was both exciting and terrifying.

I was scared as hell, fucked up, paranoid of him, and thrilling at the thought of touching his big dick, all at the same time. All I could think at that moment was, *If this is the only way to keep Kevin Landry from treating me like an enemy from now on.* And, with my inhibitions substantially lowered, I just went ahead and did it.

Blame the Quaalude, blame the booze, I was afraid to piss him off, I was stupid, whatever. I reached over and cautiously took hold of it between my thumb and index finger about halfway up the shaft and gave it a shake.

It was as heavy as it looked, and touching it set off all kinds of electric jolts in my body and mind. I still don't know why I crossed that hazy little line, but I went ahead and gripped it with my whole hand, shaking it a little, then more vigorously. I couldn't believe how fantastic his rapidly hardening dick felt in my hand! I watched the wrinkles in the loose skin steadily disappear and felt the veins and ridges become pronounced as it got rigid, thrilling me as I'd never been thrilled in my pitiful little life.

I was about to let it go when he casually said, "Keep goin' there, bruh, I dribble a lot." He grinned warmly at me, but an icy chill went down my spine as the sly narrowing of his eyes told me he had me figured out.

I should have considered that look and stopped right there, but I already had his dick in my hand, had already shook it for him, and he was just telling me to finish what I'd started. He was almost fully hard now with my whole hand gripping the pulsing shaft, making me blush and rush. His dick was shooting electrical charges up my arm and down to my groin, stopping by to give my sense of judgment a lobotomy on the way. My ears were burning, and I knew I wasn't concealing neither my excitement, nor my fear, well at all.

And, I *knew* I was committing a heinous social crime! Common sense told me that if this went wrong, it would be very, very bad – and that scared the hell out of me. But, I went ahead and shook it some more, and some more. It wouldn't flop around like it had, since it was pretty hard now, so I finally let it go then tapped the broad topside twice with my fingertips for good measure.

"There. I think that's got it." I tried to sound detached or professional, like some nurse or something, while avoiding his eyes. Then I got brave, looked up at him and added, with a hollow threat implied in my voice, "You better not make anything of this, Kevin."

He didn't even blink. Keeping our eyes locked in an intense stare, he reached over and grabbed my hand, pulling it back to his fully hard cock, wrapping my fingers around it for me. In a deeper, huskier voice, he said, "Don't worry, bruh, but go ahead 'n squeeze the last couple a drops out for me."

Oh-my-god. I didn't resist, but I didn't want to do this; but I did want to do this; but I knew I shouldn't do this. I couldn't tell from his expression if he was trying to come on to me for real or play me, so he could humiliate me and ruin my life. I got the feeling he'd smile that same smile either way.

I stared at his face with my jaw hanging open, unable to react, rushing like hell, scalp tingling. He worked my hand back and forth on his cock and leaned his head down and in close to mine, almost forehead-to-forehead as we looked down at his hand on my hand on his cock.

"Come on, Bobby, stroke it!" he stage whispered. He nodded down at my tented jeans and said, "I can see yer gettin' off to it, so go ahead 'n stroke it, bruh." He smiled what he thought was an encouraging smile.

I saw it more like a shark's smile. I thought of *Jaws*. I was all but hyperventilating, wobbling around a little. But as wary as I was of his motivations, I was simply unable to resist the first cock I'd ever held in my hand beside my own. And, that it was a really big and thick one at, easily, a good eight or nine inches, attached to this sexy, dangerous guy on my "most wanted" list, made it hard to listen to my own logic, as my libido sent jolt after jolt of excitement and pleasure through my circuits, overriding the warnings in my head.

But, I finally snapped and jerked my hand away, blushing beet red and trembling. "Uhhh … I gotta …" I mumbled and rolled out from under his arm, "… get back in there."

I couldn't believe I had just played with Kevin Landry's dick! In his own bathroom! With all these people in the house! OH FUCK!

My life is over. He's going to go back out there and have a big belly laugh as he tells everyone how Bobby Wheaton, the F-A-G, just played with his dick over the toilet. And, of course, in the telling, it will have been me groping for it without any prompting from him, I'm sure.

He kept his hand on my shoulder as I tried to get past him to leave the room, "Hey, Bobby, mellow out, dude. It's no big dope deal, bruh." He half turned and looked into my eyes, smiling that sexy smile again, "How 'bout we go party in my room – just you 'n me."

I was too freaked out to respond. Well, I guess the sheer terror in my eyes was a response of sorts. I whipped around to make my escape and tripped over the little fuzzy rug. I went down and hit my forehead smack on the edge of the partly open door. The lights went out for a second, and I wished they had stayed out longer. It fucking hurt like hell! I had expected Quaaludes and booze would have made it not hurt, but it damn sure did.

Kevin quickly came down on one knee to see how I was, "Whoa, bruh! You ok?! Oh man, that *had* to hurt! I think you dented the edge of the fuckin' door!" He chuckled. "You ok?" He turned my head and inspected it. "Oh bruh, yer gonna have a big fuckin' knot *right here* tomorrow." He poked my forehead right where I'd hit it and I winced.

"OW! Fuck!" I pulled my head away from his touch and felt to see if I was bleeding or anything. Kevin adjusted himself onto both knees and I noticed his hard dick was still sticking out of his fly. I felt my own dick jerk back to life at the sight. With my hand on my growing knot and my head tilted down he couldn't see my eyes, so I was able to stare at it. I forgot all about my throbbing injury as I stared at his big, enticing, fat dick. I wanted to suck on it so fucking bad!

I don't know what he was thinking of about that time but his dick kept twitching and bouncing itself around. It wasn't losing any hardness, and he made no attempt to put it back in his pants, thereby keeping me mesmerized. He probably knew I was staring and was doing it on purpose.

"You sure yer okay? Can ya see straight?" He took hold of his dick and aimed it at me, "How many dicks am I holding up?" He couldn't wait for my response; he busted a gut laughing and slumped against the sink cabinet. I tried to act pissed off, but busted up laughing, too.

When he got over being impressed with his own wit, he started to stand up, moving his now dangling wonder closer to me in the process. He offered his hand, and I pulled myself up by his flexing arm, getting a good whiff of his dick and inspecting his tattoos closely on the way. My ass ring spasmed as his groin scent registered in my brain.

As soon as he could tell I was somewhat stable, he grabbed my hand and put it right back on his dick again. I jerked it away and snapped at him, "Cut that shit out, man!" As it roared back to hard almost instantly.

He laughed oh-too-wisely and said, "You got just as much a boner as I do, bruh. Quit tryin' to act like ya don't like it when I can see ya do." He chuckled and jutted his pelvis forward, nudging my hip with the wide rose colored head. He tried to look in my eyes, but I refused.

"I don't … I don't … Man, fuck that shit!" I gave it my most disgusted tone, "I ain't no fucking fag!"

I slipped out the door and started walking quickly down the hall, with its dark brown sheet rock that had been floated but never painted. Kevin raced around and intercepted me halfway, pushing me up against the wall with brute strength, pinning my arms up and out from my sides and grinding his groin into mine with a big evil grin on his face. It was hard to think of him as the same age as I, being so much bigger and stronger. He looked like he could easily be twenty or twenty-one.

"Bobby, Bobby, Bobby, bruh …" He smacked his lips like he was exasperated and just didn't know what to do with me anymore. He followed my head with his to get me to look at him as I looked in every direction, steadfastly refusing eye contact as he breathed gin and Coke into my face. "Ya can't hide how ya liked my dick, bruh, so don't even *try* to pretend." He studied my face for a moment. "What, you scared I'm gonna tell anyone about this or somethin'? Ain't no fuckin' way, bruh!" He ground slowly and sensuously into my groin as he spoke. "Ain't no other reason for you to try 'n pretend like you ain't likin' it."

"I don't – I don't know what you're talkin' about, Kevin! That's bullshit! Leave me a – let me go, dude!" I was really freaking out now, feeling like some felon caught red-handed and up against the wall. And he *still* hadn't put his dick back in his pants! It was as if he couldn't care less if anyone caught him with his hard dick out of his jeans, humping on me with it in his own fucking hallway! *Anyone* at the party could have headed for the bathroom, and there was no way he could have gotten it back in his jeans before they saw it.

"Bruh, you're so into it yer about to come in your pants! Quit tryin' to act like ya don't want it, Bobby."

He was grinding his cock sensuously against my traitorous erection and had now captured my eyes, making me feel like a little kid caught on a carnival ride I was too short for, wanting, needing to take the ride, but common sense telling me I could, and probably would, get hurt. I was so fucked up, so scared of his cocky smile and his brazen fearlessness and so turned on by his very aggressive sexiness, I was having a real problem breathing.

I saw him gauging my resistance – or lack of it – at this point, and watched a smug little grin appear the moment he decided he had me. I felt my stomach flip-flop and my cock twitch, both despair and excitement flooding my drugged brain simultaneously.

"Wait right here, bruh!" He stepped away and held his arms in a semi-circle around me to underscore his point, almost sounding threatening, "Don't move a fuckin' muscle! I'll be back in a flash."

He looked down at his dick and grinned up at me like an excited kid. He was so fucking sexy when he looked up from his bowed head like that, my heart raced. He somehow managed to stuff it back in and walk away, veering off into the kitchen at the head of the hallway. I noticed he seemed to walk just fine. I guess he, umm, *recovered* from his wobbliness in the bathroom rather quickly. The rest of the group was in the living room, around the corner beyond the dining room/auto parts depot, carrying on loudly over the stereo, not missing either of us, apparently.

Three

I was totally freaking out. I had fantasized and even prayed for something like this to happen, but it was going nothing the way I had scripted. Mainly, I had no real idea how he viewed it, how he viewed me. But my imagination was going wild with images of him, now that I knew he had at least an inclination for *some* kind of guy-to-guy sex.

But, that train of thought was battling my glaring paranoia about his attitude and motives. And, both of those trains were being derailed every other second as I'd remember how his big long awesome fat hot heavy squeezable dick felt in my hand. I had never been anywhere *near* this turned on in my fucking life!

He came back around the corner with a bottle of gin in one hand and a pipe in the other. The carnivorous look in his eyes sent chills down my spine – or it was just another Quaalude rush, who knows? He strutted past me and said, "C'mon," with authority in his voice.

I followed like a condemned man into his crowded bedroom. It was filthy and smelled like a cross between a beer joint and a locker room. There were dirty dishes on the tables and beer cans and bottles everywhere, sprinkled liberally with wadded up Jack in the Box hamburger and taco wrappers among the dirty clothes and other junk. Neither Kevin's bed against a set of windows in the middle, with one busted out and boarded up, nor Stan's to the left against the wall looked as if the sheets had been changed in months.

He sat down on the left side facing Stan's bed and patted the stained sheet beside him for me to sit, then busied himself with digging out his stash to load the pipe.

I sat down beside him, mostly because I was having a head rush that left me no choice. I kept arguing with myself, asking over and over why the hell I was here, how could I be so stupid – while picturing myself sucking his big fat dick.

He said nothing as he sparked up the ten dollar an ounce Mexican weed and handed it to me after a big hit. I sucked on it and held it in. He picked up the bottle of gin and chugged some, then handed it to me.

"Chase it with this," he encouraged me. When I tipped the bottle up, he reached up and held the bottom to keep me chugging. "Yeah! Don't puss out, Bobby! Chug it!"

So I did. I knew I shouldn't drink much, but I was so nervous and paranoid I felt like I needed it really badly. On top of the Quaalude and what I'd already drunk, the pot and gin had an instant effect, mellowing me out a lot, but not really enough.

We traded hits and chugs three more times, then he got up and wedged a wooden chair up under the door handle while I watched him nervously, trembling. He swaggered over and planted his feet apart in front of me as the room began to spin out of control.

"I need ya to shake it s'more," he snickered as he undid his buttons. "I think there's another drop in there ya missed."

He let his somewhat baggy jeans fall to his ankles then twisted his hips to make his semi-hard pendulous cock sway side to side. I stared in awe and terror at it swinging menacingly, temptingly over his big hairy nuts. It looked even bigger at eye level, with no jeans obscuring its wide base. He kicked off his jeans and shoes and stood flexing in all his naked glory for me to drool over.

And damn, was he one to drool over! I truly appreciated just how awesome his body was. It was male perfection that dreams and fantasies are made of. A body just didn't come built any better, for my tastes, nor a dick more impressive. He had very little body hair, dark coppery blond around his groin, trailing silvery up his hard flat belly to his navel and lightly down his legs, and of course his armpits. There was a large tattoo of a dagger through a skull with blood dripping out the eye sockets on his perfectly sculpted left pec. I drank in the view with reverence, not quite believing this was all happening, and so fast.

But it was happening! Like a fantasy come to life, he was standing naked in front of me, telling me to play with his spectacular, already hard again dick. I was far too petrified to move a muscle, even though I already knew damn well I would do whatever he wanted me to do.

He picked up on my inability to react and stepped in close to me, putting his dickhead within two inches of my mouth. I could smell a hint of soap from an earlier shower, overpowered by summer sweat and musk from his groin, and it was intoxicating. Very intoxicating.

"Go ahead, Bobby, feel it," he urged me in a soothing tone as he put his hand on the back of my head, just holding it there.

I reached up and tentatively touched his cock. Then I wrapped my fingers around the base. They almost met my thumb. My heart had moved up into my head and was pounding so hard and loud I could barely hear him. My mouth was dry as a bone, and my hand was shaking so badly it was practically jerking him off in hyper-speed.

Oh God his dick was awesome! He gave only the slightest pull on my head, and I put the tip into my mouth, tasting the hot flesh and pre-cum leaking from it. There was no turning back now that was for sure, so I just went with it and started sucking my first cock. And, I couldn't have asked for a more wonderful cock to suck.

I eased his shaft slowly in, filling my mouth to overflowing, feeling it pulse on my tongue, tasting pre-cum, tasting male flesh. I instantly knew that all the frustration and anguish I'd experienced for the last few years were justified. I hadn't had much doubt left by this time, but with that first taste, I knew for certain I was born to suck dick, and actually felt a sense of relief, of contentment, flowing over me.

He moaned and started pumping, surprisingly gently, in and out of my hungry mouth. I lost all of my inhibitions and got more into it second by second. As I increased my enthusiasm and tempo, he did the same. Within a couple of minutes, he was fucking my face feverishly, moaning and grunting with each thrust.

By then, my only frustration was that I couldn't get that fat thing all the way into my throat. I wanted to nuzzle my face in his pubes while gagging on his dick, but it was just too thick, and he was fucking my face too hard and fast to try relaxing my throat muscles to see if I could swallow it.

He pulled out abruptly, tilted my head back and handed me the bottle. I poured the nasty no-label gin down my throat while he watched. He laughed and so did I. He took a drink himself and made me take another huge gulp.

"Hey, you're fuckin' good at that, bruh!" He nodded his head approvingly, indicating my oral skills, not my gin chugging skills.

His comment didn't register in my cock sucking dazed brain at that moment, and by then I was so fucked up I couldn't sit up any longer. I slumped back on the bed, wordlessly reaching for his dick. He laughed some more and crawled up on his knees, straddling me, letting me grab the object of my desire and stuff it back in my mouth. He fell forward onto his fists and fed me his cock, heavy balls banging against my chin with every thrust. I looked up his taut, flexing belly, past his chest and saw him looking down at his shaft sliding in and out of my mouth.

He smiled with pleasure. "Damn, Bobby, man it feels good." I smiled back with my eyes, thanking him for giving me what I'd been wanting for so long.

I was in heaven. A bit too fucked up, but I'll tell ya, lying there, with this extremely hot stud fucking my face with his huge dick was a thousand times hotter than any fantasy I'd ever had. After several minutes, he pulled out and moved off of me. I wondered why, upset that he'd taken my pacifier away.

"Take yer clothes off," he ordered.

Without a moment's hesitation, I started undoing my jeans. He re-lit the pipe while I stripped. I had to really concentrate hard to coordinate my fingers. I glanced nervously at the wooden chair wedged awkwardly under the door handle. Well, if he didn't worry about somebody catching us, then I figured I shouldn't either. The other voice in my head was ranting on and on about how stupid that thinking was.

I didn't stop to think about why he wanted me to strip until after I was naked. Was he going to play with my dick – or even suck it? I had a hard time picturing someone like him sucking on me, but was open for surprises.

I sprawled sideways across the bed near the foot, facing him on his knees while he took a couple of hits off the pipe. I looked at him and thought, *Goddamn! What a gorgeous, sexy man! He ain't no boy! I could love him. Even if he can't love me back, if he'll just let me suck his awesome dick sometimes, I'll be happy. God, I hope he'll keep this a secret. He should know he'll get it any time he wants it if he does! Surely, he'll think of that?*

Between hits, he looked down at his drooping cock, reached over and pulled my head toward it. "Suck on it," he ordered. So I did, avidly, greedily, for a minute or two. Then he pulled it out and held it up to his belly and said around the pipe stem in his mouth, "Shuck my ballz." So I did, licking, sniffing them and grinding my face into the hairy, wrinkly sac.

It struck me odd that I'd never thought about balls when I fantasized sex with guys, because I got extremely turned on by his big heavy, tasty lemons. I thought, *I could suck and lick on these beauties all night long!*

He interrupted me to give me a hit, but I pushed it away. "I don't need anymore," I mumbled and went back at it.

He aimed the stem at my lips and said, "Sure ya do, bruh. Have another toke." So I did. He watched me, looking back and forth between my face and my raging, profusely drooling cock. "You really get off to suckin' dick, don't ya." He said it as an observation, with no discernible negative to it – but still.

I froze in the middle of my hit, coughed violently and rolled out on my back. *Fuck! Why did he have to go and say something like that?* Talk about a reality check. It started soaking into my brain just what I'd been doing – or more accurately – how much I'd obviously been loving it; how openly I'd shown him my hunger for dick. I was humiliated beyond comprehension and closed my eyes to gather my thoughts, to no avail. I couldn't put anything in perspective, being this fucked up and moving in completely unknown territory.

Kevin was sharp enough to snap to my reaction and smooth enough to work me for it. "Aw man, don't freak, bruh. It's our little secret, cool?" I glared at him with fear and anger, unable to speak, feeling like my world was shutting down, going out of business.

He reached down and stroked my hair, sounding like a mom reassuring her child, "Don't be bummed out, Bobby. This is cool! We can get together like this whenever we wanna get our yayas. It's not like I care if you like dick – I'm glad ya do!" He reached over and pushed the bottle into my hands. "Drink!"

"I don't want any more," I said flatly, scowling.

"Drink!" he commanded again.

"I'm too fucked up! I don't want any more," I protested as he pushed the bottle toward my mouth.

"Drink!" He showed a little irritation in his tone, so I gave in and took a drink. Again, he held the bottle up and made me take more than I wanted.

He pulled the bottle away, looked down at me, took his cock in hand and waved it in my face, "So go ahead and suck it, Bobby. You suck it better than anyone else ever has." He was enthusiastic, and maybe I was just confused and scared enough that I latched onto his compliment, and I don't know. I was too wasted to be very rational. I just gave up, gave in, and sucked his dick some more.

I figured if my life was going to be over after this – and as far as I could calculate, it would – then I might as well get all I could of the thing that would be my downfall. I figured it was just my fate. I didn't trust him enough to believe this wouldn't get out sooner or later. My cumulative exposure to his personality just told me he likely wouldn't keep this a secret very long, since he'd done nothing 'faggotty' himself.

Sucking him for a minute was no less a condemnable offense than sucking him for an hour, so what the fuck.

I was so wasted by now that I couldn't work my head up and down very well, laying flat out on my back. He could see that, so he took my head in his hands and started fucking my face again, which I loved. And I mean I loved it! I completely gave in to my fate and was so wasted I had no trace of an inhibition left. I let him know I was loving sucking his dick and would keep on going as long as he wanted.

After several minutes of not being able to get a good breath as he jammed his cock in and out my mouth, I felt his hand burrow down between my thighs, then something cool and wet, slimy – Vaseline, to be precise – being applied to my asshole. I hadn't noticed him getting it.

I jerked my head, but he anticipated that and crammed it back on his shaft. My eyes were bugging out of their sockets as I realized what he was about to do. But I surprised myself, in that my first thought upon realizing what he was doing wasn't fear that he was doing it. My first thought was gauging how thick and long it was; I was just afraid it was going to hurt like hell. I actually realized that it didn't even cross my mind to protest. I had no inclination to resist him fucking me in the ass. My only reservation was that it was too big and would hurt.

He rubbed the gel around my hole and pushed his fingertip in. I welcomed the intrusion. He just worked the tip in to the first knuckle and wiggled it around. He kept hold of my head with his other hand, fucking my mouth slow and steady, knowing I couldn't answer him as he bent down and whispered near my ear,

"I really wanna fuck you, Bobby. It'll feel sooo good … yer gonna love it." He worked his finger in a little more. "It's what ya want, ain't it?"

I suctioned his dick fiercely and slowly spread my legs wide for his hand in way of reply. I lightly squeezed and rolled his succulent nuts with my right hand, rubbed my left hand sensuously down my stomach to my balls and pulled them up to squeeze, while steadily settling my ass down onto his finger, moaning loudly around his shaft.

After all, I had fantasized about getting fucked in the ass for a long time. Now it was about to happen. And, that it was this particular stud, whom I had so often fantasized being the one to do it, to take my cherry, was literally a dream come true. I arched my pelvis up, moaned and sucked even harder, trying to capture the feel, size and texture of his cock in my mouth to visualize when he went to fuck me.

"Ahhhh yeah, baby," he said, as he watched me wantonly yield to his manipulations, riding his finger like a cock.

His finger was thicker than average, too. It *felt* like a cock in there. I was freaking out on how easily it went in, with only slight discomfort. After a few gentle thrusts, there was no discomfort. Then it started feeling okay, kinda more than okay, as he worked it in and out.

Then he pulled his finger out of my ass and his cock out of my mouth and moved around, tugging on my hip to get me to roll over on my stomach. I looked up into his eyes as I started to roll over with his assisting hand on my hip. I know I was looking for some kind of sign that he was into *me*, some kind of tender and maybe even loving look, especially for my first time.

I saw lust; I saw hunger; I saw delight that I was willing and ready; and I knew it was foolish to hope for more. It's not as if I even thought for a second that he would fall in love with me or something – as I could do so fucking easily with him. I knew at that moment that if he showed even a hint that he felt something emotional for me I would fall head over heels in love with him.

Tender and loving or not, I wanted him to fuck me. I wanted him to take it easy, but make no mistake: I very much wanted him to fuck my ass with his big dick. I was shaking all over, even in my drugged and drunken state. Every reference I'd ever heard about getting fucked in the ass, joking or whatever, had made it sound like it would hurt. I was already short of breath from sucking, and now I was very nearly hyperventilating. I got scared, real scared, as he moved in between my legs and spread them with his knees and the reality of what was about to happen hit me.

That moment focused my mind on just how vulnerable I was, and that scared me and thrilled me at the same time. Something in my nature made itself known to me in that moment. Something about yielding, opening up for a man, some very basic need in me.

He came down over me on one elbow and aimed his shaft at my hole. Just as I felt the wide blunt head make contact, I pleaded, "Please ... go really, really slow?" I gasped as I felt the pressure. "Please?" It felt so massive at the entrance, I was trembling and trying to get some breath.

"Relax, I'll go real slow," he said tenderly as he sank his chest into my back and nuzzled my neck.

The pressure on my hole was scary, but his hairy calves and muscular thighs pushing out against mine to spread them even wider, his perfectly sculpted chest crushing down on my shoulder blades and his breath on my neck were making me tingle and want very much to consummate the picture in my mind.

Then he broke through. He probably didn't get much more than the head in – hard to say – but it felt as if he'd rammed a baseball bat all the way in my ass. I yelled or screamed, and he quickly covered my mouth.

"Shhhhh. Relax, Bobby," he whispered calmly in my ear. "Shhhhh."

I jerked my head away from his hand – because he was covering both my nose and mouth – and panted, "Oh fuck! Oh FUCK! Oh man it *hurts*! Oh fuck, Kevin!"

I hunched down into the bed, trying to get him out of me, but he pushed down enough to keep it where it was. I couldn't believe how much it hurt! "It's too fucking big, Kevin! Oh FUCK, it hurts!" I was totally panicking, sorry I had agreed to this. I was willing to take a beating, humiliation, anything, if I could make it stop.

"It'll stop hurting in a minute. Just relax, Bobby." He started a shallow pushing and pulling. "Just relax and think about how good it's gonna feel in a minute," he cooed in my ear. "You want me inside you, don't ya?"

Maybe all my drugs kicked back in, maybe his soothing voice and my long held desire for this kicked in, but before I could say no, the pain started slipping away, and that allowed me to think about just what he'd said to think about. I did a body sensation check and revived the luxury of feeling his thighs and calves against mine, his chest against my back and his breath in my ear.

It was male. It was male on top of me, and it was male fucking me in the ass. It was good. And it was getting better as he worked in more and more of that huge cock. I was so fucking grateful that he hadn't just shoved it all the way in as I'd feared he would. He was actually doing it very tenderly and carefully, which really surprised me, especially knowing how fucked up he was.

I was moaning with pleasure as he got a steady rhythm going, sinking deeper and deeper. Feeling that immense column drilling down into me and pulling back out over and over was the most powerful sensation I'd ever felt in my life. It seemed he hit bottom at one point, but he stopped pumping and pushed insistently. The pressure was really uncomfortable for me, but I was way too into it all to let it affect my ecstasy.

"Open up, Bobby. Relax your muscles," he whispered in my ear then kissed my neck. Somehow, he must have known that one little kiss of tenderness would make me do anything for him.

"I'm trying," I groaned through clenched teeth. I *wanted* him in all the way, so I really tried to relax. Suddenly, he made it through into that next channel and it was – it was – fucking intense. My breath flew out of my lungs, and my body had an incredible rush that kept rolling, wave after wave, rippling out from my bowels.

"Ahhhhhh, yeah. That feels soooo good, don't it?" he whispered in my ear.

"Y-yeah," I gasped. I really wasn't sure though. "Oh God, oh God ..." I moaned as he forcefully ground his hips down into my ass, driving his cock in as deep as it would go. I could do nothing on a conscious level. I could only feel this vast filling up of my body, unsure if I could handle the thick depth of penetration.

"Oh, Man! Ohhhhh," he moaned. "Man, you're so hot 'n tight, Bobby. Fuckin' hot 'n tight!" He started pumping, slowly, about halfway out and all the way back in, driving every last fraction into my spasming channel with every thrust. He pulled further back as he built rhythm, making me feel the column almost abandon me, only to have it forge back in, every vein, ridge and dimple of his thick cock spreading my tissues, claiming my virginal ass with every plunge.

"Huh! Huh! Huh!" I kept grunting breath out as he pumped, but wasn't aware of taking any in. It was a million times more intense than any sensation I'd ever experienced. It focused all my consciousness on that one spot, to radiate out in electric surges and jolts that blurred the fine line between pleasure and pain, begging for a new term, a new word to express the mingling of the two sensations with the raw, jagged emotions their dance ignites. Every nerve, every signal went there and sprang from there, all of them telling me that this is what I do, this is my desire, my nature, my need, to receive a man. I had just been waiting all this time.

I couldn't even tell if I was begging for it out loud or not as he massaged my prostate and plumbed my depths with a rhythmic long dicking thrust that pushed grunts and moans and cries out of my throat. But I was begging for it to not stop, whether he could hear it or not. I couldn't believe how wonderful his cock felt sliding in and out of my ass. Feeling the size and texture of it thrusting down into me, setting every nerve ending on fire, feeling like it was going all the way up into my stomach, I wanted to scream out how fantastic it felt to get fucked in the ass! Every guy should know about this!

"Yeah! UNGH! Ohhhh, fuck!" Were the first things I was consciously aware of saying. "Yeah, do it!" I demanded, mashing my face into the Kevin saturated sheets. I could smell nothing but Kevin's sweat and body odor, and it triggered my animal instinct for total surrender to the alpha in him, needing to feel him deep inside my body.

He responded to my encouragement by letting loose. He started fucking my ass like a maniac, which intensified everything even more, making it almost too much to handle at first. I wasn't sure I could take it much longer, but I wouldn't even consider asking him to stop. I quickly came to love this hard driving just as much as all the other variations he used. And he varied a lot, from fast to slow and back again. Damn, he was good at it!

As I relaxed into loving getting fucked, my drugs, gin and pot started catching up with me again. I was unable to really participate and hunch back up at him like I wanted so much to do, so I just lay there, wallowing in feeling his big dick plowing my ass like there was no tomorrow.

And it was heaven. It was all my dreams and fantasies come true – well, except for the part where he falls in love with me – to have one of the main objects of my desire fucking me. Between the fact that it felt so wonderful to get fucked in the ass, and that it was Kevin Landry doing it, my head was about to explode in a blaze of ecstasy.

Four

I still can't believe I passed out while he fucked my ass with that huge cock! I would have thought that would be impossible, with the incredibly powerful and stimulating invasion of my body rocking and bouncing me around like a rag doll. When I came back around, I had no idea how long I'd been gone, but was enraged at myself for missing even one second of the most wonderful thing that had ever happened to me.

What brought me out of my blackout was persistent knocking on the door, and Billy West sounding all concerned on the other side – or maybe it was Kevin pulling out of my ass that snapped me to.

"Well what're you doin' in there, man?" Billy was asking. "Most everyone's left already. Is that Bobby dude in there with you?"

"Yeah, he's passed out." Kevin scooted up near my right side on the foot of the bed and sat with his right foot on the floor and the other crossed under his thigh, his cock sticking straight up proud and shiny as he looked back and forth between me and the door.

"Donald was looking for him, but he went ahead 'n left with those other losers. So what're y'all doin' in there? Why you got the door locked?"

"I ain't doin' nuttin', bruh, just chillin'."

"Then let me in!" he whined.

I look groggily up at Kevin, thinking we ought to be getting dressed, though I wasn't even capable of raising my head, let alone attempting something like that. I was barely able to keep my eyes open. He looked down at me blankly.

"I'll be out in a minute, bruh," he said nonchalantly.

"Why can't I come in?" Billy sounded too curious and frustrated as if it was imperative that he see what Kevin was up to.

"Fuck, Billy!" Kevin let the irritation show in his voice.

"What y'all doin' that's so fuckin' *secret* in there, dude?"

"Nuttin'! I'll be out in a fuckin' minute, bitch!" He looked reluctantly around behind him on the floor for his clothes. I was pretty sure he hadn't come yet, and I figured he was trying to think of a way to get Billy to leave, so he could finish. I was praying Billy would give up and go back up front, even if we didn't finish our sex.

"Well then it's no big deal if I come on in!" He jiggled the handle again.

"Aww, fuck it!" Kevin said with exasperation. He got up, pulled the chair away and opened the fucking door! I went into shock.

I tried to pick my head up to protest, but could only manage a weak plea, "What're you *doing*?! Don't ..."

"S'what's goin' on in here?" Billy barged past Kevin and froze in his tracks when he saw we were both naked as jaybirds, with Kevin's joystick swingin' big and hard. His eyes got big as saucers and his mouth gaped open.

Kevin closed the door, moved in quickly beside the speechless boy with a casual, confident look on his face and started talking. They both looked down at me lying on my stomach with my legs spread wide, unable to move to erase the impression. So I gave up and stayed just as I was. I was so shocked and embarrassed I was near tears. Wondering why the hell he would let Billy in at all confounded my embarrassment over Billy seeing me in my obviously servile position, leaving me wondering how Kevin would explain this scene.

Kevin put his arm around Billy's shoulders and cocked his head, looking at me as he casually asked, "Want some? He gives hellatious head."

Billy looked at Kevin like he was crazy – for about three seconds. Then he grinned cautiously and asked, "For real?" He kept glancing down at Kevin's pendulous meat, obviously impressed.

I was stunned comatose. I absolutely could not believe my ears and eyes. My mouth must have looked like I was inviting his dick in or something 'cause it was as wide as it could go.

"He can't get enough, bruh." He made eye contact with me as he nodded my way. "You'll fuckin' love it." I wasn't sure if he said that to me or Billy.

I was utterly speechless, but pleaded with my eyes to know why he was doing this to me. *How could he?!* How could he think I would even *consider* sucking Billy West's dick?! He grinned at Billy, who looked at me then back to Kevin for the okay to proceed. Kevin gestured toward me with his blessing.

I wanted to die. I couldn't believe this was happening! I couldn't believe Kevin would do this to me! After he'd said there was no way he'd ever tell anybody about it! I didn't just want to die; I wanted to kill Kevin, too. Even though I had assumed he would eventually tell someone about what we did, I just couldn't handle him doing this here and now – when I was so fucked up I had passed out while he was fucking me, and was not at all capable of resisting this development. *Fuck him, goddammit!*

And, it was Billy West! Wiry, skinny little fucker who wouldn't even be a part of the "inner circle" if it weren't for the fact that he had an unfailingly reliable drug connection that was even steadier than Brian Steinholz's. He was probably less socially viable than I was, but for that factor. He was kinda cute, I guess, but not at all appealing to me, cuz he was a cocky fucker, the kind who always gave shitty attitude to us hangers. He had pretty, naturally wavy blonde hair down the middle of his back and a pug nose that made him look like he was sixteen instead of eighteen. I'd never much liked him and did *not* want to suck his dick.

Billy took a step toward me with a hungry but apprehensive look in his eyes. I stared unblinking at him. I was still too devastatingly stunned to act or react. When he saw no sign of resistance from me – besides the look of horror on my face – he got excited and started undoing his jeans while moving to the foot of the bed. Kevin did an end-run around him and climbed in on my left side. Just as I thought I was about to be able to say NO WAY! Kevin grabbed my head and turned it to face him, ramming his now drooping cock into my mouth.

"See? And he's really good at it, too!" He sounded like a kid showing off his new toy, but Billy didn't need a sales demonstration. He dropped his pants and boxers around his ankles and slid onto the foot of the bed with his knees spread wide. He took my head out of Kevin's hands and turned it back toward him as he pulled on his dick to get it hard. I felt utterly helpless, physically unable to do anything in protest.

He didn't wait for an erection. I just got the "n" in no out, "N …" when he jammed his cock in my mouth and started fucking. He got rigid hard within seconds. I was constantly in jeopardy of drifting into unconsciousness again, even as he forced his dick down my throat.

He had a nice enough dick, much smaller than Kevin's, not a whole lot shorter, but pretty thin; actually, very similar to mine, probably around six-and-a-half inches and curving to the left. I was disgusted and feeling sick with this turn of events. I was humiliated beyond comprehension again, that Kevin had just brazenly handed me off to Billy to use.

Now Billy knew. Everyone would know now. Billy was a loudmouthed little fucker. He would definitely tell everyone. I couldn't imagine him not telling everyone. I thought, *It's over. Fuck, my life is definitely over. Can't say it was a good life, can't say it was so bad – until this. But it's over now.*

Then a light bulb came on, and I thought, *Hey, wait a minute! I've just graduated high school, and I am planning on moving to Houston to go to U of H anyway. I can just move away and never show my face here again. Yeah! Fuck this place anyway!*

That realization helped me a lot. I was already on the threshold of the rest of my life, and this would give me a kick in the ass (or dick in the ass, if you prefer) to really make a complete change – maybe even come out and live openly gay in Houston. It wasn't like these people were lifelong friends I'd be leaving behind or anything. I wouldn't miss them at all. And I'd been fantasizing lately about living in the Montrose area of Houston, among all the queers, my people, my tribe, as I was beginning to think of them – us.

As Billy got a rhythm going, Kevin crawled around and got back in between my legs. He wasted no time plunging his cock in, quickly matching Billy's rhythm.

"Oh dude! You been fuckin' 'im in the ass, too?!" Billy was incredulous. I squirmed.

"Yeah, and it's fuckin' awesome – but he passed out on me," he said as casually as if he was talking about some car he was test driving; actually, probably with less concern.

They banged away at both ends for a couple of minutes then I heard the door open.

"Whoa! Fuck me ragged! What the fuck's goin' on in here?!" I could hear Darius Sterling, but could only see pubic hair and the shaft sliding in and out between my lips. Kevin had forgotten to put the goddamn chair back under the door handle.

What's one fucking more? Well I *did* still have to face most of these guys for a while, at least sometimes, since I wouldn't be able to afford moving until just before the fall semester. And regardless of how things worked out later, this was humiliating as hell *now*, to have people just randomly wandering in on this scene. I thought of all the people who'd been here tonight. I had no idea who was left and who might wander back here – but I was pretty sure Jimmy would have left with Donald, so at least my best friend wouldn't see this.

"Aww man! Shut the fuckin' door 'n put that chair against it!" Kevin hissed.

"What the fuck you doing?!" Darius insisted, even though it was quite obvious he was fucking someone in the ass. He was just shocked – probably because he knew that the only female back at this end of the house was Kevin's mother.

"Shut the fucking door!" Kevin retorted. "Shut it, 'n you can get some, too."

"Who *is* that?" Billy's back was to him, so he stepped around where he could see my face being stuffed with cock. I tried – and I don't know why I bothered, with Kevin humping away on my ass, too – to pull away, but Billy held my head firmly with both hands. "Is that

Bobby Wheaton?! WHOA, DUDE!" he yelled, understandably shocked.

"Shut the fucking door, Darius!" Kevin bellowed. "Then you can get some."

"No way, dude!" He didn't dare show too much disgust at anything Kevin was doing, but he wasn't going to go along with it either. "I ain't into *that* shit," was about as strong as he was willing to get.

Personally, I would rather have had Darius Sterling fucking my face than scrawny Billy West any day of the fucking week! Darius was ultimate cool and one fucking big hot hunk of a guy. He had long been on my "top ten most wanted" list along with Kevin. Now, *he* was gorgeous, too! He was a big fucking jock, and LaPorte High School was different than any other school I'd gone to, in that it was the only one where the jocks were almost all cool and got high like everyone else who mattered, so there was none of that "jocks versus stoners" type attitude that was in every other high school I knew of. Anyway, he was hot, hot, hot. Short dark brown hair and eyes, a good six-two but kinda thin, and quarterback or some shit on the LaPorte football team. He was fucked up most of the time he wasn't on the field, and he just looked like he'd have a really big dick, too, with those big ol' hands and feet.

"Then get outta here 'n shut the fuckin' door!" Kevin was exasperated, but still fucking my butt.

"Uhhh, Matt might want some," Darius offered – I guess to sound like he wasn't disgusted with them.

The conversation was blowing my mind. Billy wasn't saying a word, content that if bad-ass Kevin Landry was having sex with a guy like it was no big deal, then he could, too, without catching any flack.

"Ok, but don't fuckin' tell Stan. Don't fuckin' tell *anyone* else!" he commanded as he kept fucking my ass like it was the thing to do while carrying on a conversation and inviting more people to use me. Darius mumbled something and closed the door behind himself.

Billy didn't miss more than a stroke or two, either. The physical stimulation at both ends was so amazing my thoughts wouldn't stay on my humiliation. I was disgusted with myself, but I had already conceded the fact that my life was over in this town; nothing mattered anymore. I was fucked up to nearly incapacitated and couldn't prevent these guys from using me like a whore, so I might as well get what pleasure I could out of it. Fuck the consequences! I was getting fucked at both ends – something I'd never even fantasized about – and it was too incredible a sensation to let the foregone end of my present world detract from it.

With the distraction gone, Kevin and Billy really let go, encouraging each other. "Yeah! This is hot!" Billy exclaimed. After another minute of hard driving, he asked, "So, uh, is his ass pretty tight? He ain't puttin' as good a suction to it now as he was." He jiggled my head like a flashlight a couple of times as if he thought that would make my suction kick back in like it was on batteries or something. My mouth was full of him or I would have told him I couldn't concentrate on his punk-ass dick with a whopper like Kevin's in my ass sending me into orbit.

"Man, I gotta tell ya ... it's tighter than any pussy I ever had," Kevin admitted, grunting between words as he fucked my ass and made me see stars. "Sorry man, but that's the fuckin' truth." I guess he felt like he had to apologize for admitting sex with a guy was better than any girl. His words made me tingle anyway.

Curiously, at that moment, I was wondering how he could get sucked and fuck my ass for so long, talking about how it was the best he ever had, without coming. Must have been the drugs, booze and pot, plus all the interruptions.

"No shit? Lemme try it, dude."

The door opened and in stepped Matt Swider. Kevin was just pulling out of my ass to let Billy sample it. "Shut the door and put that chair under the handle," he snapped at a wide-eyed Matt.

"Oh man, y'all really ARE gettin' it on with a dude! Oh FUCK, man! *Bobby Wheaton?!* Fuuuck, it's really true?!" Matt was having a hard time believing what he was seeing, but sounded excited at the scene anyway.

Kevin showed his irritation again as he sat on his heels under the window at the head of the bed, "Goddammit, either get in here 'n shut the fuckin' door, or get the fuck out, Matt! And put that chair up under the handle."

Billy hurriedly got the rest of the way undressed and was moving around to take Kevin's place, so I was able to watch Matt jump and hastily close the door. He was fucked up enough that it took him a bit to get the chair wedged properly under the handle. When he finished, he turned and looked at me.

He showed excitement, but he also showed real uncertainty. I figured from the look on his face that in his mind no guy he knew would be letting himself be used like this willingly. I had always liked Matt. He was always nice to me. He stood there with his hand on his zipper, his eyes darting between my eyes, Kevin's big dick and Billy positioning himself to fuck me.

Billy rammed into my ass, and I jerked forward from the impact, moaning at the different feel of his dick compared to Kevin's. It wasn't nearly as big, but I felt it in surprising detail, even through the semi-numbness of my whole body.

"Ahhhhh, yeah!" Billy exclaimed and started rabbit fucking my ass hard and fast with no skill whatsoever. Matt stood with his mouth gaping, watching Billy. It felt good anyway, and all I could think of besides it was that my mouth was devoid of dick for the first time in a while. So I closed my eyes and concentrated on enjoying the fucking I was getting.

"Ya want some or not?" Kevin demanded of Matt impatiently.

Matt wasn't part of the upper clique, like Kevin and Billy, and Darius – who was top of the heap, prime citizen of Kelly's Cue. But, he was generally treated well enough by them, as he was a cool guy. I opened my eyes and watched him get naked. He was bigger than Billy and his body was sleek and smooth, not as big or defined as Kevin's, but perfect in its youth. His olive complexion made his emerald eyes seem to glow and his long auburn shag hairstyle softened his sharply cut features, that I always thought of as Russian for some reason. Very handsome boy.

"Yeah! Yeah, I want some!" he said, grinning wide with anticipation. He started stroking his dick, which was hard before he even got his clothes all the way off.

"Oh, man! This is fuckin' good!" Billy was banging my ass harder and faster with short jabs, sounding like he was getting close.

Matt had a nice dick, too. Slightly longer than Billy's and much thicker, though not nearly as thick as Kevin's. It tapered at the head some and got thickest in the middle, while not being thin at all at the base. He positioned himself with one knee by my shoulder and one by the top of my head. Sitting back on his haunches, he put his dick in my face, waiting for me to suck it.

"Ya gotta feed it to 'im. He's pretty wasted," Kevin instructed and took another hit off the pipe.

Matt asked, as if Kevin owned me, as if I couldn't think for myself, "He likes it? He's cool with this?" But I guess since I hadn't reacted or said anything up to now it wasn't that callous, and Kevin was obviously running the show.

"Fuckin' loves it, dude, 'n he's really good at it, too."

"Fuckin' A, man!" Billy chimed in breathlessly.

"Awesome!" He raised my head to his dick and pushed it in cautiously. I wrapped my lips around it and started sucking, while jerking and grunting at Billy's furious pounding of my ass. As soon as he felt me actually suck on him, he started fucking my face.

Matt seemed to be much more into the experience of it, as opposed to Billy, who was just wanting to stick his dick in something until he came. Matt fed it to me slowly, watching intently as it slid in and out, eventually going all the way into my throat. I looked up from the corner of my eye and watched him watch me. He saw me looking and smiled encouragingly at me. I saw his eyes darting over every little bit to watch Billy's dick going in and out of my ass, and over to Kevin's dick, too.

I sucked him with more energy and enthusiasm, grateful that he seemed to think of me more like a person he was having sex with, rather than merely a hole to use. I kept my eyes trained on his and after a bit he just looked back and forth between my eyes and his dick sliding in and out of my bruised lips.

Matt was always one of those people who would look you in the eye when he talked to you. He was so easy going and nice to me I'd always wanted to be his friend but just never seemed to get the right opportunity to really get to know him. As I said, I usually irritated people, so he had probably never been interested in being my friend. But I liked him and really liked his dick for that matter, mainly because he seemed really into this with me, enough so that I was starting to get a little control back over my body just to respond to him.

"Man, that feels fuckin' good, Bobby," he said with tenderness and appreciation. He smiled at me, then frowned as he traced the knot on my forehead. "Uh, what happened to your head?"

Kevin chuckled, "He fell right fuckin' into the bathroom door edge."

"Aw man, that looks like it hurt, huh?" He showed concern as he worked my face on and off his meat.

I found the muscle control to pull my head off and he let me. I pushed my face in between his thighs and started licking his sweaty nuts.

"Ahhhhh, fuck yeah! Oh man, that's so fuckin' good!" He moaned, spread his knees wide and tilted his pelvis up to give me better access. His nuts weren't as big and heavy as Kevin's, but they were still wonderful and tasty. I discovered that ball sweat has an acrid, musky and delicious flavor that seems to be unique to balls alone, different than the taste of the cock right above them.

"AHHH! AHHH! OH FUCK YEAH!" Billy shouted as he started unloading in my ass. Kevin tried to shush him but gave up. He slammed it home really hard as he spasmed, bending my neck up into Matt's groin. Luckily for Matt, I was only licking around at that moment and didn't have either of his nuts in my mouth.

Billy collapsed on my back and heaved his ragged breath in my ear as he jerked around with his last shots. Kevin climbed off the bed and came around behind Matt.

"Okay. My turn again," he said matter-of-factly.

He effortlessly lifted Matt up by the armpits from behind and stood him on the floor. I saw Matt's eyes bulge when Kevin's hard cock pressed against his ass in the process. Then Kevin pushed Billy off my back and aimed his cock at my mouth. It was hard, and I had missed it. I looked up his fantastic body and wished like hell this could just be something we all did and loved, with no negatives attached to it. Since I was wishing, I wished Kevin wasn't a coldhearted user and wished he could love me. If wishes were …

"Get some ass while ya can, bruh," Kevin warned Matt. "I'm gonna be back there in a minute."

Matt stepped around and mounted me. I guess he knew there was no need to be gentle going in, with Billy just having pulled out, so he shoved it in and it felt really good. It was enough bigger than Billy's to really feel the difference and with Kevin fucking my face again with his heavy sausage, I was in hog heaven.

Actually, I wanted Kevin fucking me while I sucked on Matt, 'cause Kevin filled my ass to incredible proportions, and I could get Matt's cock down my throat. I figured they would switch soon enough though.

In the meantime, I tried to relax my throat muscles and signal Kevin that I was trying something, as I was getting more and more muscle control back. He seemed to get it and let me work it myself. I consciously relaxed my throat and pushed my head against him. He figured out what I was trying to do and held the back of my head while pulling slowly but forcefully.

I did it! It felt like it ripped my throat muscles, but it was in! I still wasn't quite nuzzled into his pubes, but I was close. It felt like it was spreading all the little bones in my neck to where they'd never settle back in place, but it was satisfying as hell. Kevin pulled back and pushed in again slowly, steadily, and sank it all the way this time. He ground my face into his pubes and moaned loudly with approval. I gagged and concentrated on relaxing my throat muscles.

"Ahhhhhh, yeah! Ahhh, that's it baby, that's it, yeahhhh." He started a slow in and out, going all the way in each time, watching intently. "Fuck! He's taking it all the way to the bone! No bitch has *ever* been able to take the whole thing to the bone!" he bragged to the others.

"That's smokin' if he can take that big fuckin' donkey dick all the way down to the short 'n curlies, dude," Billy said from somewhere on the bed. "You got the biggest fuckin' dick I ever seen!"

"No shit!" Matt enthused, as he put his face in close to mine to watch Kevin's cock slide in and out of my throat. "Fuuuuck! He *is* takin' it all the way down! I can see his fuckin' throat stretching! Fuuuuck."

I was thrilled that I could swallow his entire cock, finally. It felt like a huge accomplishment! Getting his cock all the way in while Matt fucked me with a good long dicking pace was sending me into orbit. As for all of their praise at my accomplishment – it was too fucking bizarre to even think about. I didn't know whether to laugh or cry about how this was going.

Kevin was enjoying it so much he stayed with my mouth longer than he probably would have. He was mumbling compliments and encouragements to me in between his moans. I was even able to hunch back up into Matt a little by this point, and he murmured his appreciation as he held his face practically cheek to cheek with mine to watch Kevin's dick in action up close. I even thought how cool it would be if Kevin pulled out of my mouth and shoved it into Matt's real quick, since it was right there. That would have thrilled me to no end, and somehow I got the feeling Matt wouldn't object all that strongly either.

But Kevin wanted to get back to my ass, so he eventually pulled out and stepped around behind Matt and I. Matt damn sure didn't want to stay in the position he was in on me, with Kevin's big slimy cock aimed at his ass, so he wordlessly pulled out and slid off sideways, yielding to the alpha male in the room. Kevin climbed on and sank his wonderful shaft in my hole. After Billy and Matt being in there for awhile, it was an exquisite shock to my ass to have his massive eight or nine inch cock sink deeper and so much fuller than theirs.

I moaned with pleasure and arched my ass up into him. I wanted to tell them all what they were missing, how fantastic it felt to have a dick in your ass, but, you know …

Matt, meanwhile, wiped his dick off with the top sheet and moved back into position in front of my face. I couldn't see Billy, so I had no idea what he was doing. Oh, this was perfect! Having Matt fuck my face and Kevin fuck my ass at the same time was truly heaven. I just assumed my ass should be getting really sore, but it wasn't – at least not that I could tell. I was still really fucked up.

I sucked Matt with a vengeance. Within a few minutes, at my prompting, he started really fucking my face hard. He warned me, "I'm gonna come!" I sucked harder and grasped his thigh to let him know I didn't want him to pull out. "I'm gonna come!" he repeated. I reached up and lightly squeezed his nuts and pulled his groin toward me.

I wanted to taste some cum. Matt's would be as good as any.

He grunted loudly and fired his first jet in my mouth. I whimpered around his cock and clenched my ass around Kevin's. Kevin increased the force and pace of his thrusts. Matt jammed the next shot or two down my throat, but I wanted to taste more of it, so I jerked my head back and let the next few jets – and there were many – hit my tongue. I swallowed and got a couple of shots on my nose and cheek while I did, then opened up for the last few shots of his enormous load.

It was so mind blowing, I just convulsed at the sensations of Matt's cock coming in my mouth and Kevin drilling my ass with his huge tool, making my own cock grind into the mattress with each determined thrust. I flooded the Kevin saturated sheets with my own seed, gasping and heaving while they both banged away at each end. I was so drunk with animal lust it was like my orgasm just made me want more –- more dick, more dick, and more dick.

Five

Matt was just starting to slump a little when there was pounding on the door as the handle was jiggled. This wasn't knocking like Billy had done; it was pounding.

"What the fuck you got the door blocked for?!" Stan demanded. "Open up, pussy face!"

Kevin stopped pumping and muttered under his breath, "Aw maaaan, I was *just* about to come, goddammit." Then he shouted, "Fuck off, bitch! Sleep in Mark's room tonight!"

"Fuck you! Open the door, mother fucker!"

"Get the fuck outta here! Me 'n my friends are busy 'n don't need you fuckin' around in here!"

"You better open up or I'll kick the fuckin' door down and kick your fuckin' ass, Kevin!" He kicked it and made the chair move a little.

Matt and Billy frantically scrambled for their clothes. I could do nothing, with Kevin's cock still in my ass and his midsection pinning me to the bed. I was terrified! With four sets of clothes strewn about the room, mingled with Kevin and Stan's dirty clothes everywhere, Matt and Billy were so fucked up and terrified they couldn't seem to find their clothes. Kevin was the only one who didn't seem freaked out at the prospect of Stan possibly discovering what we were doing.

He pulled out of me and stood up swaying. Just then, Stan kicked the door really hard. The chair slipped out from under the handle and fell to the grungy floor, bouncing noisily a couple of times. Stan plowed into the room and came up face-to-face with a naked and hard Kevin.

"WHAT THE FUCK YOU WANT, BITCH!" Kevin yelled with a nasty scowl on his face. I though he'd wake the neighbors, and surely even his parents across the hall at the other end.

"I want in my fucking room, cunt lips; what the fuck you *think* I want!" He shoved Kevin backward over the chair. Kevin fell into several stacks of eight track tapes on the stereo table, sending them clattering all over a pile of junk on the floor.

Stan stopped and took in all of our naked bodies, Billy struggling to get his foot into his jeans, Matt with his tee shirt only partway on, both frozen stiff with fear. Me, of course, lying spread eagle with cum on my face and running out over the Vaseline all over my ass, eyes like ping pong balls and mouth like an "O."

Stan sneered with disgust, "Well whatta we got here, a bunch a fuckin' faggots?" He looked at Matt and Billy, "Y'all been suckin' dick and fuckin' each other up the ass?!" Neither moved a single muscle, their faces just as stricken white as mine. "Hmmph," he grunted with contempt.

Kevin uprighted himself and grabbed Stan's shoulder, spinning him to face him. "Fuck you, bitch! We're all just gettin' some from him! *He's* the fag!" he justified, pointing down at me.

Made me feel special. Asshole.

"Like I said, yer all faggin' out together in here." He shook his head in revulsion, like he just couldn't believe what he'd walked in on. "My bedroom, fuckin' full a queers! Shit."

"FUCK YOU, Stan! Don't you be callin' *me* a queer, when you told me what you did all the time in jail with that kid, how you fucked him twice a day and told me it was the best ass you ever had!"

Ah hah! Was *that* why he'd been so into trying this with me? He wanted to know what it was like to fuck a guy in the ass like his brother had bragged about?

Stan jabbed his palm hard in the middle of Kevin's bare chest, shoving him right back over the same chair. Kevin sprawled over it and rolled into the pile of eight-tracks and junk.

"That's different, fuck head. Jail's a whole different thing and you know it!"

Kevin gathered himself, jumped up and landed a powerful punch on the side of Stan's head, sending the very fucked-up brother into Matt, both falling in a tangle of arms and legs onto Stan's bed.

While Stan recovered from the blow, glaring menacingly at poor naked and terrified Matt – who was frantically scrambling to untangle himself from their accidental embrace – Kevin spat at him.

"Well it ain't no different thing at home," he wasn't yelling now, "with you 'n Mark fuckin' Peter all the time – and why the hell won't he let ME fuck him!" He sounded bitter and jealous, rather than accusatory.

Stan jumped up, red faced and glaring daggers at him, fist reared back to strike, "SHUT THE FUCK UP! I CAN'T BELIEVE YOU JUST SAID THAT IN FRONT OF THEM!" he shouted in a rage that made us all cringe. He pointed at Kevin, jabbing the air, "You're dead meat, mother fucker!" Then he realized that he had just confirmed it, so it wouldn't do him any good to deny it now. "When Mark finds out you said that ..." he sputtered. "If I don't kill you first ... You fuckin' stupid bitch!"

Kevin glanced guiltily around the room at all of us and aimed his red face angrily at the filthy floor, looking guilty as all hell. There was silence for a moment, then Stan kinda shook himself and pointed his finger at each one of us in turn. He was clenching and unclenching his jaw and the veins in his temples were bulging. He spoke evenly, with a barely controlled quiver in his voice.

"Tell you what, mother fuckers: If I ever hear ANYTHING get back to me about this, you're dead. And I don't mean play like. I mean I'll kill all three of you. I don't care who said what – you're all three dead." We all instinctively felt that he meant it literally, and all of us were reasonably sure he was capable of carrying out the threat without a second thought.

He turned to Kevin and looked at him with utter contempt, "Now, you want me to kick your ass in front a your friends? Or you wanna step outside 'n I'll do it in private, so you don't look like the little fag you are?"

Kevin jerked his head up, his whole body shaking with his rage and humiliation. I watched real, undiluted hatred bubble up and pour out of him like lava, "YOU GO FUCK YOURSELF MOTHER FUCKER!" Which just *had* to wake the neighbors.

"Wouldn't you rather have me fuckin' *you* in the ass?" Stan retorted with a sneer.

We watched in horror as they both lunged at each other in the same instant. I scrambled up the bed toward the window next to Billy to get out of the way. Matt and Billy both tried to make themselves invisible and stay out of the way as well. My high had been pretty much scared out of me, and I tried to see where my clothes were without moving enough to draw attention. I noticed neither Billy nor Matt dared to move enough to try and finish finding or putting their clothes on.

Stan and Kevin literally bounced off each other on the first lunge, with Kevin landing a fist in Stan's gut as they met, but tripping over somebody's clothes and his own feet, falling right back into the junk pile yet again. Stan had glanced a blow off Kevin's jaw, stumbled backward until his calves were against his own bed, and he teetered, rowing his arms for balance to remain standing. He was very high, too. Matt shrunk back against the wall on the bed, holding his hands up to stop Stan's fall if he were to lose his balance.

Kevin came up out of the pile of junk with an empty Bud longneck bottle in his hand. Stan, I gauged, was just enough bigger than Kevin that he probably won most of their fights. I figured that was why Kevin was willing to use a weapon, probably hoping Stan would back out and maybe leave us alone. At the same time, I thought maybe Kevin was really afraid Stan would start telling people – especially his brothers or parents – that he was a fag, so he wanted to threaten him with real violence to stop that before it started. But then, I thought of how he hadn't seemed to care that this many people knew he was fucking me. But I guess it would be different if Stan were to say he was "participating," implying or saying he reciprocated.

And of course, the revelation that Stan and Mark were fucking their own little brother Peter in the ass, apparently for a long time now, was playing into all of this, big time.

Kevin crouched with his arms spread wide, daring Stan to come after him. Stan took the dare and moved toward him confidently, eyes darting side-to-side to look for a weapon of his own.

Stan taunted Kevin, holding his hands out, beckoning, "Come on, pussy-fag-boy! Go for it!"

So, Kevin darted his hand out to the side and slammed the bottle over the metal side edge of, presumably, Stan's stereo, denting it and breaking about the bottom third of the bottle off. With a mocking grin, he menaced Stan with the jagged weapon. Stan didn't even flinch. He eyed the bottle then judged the distance and tried a very swift kick at Kevin's hand with his steel-toed work boots but missed, losing his balance and lurching into Kevin in the process.

I couldn't decide, in that split second, whether Kevin reacted instinctively, or whether he consciously took advantage of his brother's mistake, but he fucking stabbed him in the stomach!

HE STABBED HIS BROTHER IN THE STOMACH RIGHT THERE IN FRONT OF THE THREE OF US! Well, he actually just kinda held the bottleneck firmly in place and Stan fell into it – but he could have let it give way.

Billy screamed, jerked open the window and jumped out, naked, jeans in hand, and ran like hell into the night. I cried out and just about pissed the bed. Matt kinda yelped and curled himself up against the wall over on Stan's bed, staring at them in total shock, shaking like crazy.

Stan stopped in mid-motion when the glass cut into his flesh. He stared open mouthed at Kevin. I watched his lips and cheeks twitch, eyes wide in disbelief. His face looked as bleached white as each of ours had when he threatened us, but it was shock rather than fear.

Kevin looked stunned. He slowly looked down and saw how far it went in. Stan grabbed Kevin's hand over the bottleneck, looking down at it, his lips moving but no sound making it out. They stood there with their legs spread in between each other's like an incestuous Tango, Kevin's slimy limp dick and balls draped over Stan's jean clad thigh. They stared at the top of the king of beers label lodged in his abdomen, twitching as the muscles around it began to understand what had just happened to them.

An eerie silence filled the room, and time stood still. A sinking feeling overtook me, and I could see the same on everyone else's faces as well. Nobody moved a muscle for several very long seconds, except for Stan's silent lips.

The sheer volume of thoughts that ran through my head in that span of time is still amazing to me. I had this whole scenario of the history of this family, the love/hate relationships they all had, the violence that was such an everyday part of their existence. The stories I'd heard, the things I'd seen, just the way their conversations were violent. In that moment, I was surprised they hadn't killed each other long ago.

And I surprised myself when I realized I was curious, morbidly curious, to see how Stan would act and what he would look like, dying. I had no idea if the wound was life threatening or not. It was in his stomach and to his left side a little, so I didn't think it hit any vital organs, but I didn't know. It was definitely a massive and very serious wound.

Like me, Matt was scared shitless. He wasn't even breathing. I don't guess I was either, as we watched Kevin and Stan both look at their hands over the bottleneck, blood just starting to trickle out.

It would have seemed a lot different if he'd been wearing a shirt. It wouldn't have been so *real*. We could *see* the flesh yield, could *hear* it when the glass sliced into him, could see it sink in devastatingly deep. It wasn't just a point. It was the whole damn circumference of the jagged bottle half, and I actually wondered if the circle of flesh would come out with the bottle like a cookie cutter when they pulled it out.

The first sound I heard was Stan, like a hack in his throat, then a little moan. I watched his eyelids flutter then his eyes rolled mostly back in his head. He brought his other hand up to Kevin's shoulder and grasped it for stability, wobbled a little, but stayed in place for the moment. Kevin was in shock and didn't move. Then he looked up from their hands into his brother's face and went white as a ghost.

"I didn't … Stan! I didn't mean to … Oh God! Oh God!" He started hyperventilating, but didn't move.

I heard footsteps, and Darius came around the corner, asking what all the yelling was about. Then he saw the embedded bottle with blood trickling out and both their hands over the neck. He sprang backwards like a cat about three feet into the hallway.

He stomped his foot and put his hands over his ears as he yelled in horror, "OH FUCK DUDE! OH FUCK! WHA'D YOU DO?! OH, FUCK!"

"I didn't mean to …" Kevin offered weakly, sounding like he was about to cry. Everyone looked at the bottleneck, and Kevin made a movement like he was going to pull it out.

Darius waved his hands frantically and yelled at him, "NO! DON'T PULL IT OUT!" He glanced at Matt and pointed backwards down the hall, "Go call 911! NOW!" We had only recently gotten 911 service in our area.

Matt jerked out of his shock, bounced in place for a moment, then crawled off the bed and slunk cautiously, fearfully around the brothers and ran down the hall butt naked, with his tee shirt half on, one arm in and his head through the neck hole. Darius stepped up to the brothers and put one hand on Stan's back and one hand on his chest, very gently getting him to step backwards.

"Don't move big or fast. Step back over here and sit on the bed real fuckin' slowly." He guided Stan back to his bed and helped him sit as slowly and evenly as possible. As they moved away from him, Kevin's hand stayed where it had been around the bottleneck, fingers still wrapped around empty air. Darius motioned with his head for me to help, "Come put all the pillows behind him, so he can lay back a little." I was still stunned, not moving and he snapped at me, "DO IT!"

I scrambled off Kevin's bed and frantically gathered pillows, sheets, dirty clothes, everything soft I could find to pile behind him. Kevin sank to his knees and started crying.

"I'm so sorry, Stan! I didn't mean to do it! I'm so sorry!" He cried as he crawled on his hands and knees over to Stan, "Please don't die! Please don't fucking die!"

Stan was keeping his eyes closed, mostly. He didn't acknowledge Kevin's pleading. He looked up at Darius with a grimace on his face, "Man, this fuckin' hurts, dude. Goddamn it hurts!" His voice was weak, and he was breathing hard, which I could see was making it hurt even more, and causing blood to flow pretty freely around the bottle now, and I could even see it puddling inside the amber glass.

I was extremely impressed with Darius, the way he stayed so calm and took control. "Don't talk Stan. Try to breathe as evenly as you can." He looked around at me and said, "Bobby, get dressed and go wake up his parents."

In unison, both Stan and Kevin barked an emphatic, "NO!"

Darius and I both looked at them in stunned disbelief. "What?!"

Kevin talked fast, "No! Don't wake them up! They'll kill us!"

Darius shook his head in piteous wonder, speaking like he was explaining to a small child, "Dude, Stan could *die* here! Don't you think you oughtta wake your parents up for this? I mean, we're a ways away from any hospital. I can't even think of where the closest one is, man. By the time they get here 'n get him to a hospital …"

Stan spoke up, "It don't matter, Darius. We just don't wake 'em up for nothin'. We've had worse than this happen. Ya just don't wake 'em up."

"I don't *believe* this shit! You tellin' me you would sit here and fuckin' DIE and not even wake your parents up and tell 'em?! You fuckin' crazy mother fuckers! You're both fucking insane!"

"It's just the way it is, Darius," Kevin said to Stan's knee. "It's always just been that way. We don't wake 'em up no matter what's goin' on. Dad'll go apeshit fuckin' crazy if we wake him up for any fuckin' reason."

Darius threw his hands up in frustration and sighed. "Okay, whatever! I can't believe this shit, but …" His mind at least was working clearly though. After a moment of silence, he looked at me and said, "Go ahead and get dressed and go out in the living room and get all the roaches and pipes 'n shit and bring 'em back here to put away. The cops'll come with 'em, and we don't need that shit sittin' around. You're eighteen, right?" I nodded yes, so he didn't have to worry about underage drinkers being present.

Matt came back in the room about that time and breathlessly announced, "They're on their way!" He was white as a sheet and trembling, just like me, just like Kevin – but Kevin was crying, too. I couldn't help but wonder if he was crying because he stabbed his brother or if he was crying at the thought of what his brother would do to him if he lived. Or for that matter, what Mark or his dad might do to him for this.

"Get dressed and help Bobby clean up shit," Darius barked at Matt. He looked back to Stan and asked in a soothing voice, "How ya doin'?"

I stood in the doorway with my pants in hand, trying to see around Darius to see Stan's face. He was trembling, and his voice was even weaker than it had been moments ago.

"I'm kinda cold," was all he said. The blood was starting to soak into the sheets around him, and he lay back further into the pile of pillows and closed his eyes.

"Don't close your eyes, Stan!" Darius all but yelled to get him to look at him, then toned back down to soothing, "Hang in there, dude. Just hang in there. I was full a shit a bit ago when I said you could die from this. It's in your stomach. It won't kill you, okay? You're gonna be alright. Keep your eyes open and talk to us."

Kevin was groveling at Stan's knees and begging him to forgive him and begging him to live. Matt and I finished dressing and went out to the living room, gathering up all the paraphernalia, too stunned to talk at first. I turned off the stereo and started emptying ashtrays into a Big Gulp cup as Matt picked up things and sat them right back down where they had been. He was still just too stunned to function. He jumped when I spoke.

"Isn't that bong the only kinda pipe y'all were using?"

"Uhhhhh … Yeah, I think so. Where'd Billy go?" He asked as if I would know.

"I dunno. I guess home. I think he came in his own car."

"I can't believe he fuckin' stabbed him with a broken fuckin' bottle, dude." He stood in the middle of the room, shaking his head, tears welling in his eyes but not leaking out. "His own fuckin' brother. Fuuuuck."

I stopped and stood facing him, shaking my head as well. "No shit, man. Uh … you think he's gonna die?"

"Oh man, I dunno. Oh man, I hope not. Fuuuuck."

We heard a siren way off in the distance and snapped our heads up at the same instant. I remembered there was a fire station actually not that far away in Fairmont Park. We both looked at each other with fear in our eyes. We knew the cops would be coming, too. We were all of age for drinking, at eighteen, but even though we'd had the high scared out of us, we didn't know if the cops could tell we'd been on pot and Quaaludes, too.

We both ran toward the back, and Matt stopped and shoved the bong into a kitchen cabinet. I stopped and looked at him like he was stupid. He looked back at me like, *what?* and snapped, taking the bong back out and bringing it with him.

I thought I was prepared, thought I had already seen enough that I wouldn't be any more affected by it, but when I came around the corner and saw how much blood was all over Stan, his jeans soaked nearly all the way down over his work boots, and the bed, all the sheets for nearly two feet around him and the floor, puddling in the only clear spot around, I just about lost it.

So much deep crimson. The rich color overwhelms every color around it. Knowing that it's living liquid, having watched it under a microscope in biology class, I had a mental image of the blood draining life away from Stan and infusing the sheets around him with that spark, that essence.

Matt was right behind me, saying, "They're almost here. So what're we gonna tell 'em?"

He rounded the corner, almost knocking me over and froze, kinda behind me looking over my shoulder. Darius was speaking a continuous stream of soothing words in Stan's ear, stroking his forehead softly. I couldn't believe my eyes, but Stan was smiling. Darius had his other hand on the topside of the bottle, meeting Kevin's left hand around the underside, both pressing a shirt or something around it, trying to stem the flow of blood – unsuccessfully.

The blood had filled the bottleneck and was running out over the rim, which for some reason freaked me out worse than anything else I'd seen so far. It was like a keg tap, steadily running the red brew over the rim and down over Kevin's hand. Kevin was a basket case, feeling the warm blood flow over his knuckles, crying and mumbling incoherently into Stan's knee.

Darius interrupted his stream of words to Stan and looked back at us. He nodded his head down at Kevin, "Help him get dressed. Let me do all the talking. If they question us separately … uh…. Say they got in an argument. Nobody knows … well … over the stereo, yeah, over the stereo. Got that, Kevin? Over-the-stereo!" he said each word extra clearly, so Kevin would absorb it through his quiet hysteria. "So they started fighting, and it escalated and the rest happened just like it did. It was an accident that Stan kinda fell into the bottle. Kevin didn't stab him with it, he just fell into it."

I said, "Well he did. I mean, he did kinda fall into it."

"Yeah," Matt added.

"Cool. Uh, where's Billy?"

Matt buried the bong under a pile of dirty, moldy clothes in the closet and chuckled, "He fuckin' screamed like a girl and went out the fuckin' window the second it happened and ran like a pussy." The three of us had a slightly tension relieving little laugh.

Kevin had his face right up in Stan's now, telling him to hang in there, the ambulance is almost here. Stan was still smiling, eyes closed. Kevin took Stan's bloody hand and squeezed. Stan twitched his fingers. Kevin kissed his cheek and asked him once again not to die. I blinked at that.

Matt and I pulled Kevin away, got him standing and got him dressed. He was dazed, almost as lifeless as Stan, so we had to do it all for him. I was the one who had to stuff his ample genitals into his pants, thinking back on the bizarre night as I did.

I couldn't really wrap my mind around it at that point, not even a little. I was shell-shocked, stealing glances at a blood drenched dying man while dressing his killer, his own brother, who had fucked my virgin ass and passed me around like a toy. I guess it's not really surprising my naïve eighteen-year-old mind couldn't quite deal.

Three different versions of sirens out front, each dying at its own pace, poured in with the humidity through the open window, mosquitoes honing in on the rich metallic smell of blood in the air, pulling us all out of our private thoughts and back into the stark reality of the moment. I looked at Stan, barely any sign of life, the rise and fall of his chest almost imperceptible. So much blood. So fucking much blood. Darius stood, wiped his bloody hands on someone's discarded shirt and headed up front to direct the paramedics back to us.

Epilogue

That night was a major turning point in my life for many reasons, the glaring and the subtle, the base and the cerebral. I came face-to-face with mortality that night for the first time in my young life. Stan came within a heartbeat of dying, pulling through miraculously. But, we didn't find that out until the next afternoon. The paramedics talking to each other at the scene made it sound like they quite frankly didn't think he would live, having lost so much blood from the deep laceration. One of them did tell us that if we had pulled the bottleneck out, he would most definitely have been dead before they arrived.

So by the time Darius, Matt and I left the house after three in the morning, we were all pretty sure he had died. Amazingly, or stupidly if you prefer, none of us thought of calling the hospital to find out. Hell, we didn't even know what hospital they took him to. I sensed that none of us really wanted any further involvement with the Landry Boys. I knew I didn't.

Thinking I'd witnessed a man's death throes up close and personal, in crimson Technicolor, did a real number on my head, and I know it did on the others' as well. Ridiculous as it was, I felt partly responsible. If I hadn't been there, or at least if I hadn't let Kevin manipulate me into sex, none of this would have happened. But, then I realized something like this would probably have happened sooner or later, and it certainly wasn't in any way my fault Kevin stabbed his brother.

I tried to comprehend, at least a little, life for this family that was so foreign to me, how there could be so much anger and violence and yet be bonded with some kind of love. I pitied them their little culture of closeted love, yet I admired some things about them at the same time.

And of course, there were my numerous and life altering revelations *before* the fight. I had only a vague and fleeting sense that night of how irretrievably I was swept into a tide that would ultimately wash me clean and then let me get dirty again on my own terms. That night replayed itself occasionally in quiet moments for the rest of my days.

Darius was the obvious hero of the night. He convinced the Harris County Sheriffs it was an accident and that their parents weren't home. They had been called to the house on numerous enough occasions to not be surprised at anything they found. Their parents never woke up, even with the sirens and paramedics banging the stretcher down the hallway and back. Fucking amazing.

When everyone was gone, Darius instructed that none of us would tell anyone what had happened that night, including what had brought this fight on. Kevin rode with Stan in the ambulance, so he and Billy were told the next day about the pact. I know everyone was more than happy to comply.

I was so grateful to Darius for both saving the day and handing my life back to me relatively intact by swearing everyone to silence, that I fell in love with him, in a way – I mean, I knew better, but I've always been drawn to strong men. So, I worshipped him from afar for awhile. He was actually nicer and paid more attention to me after that night, and that made me admire him even more.

Let's see – before meeting his future wife in '78, Matt and I got together a few times after that night and had awesome, memorable sex that I still think of as "making love." And, we both went all the way with each other, me taking his cherry about the third time we were together. He was a really special guy. He was tender and sensual and sexy and sweet, and I came *this* close to falling deeply in love with him.

But, he made it very clear that he was "Bi, but more straight. I just can't fall in love with a guy, okay? I enjoy what we do, but I don't feel 'that kind' of love for you, like relationship love, know what I mean? But I really do like you a lot and, well … I do love you in some real and meaningful way, just not in a 'mate' way." And, I accepted that. I appreciated him for being the beautiful person he was and is. We lost contact with each other years ago, but I still think of him fairly often and get a warm glow in my heart, and yes, a stirring in my groin as well.

Matt told me Billy was really freaked out about that whole night, and talked for hours with him about it one time only. But, Billy never spoke to me about it. He didn't speak much to me anyway after that. He wasn't hostile or anything; he just avoided me, and that was fine with me.

I never even spoke to Kevin again. He hardly ever came to Kelly's Cue that summer. When we did see each other, we just acted as if we didn't really know each other. And the few times I did see him, he looked like a changed man, quieter, kinda mellow. He went to work in the refineries along the ship channel as a pipe fitter.

I'm glad I didn't hate or even resent Kevin, and I always felt somehow that if circumstances had been different that night – in other words, alone – we could have had a mutually satisfying sexual relationship that summer. Is it pathetic to think that way? Who's to say? I mean, he was so hot, and if we hadn't been interrupted, we probably would have just had awesome sex with no real complications – even though I passed out for a while.

From what Darius told me, Stan didn't retaliate for the stabbing and even told people it was an accident. He said Stan told him he had a "near death experience" on the way to the hospital – tunnel with white light and all – and looked at life differently from then on. He got married in '79, to a girl none of us knew, and seemed to really take to the whole family life thing. He, his wife and four-year-old girl were all killed in a car wreck in '84, up by Austin on Labor Day, so they became a holiday statistic. Kevin moved out to California right after Stan and his family died. It seems as if no one's heard from him since.

I guess none of the citizens of Kelly's Cue, which is long since closed, has any desire to ever go by their house to ask his folks how Kevin is doing, and none of our crowd knew their other brothers well enough to go by and see any of them. I did hear that Peter went to New York and achieved some notoriety for his artwork, and someone said he came out as gay, but the source was a ditzy girl, so I don't know for sure.

As I said, that night changed my life. And I honestly don't regret it at all. Sure, I'd like for things to have gone differently, but I grew up a lot in those few eventful hours. By the next day, I knew my life had changed forever. One very significant thing I noticed, gradually, was that after that night, something in my personality changed. I no longer seemed to irritate people. I couldn't tell you what the difference was. I just found it easy to make friends, and people seemed to like me. Maybe it had something to do with coming out. Not having to hide anything let me open up and lose my anger at the world.

In the fall of 1977, I enrolled at the University of Houston and moved to the Montrose, where I rapidly immersed myself in the gay community and had a few blissful years as a sex pig slut. In the middle of that period, I met an amazing and wonderful man named Dennis, and we fell madly in love in 1980. We were both into the leather scene and into just about any and everything you can think of – you name it, we tried it, more than once. I told him about that night in detail, and we debated whether that event caused me to become the sex pig I became, or whether I was born to be that way. It didn't really matter.

By 1987, ten years after that night in Spinwick, I had already watched Dennis, the love of my life, die of AIDS, along with most of our friends, and I was full-blown as well. I dedicated the rest of my life to fighting for PWA care and funding and safe sex education.

Author's Note

Bobby told me his story, and I've tried to relay it in his words, with his thoughts and his emotions as much as I could. It was hard to watch his deterioration happen before my eyes over the months at the end. He was bedridden by the time he told me this story, and I got a few of the details from Matt a couple of years later.

Robert Alvin Wheaton died of AIDS complications in 1990, two weeks before his thirty-first birthday, as his mother and several of his closest remaining friends and I sat in vigil. He was a brave, kind and generous man, full of love and life, poignantly displaying himself as a brutal reminder of why we should all have safe sex. I count myself lucky to have known him, to have been his friend. I really miss him.

ABOUT THE AUTHORS

DESERTMAC – Soon to be married to his partner of twenty-six years, DesertMac lives in Palm Springs doing specialty landscape design. Since meeting Jae, they've had a variety of businesses from restaurants to ballroom dance studios, truck stops to promotions, from New Orleans to Honolulu. Mac has two stories in a recent STARbooks anthology, *Unmasked – Erotic Tales of Gay Superheroes*, edited by Eric Summers.

JAY STARRE – From Vancouver, Jay Starre has written for numerous gay men's magazines including *Men*, *Mandate*, and *Torso*. His torrid stories have also been included in more than forty-five gay anthologies such as *Daddy's Boyz*, *Kink*, *View to a Thrill* and *Love in a Lock-up*. His steamy gay novel from STARbooks, *The Erotic Tales of the Knights Templar,* was released in autumn of 2007 to rave reviews.

JAYDEN BLAKE – Jayden Blake lives and writes in western Massachusetts with her partner, dogs, and gerbils. Her writing has appeared in the anthologies *Swing!*, *Best Women's Erotica*, *Mammoth Book of Women's Fantasies*, *Bi Guys*, and *Flesh to Flesh* and on the Web sites *Three Pillows*, *Clean Sheets*, *The Erotic Woman*, *New Camp Horror*, and *The Shadow Sacrament*. A reference librarian by day, Blake's colleagues have no idea she moonlights as a writer of erotica.

JUSTIN SHEPHERD – Born in eastern Canada and raised in western Canada, Justin now lives in Brooklyn, New York. A graduate of Yale University, his interests and pursuits cover a wide spectrum, including competitive road cycling, music and fine arts, photography, writing and not-for-profit board work. As with most of his writing, this story has some autobiographical content and explores some of the challenges and questions that gay people encounter within the institutional church.

LANDON DIXON – Dixon's writing credits include *In Touch/Indulge*, *Men*, *Freshmen*, *Mandate*, *Torso*, *Honcho*, and stories in the anthologies *Straight? Volume 2*, *Friction 7*, *Working Stiff*, *Hard Hats*, *Sex by the Book*, and *Ultimate Gay Erotica* 2005, 2007, and 2008.

LOGAN ZACHARY – Logan Zachary is an author living in Minneapolis, where he is an avid reader and book collector. He enjoys movies, concerts, plays, and all the other cultural events that the Twin Cities have to offer. His friends, his partner, Paul, and his two dogs inspire his writing.

ROB ROSEN – Rob Rosen is the author of the critically acclaimed novel, *Sparkle: The Queerest Book You'll Ever Love*. His short stories have appeared in more than 50 anthologies, and his erotic fiction can frequently be found in the pages of *Men*, *Freshmen*, and magazines. Please visit him at his Website, www.therobrosen.com, or email him at robrosen@therobrosen.com.

RYAN FIELD – Ryan Field is a thirty-five-year-old freelance writer with many published short stories in anthologies and collections. He lives and works in both Los Angeles and New Hope, Pennsylvania, and he's currently working on a novel.

SCOTT JAMES – Scott James lives in Vancouver, where he is a ski-instructor at the nearby Whistler resort. He is currently at work on a novel – *Sex on the Slopes* – based on his experiences there. He would like to dedicate "Betrayal" to his long time partner, Ben.

SHANE ALLISON – Shane Allison has been called a fag, a nigger, and a genius. His stories have been published in such anthologies as *Muscle Worshipers*, *Wild and Willing*, *Don't Ask, Don't Tie Me Up*, *Best Black Gay Erotica*, *Ultimate Gay Erotica* and *Best Gay Erotica*. He is the editor of *Hot Cops: Gay Erotic Stories* and *Back Draft: Fireman Erotica*.

STEPHEN OSBORNE – Stephen Osborne has been published in *Unmasked – Erotic Tales of Gay Superheroes*, *Ride Me Cowboy*, *Hard Hats*, *Ultimate Gay Erotica 2008*, *Best Gay Love Stories: Summer Flings*, *Dorm Porn 2*, *Best Date Ever* and many others. He lives in Indianapolis with two cats, his fantastic roommate Frank, and Jadzia the Wonder Dog. He is currently working on a book of ghost stories and legends called *South Bend Ghosts*.

WAYNE MANSFIELD – Wayne Mansfield was born and raised in rural Western Australia. He currently lives and works in Perth. Apart from writing, he enjoys going to the local nude beach and giving private nude yoga sessions.

ABOUT THE EDITOR

MICKEY ERLACH – This is Mickey's second anthology for STARbooks Press. Although he has made every attempt, he has never been caught in the act.

...earing any underwear. "Excuse me," I said, having a hard time lo...

...inded by that bulge in his crotch. "but don't I know you?" "May...

...ind of t [ad] bou

with Ray [ad] God

t loser? [ad] in?"

...id. "Lik [ad] s stro

...ce body [ad] e on

...lly, he l [ad] I ev

...i up to t [ad] any

...staking [ad] ne sa

...i, I coul [ad] ery

...ood rac [ad] ne s

...ing with [ad] e in

we go [ad] bef

...ill see [ad] in

...ed?" he [ad] ven

...rivacy. [ad] gra

...hard. I [ad]

...k, traci [ad] t, s

...ed it, ha [ad]

with m [ad] bin

...bbing, I [ad] n co

...he sound of unzipping filled the small space. I don't know who'...

..., but before I knew it, I had his rod in my hand, and mine was in...

...it to do?" he asked, his tone challenging. I knew exactly, and sa...

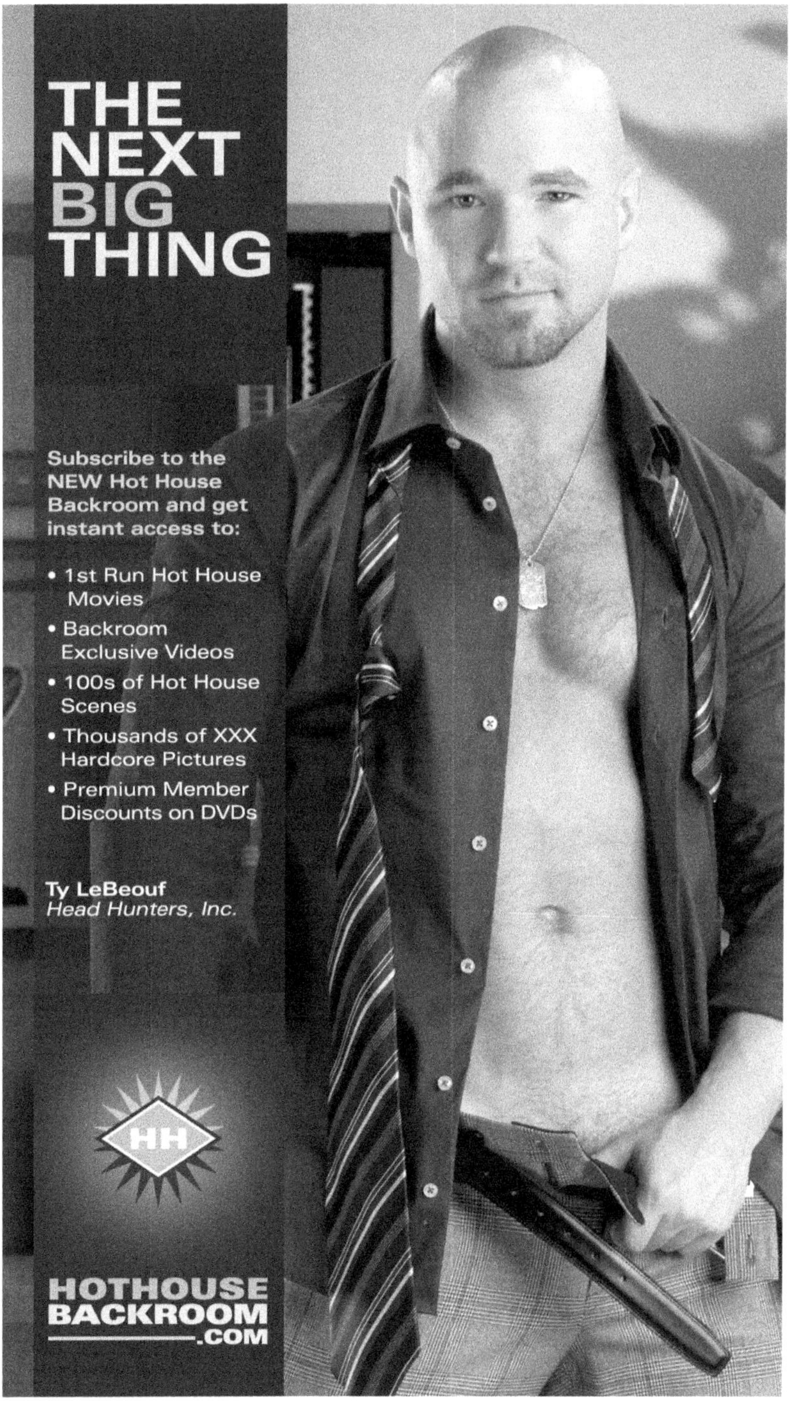
THE NEXT BIG THING
Subscribe to the NEW Hot House Backroom and get instant access to:
• 1st Run Hot House Movies
• Backroom Exclusive Videos
• 100s of Hot House Scenes
• Thousands of XXX Hardcore Pictures
• Premium Member Discounts on DVDs
Ty LeBeouf
Head Hunters, Inc.
HH
HOTHOUSE BACKROOM .COM

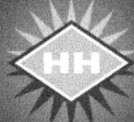